Secrets On Wenshen

by

Earl T. Roske

Thank You:

Nicole, Andrew, & Erin for your ears and your feedback.

Tim for all the proofreading and feedback.

Mike for the awesome covers.

For my wife and daughter.

And my mom.

Never forgotten. Always remembered.

Other titles by Earl T. Roske:

Orphan Corps Shepherds: Lost Sheep
Diversion in Raziel
Reckoning in Samael
Liberated in Ikenga

Stories of the Orphan Corps
Rescue on Gimhae
Deceit on Panchala
Standoff on Oulu
Counter Offensive on Arda
Defiance on Vargo

Other Works:
Tale of the Music-Thief
Last Wave
Ofendra (short story collection)

P.S.
At the end of the book, you'll have a chance to get a free story and join the newsletter to learn more about the Hospitallers.

01

It always happened when things were quiet. Lieutenant Dewey Tyler knew it, and yet he dared to pick up his tablet. He dared to open a book in it to read. Two pages in, his feet free of his boots, and things weren't quiet anymore.

"Lt Tyler? Major wants to see you."

"On my way, Dunn."

"I'll let the major know."

Private First Class Dunn's footsteps banged on the metal floor of the corridor as she jogged back to the bridge.

Dewey stared at the words on the tablet. A part of him said that another paragraph couldn't hurt. A larger part of him was already sitting, his toes finding the top edges of his boots, and sliding home. He tapped the screen to put the tablet to sleep and then pocketed it. Maybe it wasn't a big thing. Something simple that he could accomplish quickly and get back to reading. He wouldn't even take off his boots, wouldn't lie down. Just sit on the edge of his bunk, and read.

"Right, Dewey, cause that's always how it works." He checked himself in the metal mirror, and then marched into the corridor and forward to the bridge.

It wasn't a long walk to the bridge of a Hospitaller patrol ship. His quarters were past medical, and near the stairs that led down to the response platoon's quarters, and training. The other way led to loading bay 2, and then the engine compartments. Not a long walk, but long enough to give Dewey time to wonder about the request to report to the bridge.

And they didn't request his presence over the comm. That, too, was curious.

"Major Simmons," Dewey said. "Lt Tyler reporting as ordered."

Major Helen Simmons looked up from where she was bent over the comm station operated by Cpl Marcia Robertson, and Pfc Camille Dunn.

"Lieutenant," the major said. She added a nod to her return greeting. "We received an incoming message. A distress signal."

Dewey regretted trying to read his book. "Is it local? I was under the impression the in-system marauders had been quelled."

That was why it had become so quiet throughout the system. After four months of attacks and forced boardings of enemy ships, the quiet had been welled-earned. But apparently not quite enough to read a book.

"No, Lt Tyler," said Cpl Roberston. "It's coming in from the Kongxu system."

That was why the Major had called him up to the bridge. "The Kongxu system is uninhabited. Five planets, four of them are gas giants. Well, there's a sixth body, but it's a burnt rock so close to the sun we'd burn to a crisp the moment we touched the surface."

"So, the fifth planet?" Maj Simmons's eyebrows were arched, hinting at the lack of patience she was feeling.

"Yes, of course, Major," Dewey said. "There's a standard-size rocky planet. Someone actually bothered to name it: Wenshen. But no one ever colonized it because the atmosphere is just acidic enough to burn skin and lungs after a short exposure to it. Oh, and of course, it would permanently blind people, too."

"Sounds like a fun place," said Pfc Dunn. "Couldn't they have terraformed it?"

"Supposedly they tried in the first expansion," Dewey said. "But the atmosphere corroded the equipment before it could make a significant difference."

"So there's no reason to be there," said the major. It was a statement, not a question.

"Shouldn't be. Oh, there was some research done on the planet just about the time the Radial War began. The information is thin, but it seems that the researchers were pulled as the war picked up speed."

Dewey liked to read. When he read, he read a lot. His brain was a sponge when it came to information. His level of recall, once he read something, was nearly as good as that of the handlers who worked with the Wutenigels. Dewey could talk about the history of those creatures, too, if given a chance. Which he wasn't going to get right now.

"Okay," the major said. She walked back to her seat. "We have a distress signal in an unoccupied, unclaimed system. Cpl Robertson, send a request to respond over to system command. Lt Tyler, you might want to prep your teams. Just in case."

"Will do, Major."

Dewey left the bridge with one backward look at the comm station. Cpl Robertson had a comm mic, what they called a plunger, over her mouth as she communicated with system command. This was just a lowly patrol ship that had specific permissions and responsibilities. Jumping out of system, even to respond to a distress signal, was not one of them. Command could elect to send someone else. Though, based on their ship's position, they were the likely candidate.

Admittedly, Dewey wouldn't mind if someone else went. Maybe then he could get back to his book.

"What's going on, Lieutenant?"

Dewey paused and looked left. He was in the corridor that led aft to the crew quarters, the mess hall, and the stairs down to his platoon. His quarters were to port along with MSgt Roberson, and several empty rooms for visiting officers. Parallel with his quarters were the medical offices. MedTech1 Terrence Phillips was sitting on one of the examination tables, his own tablet in his hands. Was he getting time to read? What was he reading? Dewey might not ever know.

He poked a thumb back toward the bridge. "Distress call just came through."

MedTech Phillips hopped off the table. "I thought the system was cleaned up?"

"It's coming from another system." Dewey nodded in the direction of the mess hall. "I need to go brief my teams."

"Understand, Lieutenant."

Dewey returned to walking the length of the ship, passing through the ship's crew quarters, and then through the mess hall where he could smell the spices and oils that would be part of lunch. Past the mess hall, the corridor continued with an initial interruption by wide spiral stairs leading to lower levels. Dewey followed them to the next level, where they opened onto the Response Platoon's quarters.

The platoon was modified by attrition such that there were now only two squads rather than three. A new squad was scheduled to transfer over within seventy-two hours. If the ship was sent to investigate the distress signal, they'd be doing it shorthanded.

"Attention on deck!" The voice boomed through the platoon quarters as Dewey stepped through the hatchway. A dozen Hospitallers leaped from bunks, jumped up from tables, snapping to attention at Sergeant Shelley Perry's command.

"Stand easy, everyone," Dewey said. Around him, the Hospitallers took a more relaxed stance but did not resume whatever it was they'd been doing previously. Dewey looked around. "Everyone here? Where's the staff sergeant? Who else is missing?"

"I'm here, LT."

Dewey turned to see SSgt Diane Castro exiting her private quarters to starboard. As a Staff NCO, she had her own space, though it wasn't a lot of space, about half of what Dewey had, and no private head.

"Pfc Ramirez is in the shower," said Sgt Perry. Ramirez was one of her charges.

"Pfc Burke and Pvt Becker are forward, in the cargo bay," added Sgt Parks, 1st squad's leader.

"Get everyone, please," Dewey said. He didn't have to say please. His words were orders. When he'd been a private, he'd jumped when asked to jump, and no one had to say please. It was just his own habit.

Two Hospitallers instantly bolted from the room.

"What's going on, Lieutenant?" asked SSgt Castro.

"Message. May mean action. Let's wait."

They all stood around in an awkward silence that was slowly filled with the sounds of three pairs of boots sprinting in from the loading bay.

"Pfc Burke reporting, Lieutenant."

"Pvt Becker reporting, Lieutenant."

"Stand easy. Where's…? Ah, Ramirez, good. We can start."

Ramirez had appeared from the directions of the showers. She had a towel wrapped around her torso, and a second one hanging on her head.

"Sorry, Lieutenant," she said.

"No need, Ramirez. No need." Dewey paused and looked around. "All right. There's been a distress signal. It's come from out of the system. From an unoccupied, uninhabited system."

"Pirates?" someone asked.

"Don't know yet," said Dewey. "Don't even know if we're going to be the ones that respond. But as we might, I need everyone to gear up. Assume hostiles. Plan for the worst."

"Business as usual, Lieutenant."

Dewey grinned. "That's right, Cpl Mitchell, business as usual."

"SSgt Castro, get them suited and booted. Let me know when everyone's ready."

"Will do, Lt Tyler." Castro turned to the platoon. "Suit up kids. Let's have some fun."

Cheers and joviality filled the air. Dewey headed back to the stairs until the ship-wide comm pinged for everyone's attention.

"This is Maj Simmons. Prepare for action. Stand by for jump."

"That answers that," Dewey said as he turned back to face his platoon. "We're going to the rescue."

Lt Tyler's platoon quickly suited up. Some, like Pfc Ramirez, had to move a little faster than others. However, before the last warning for jump, everyone was dressed and ready. Those who felt queasy during jump were already lying in their bunks. The rest were seated and buckled in. Sometimes dropping out of jump came with surprises. Nothing more embarrassing than being thrown across the dorm room because the ship fell out of jump and ran into an ambush or an uncharted asteroid field.

As Dewey was some distance from his own quarters, he sat in a nearby chair and buckled in.

"Two, one...." Maj Simmons's voice stopped, and the shiver of entering jump completed her sentence.

The jump was short. The ship only had to move over to the next system, four light-years away as the photon flies. No one had time to fall asleep or tell a tried-and-true corny joke before the ship dropped out of jump.

Dewey looked around, catching SSgt Castro's eye. He gave her a nod.

Castro grinned, and said, "Well, that was anticlimactic."

"I've been through the opposite," said Sgt Perry. "I prefer the anticlimactic any day."

The comm buzzed, signaling that a message was forthcoming.

"Lt Tyler to the bridge." Pfc, Anderson, or Dunn, Dewey wasn't entirely sure. Except for the noses, they could have passed as twins.

"Don't keep us in the dark long, L.T."

Dewey flipped the latch on his lap restraint. "Never, Cpl Garner."

Several people chuckled at the exchange. Dewey left the bunk room, and made his way up the stairs, and then forward to bridge. Besides Maj Simmons and MSgt Roberson, Cpl Theresa Knight was on nav with Pfc Fox. Pfc Angel Anderson was at the comm station. Weapons station was currently unoccupied. If needed, Dewey would have one of his fireteams in place.

"Lt Tyler reporting."

"Thank you for joining us," Maj Simmons said. "Have a seat. We've images coming on the screens momentarily."

Dewey took the empty seat behind the major. MSgt Roberson was in the other and gave Dewey a welcome nod.

There were no portholes or windows on the bridge. The bridge wasn't even at the front of the ship. Instead, weapons and stowage were forward. Command was nearly in the center of the ship, protected by other sections, and extra layers of ballistic, and steel shielding. Hundreds of cams, embedded in the outer skin of the ship, provided the view displayed on the screens. Five screens provided the illusion of windows.

Dewey watched the center three screens that were currently displaying a starfield. A filtered image of the Kongxu system's star was visible to the left. Several discs in the center screen were the gas giants. Wenshen, the almost-habitable planet, was not visible to the naked eye, and might not even be on this side of the system. Dewey's mind held facts, the math took a lot more work.

"Data coming in, Major," said Pfc Fox. She'd turned in her seat to speak, and then spun back to her station, her fingers attacking the keys, and touchscreens.

"Thank you, Fox," said Maj Simmons.

The image on the center screen winked. The starfield was gone, replaced by a slightly blurred image of a transport ship.

"What do we have? MSgt Roberson?"

"Modified transport, Major," Roberson said after a short pause to consult a small screen to his right.

"Damage?"

"Engines are offline."

"Anderson," Maj Simmons said. "That the source of our distress signal?"

"Yes, Major."

"Hail them?"

There was a long pause while Pfc Anderson spoke into the plunger. It filtered out sounds that the ship might not want anyone else to hear and kept the speaker's voice clear and isolated. Several times she shook her head. She made a series of adjustments on her station's controls while she continued to talk. At least, Dewey had to assume she was talking, based on the motion of the muscles in her cheeks.

"There's something, Maj Simmons," Anderson said after several more adjustments to the controls at her station. "I think they can hear me, but I think they've lost too much power to boost a comm signal."

"Any other ships in the system? Cpl Knight?"

"Nothing, Major." Cpl Knight looked up at the screen to her right.

Dewey followed her lead.

The screen showed a simple version of the system with over-sized circles for the planets. White lines arcing out from the circles traced their orbits around the Kongxu star. Two other dots were present. The green one Dewey knew was their ship, the Shnel Shnek. The red dot was the transport ship.

"All right, then," said Maj Simmons. "Bring us closer."

For the next two hours, Dewey watched as they moved closer to the other ship. At some point, crew brought boxed lunches from the mess hall. Dewey recognized them as the second fireteam from first squad. Shultz, Burke, and Becker. Each of them gave Dewey a questioning look as they passed by. Dewey signaled for them to remain quiet, and to fall back, which they did after dispersing the meals.

As the ship continued its approach, the bridge became tinted with the smell of protein spread from the sandwiches in the lunch. It was one of the better flavors, Dewey considered, which meant the smell was bearable. If he'd been in charge, they'd never open a container of spread while onboard. Stick with pouches and bars was his opinion.

"We have comms, Maj Simmons," Pfc Anderson said.

"Fox? We have ID on that ship?"

"Sort of, Major." Pfc Fox wobbled her head, mimicking confusion. "It's the Tunkum Panri, but it doesn't show up in any registry."

"So they're running gray," Maj Simmons said. "Weapons?"

Dewey tapped on the screen to his right. It was small, and could be flipped on a hinge, and slid out of the way as necessary. It took him several seconds to pull up the right window and scan through the readings.

"They have self-defense," Dewey said. "But it's either down or offline."

"Fun," Maj Simmons said. "Okay, Anderson, let me talk to them."

Pfc, Anderson set her plunger on the comm station and tapped the monitor screen in several places. "All yours, Major."

"Tunkum Panri, this is the Shnel Shnek of the Hospitallers. You copy?"

The reply was quick, though the comm sounded distant. "Copy,

Shnel Shnek."

Maj Simmons motioned upward with a thumb, and Pfc Fox made adjustments at her station that brought the distant voice closer.

"This is Maj Simmons. What seems to be the nature of your distress?"

It was more than a mere formality. They had already managed to assess the external damage. But there might be problems inside that were of greater concern. For example, a failing life-support system.

"Thank you for coming, Major." The other voice took a deep breath. Whispers of others somewhere near the comm on the other ship were heard. "We've lost engines, defenses, and our escape pods, and airlocks are damaged."

Maj Simmons tapped a circle on her chair's screen, muting the comm. She turned, and looked at MSgt Roberson, and then in Dewey's direction.

"That's some interesting damage," she said.

MSgt Roberson nodded. "It's almost like someone didn't want them to escape."

"Might be coming back," Dewey ventured.

"Good point, both of you." Simmons turned back to the front. "Fox, set up a wide scan. Let me know if anything pops in from another system. Cpl Knight, bring us closer to the Tunkum Panri."

"Yes, Major," Knight said.

The major tapped the button to unmute the comm. "That's pretty selective damage, Tunkum Panri. Any chance you know how this happened?"

The laugh on the other side was bitter. "That we do, Major. It was an allied planet attack ship."

"Well, that is interesting," said MSgt Roberson.

"Yes, it is," Maj Simmons said after a short pause with the mute button. To the other ship, she said, "Why would an A.P. attack ship come after you?"

It was standard procedure, if dealing with smugglers, to order them to stand down. Most did. The others had their engines disabled. But only a desperate smuggler would resist a military ship. The defensive weapons on the ship, from Dewey's quick survey, would do little damage to a military-grade ship. So why, indeed?

"'Why?' To kill us, Major."

02

Dewey could feel the collective holding of breath across the bridge. Even in battle, the goal wasn't to kill the enemy but to disable their ship, to force them to surrender. Yes, people died in war. Space was a terrible place to engage in combat. One lucky shot could destroy an entire ship and its crew. But to set out with the intent of killing? If that was the goal, there had to be a lot more going on.

All of that went through Dewey's head in a flash, likely something similar went through the major's, and MSgt Roberson's.

"Hyperbole?" It was a suggestion on MSgt Roberson's part. Though, from his facial expression, it looked to Dewey as if the master sergeant doubted his own question.

"If they wanted them dead," Dewey said. "Why didn't they just blow the ship instead of disabling it."

Maj Simmons nodded. "They would have recognized the distress signal going out," she said. Her voice was slow and thoughtful. "But they wouldn't have destroyed airlocks, and escape pods before leaving the area. They wouldn't be able to count on having the time."

"They also didn't finish their job," said MSgt Roberson. "If they had to leave, why not just launch a barrage of missiles, and go."

"Because they are coming back." Maj Simmons scooted forward on her seat. "Cpl Knight, push the power on that scan. We need to know the moment they come back."

"Yes, Major." Knight started making adjustments on her screens.

Maj Simmons turned in her seat. "Lt Tyler. We're going to do an evac of that ship, the Tunkum Panri."

From the way the major had been acting, Dewey didn't think they were going to do this like a regular boarding. "Ship to ship, Major?"

"Ship to ship," said Maj Simmons with a quick nod. "Put everyone in EVA gear. Helmets sealed."

"Tethered."

"Yes, Lieutenant, and two fireteams on weapons."

The major wasn't taking chances. Dewey jumped out of his seat. "On it, Major."

Dewey ran, just as Pfc Dunn had earlier in the day. The book Dewey had planned to read was temporarily forgotten. He passed medical without a glance, and then through the mess hall. As he took the stairs, he began shouting orders.

"Gear up! EVA squad one. Ship to ship extraction!"

Ordered chaos was already in progress as Dewey leaped over the last step, and jogged to a stop in the Response Platoon's quarters.

"Hostile boarding, Lieutenant?" asked Sgt Parks. She had the EVA lockers for squad one open, and the Hospitallers were already pulling out their gear, and suiting up. Next to her, SSgt Castro was in her suit, helping others.

Dewey shook his head as he looked around. "Sgt Perry, your squad on weapons."

"Yes, Lieutenant," said Sgt Perry. She started barking her own commands. "Cpl Chavez. Your team to bridge weapons control. Cpl Mitchell, your team is forward."

There were several shouts of acknowledgment, and then a fireteam ran towards Dewey.

"By your leave, Lieutenant," said Cpl Chavez. Her fireteam was forming up behind her.

"Carry on, Corporal," Dewey said. He moved to the side, and the fireteam bolted up the stairs like they were the last ones to chow call and there was a shortage on dessert.

On the other side of the platoon's quarters, Cpl Mitchell's fireteam was disappearing through the door that took them to the training area. At the other end was the second weapons control station and the airlock to the forward loading bay.

Dewey went over and began to do safety checks on the first squad.

Overhead, the comm pinged for everyone's attention. "This is Maj Simmons. We're about to make ship-to-ship contact for an emergency extraction. Boarding protocols are to be followed, except do not shoot on contact."

"Like we would," said Sgt Castro. Her voice came through the speaker on her EVA suit, but Dewey could still hear the humor that tinged her voice.

When a hole was cut into a ship for boarding, the Hospitallers moved forward with ballistic shields presented. The enemy was always allowed to surrender. But once they started shooting, the Hospitallers did not hesitate to defend themselves. The more aggressive the reception, the more aggressive the response.

The major continued, saying, "We need to evacuate the other ship as quickly as possible. Hostiles may be incoming. Everyone needs to be alert. Lt Tyler, contact in five minutes. Forward loading bay. Starboard."

The rear loading bay held the boarding boats they would typically use to enter another ship. However, the Shnel Shnek was designed to initiate a boarding, too. There were two special airlocks to either side of the ship. Much like a salvage boat or one of the boarding boats, they were capable of connecting to varied surfaces. Once connected, they would cut a hole into the other ship, and then seal the passage, creating an airlock much like one would use to transit from ship to station. Like the others, the Shnel Shnek was then capable of re-sealing the entrance to preserve the internal integrity of the boarded ship.

"You heard the major. We've got less than five minutes to move forward and prepare to board."

"You heard the lieutenant," said SSgt Castro. "Move out."

In their EVA suits, Sgt Parks and her squad did not move with the same speed the two fireteams of second squad had employed as they left the platoon's quarters. The EVA suits were heavy, though not bulky. They had deck boots with their automatic magnetic engagement should gravity be cut on the enemy ship. Those had a lot of weight to them. The suits were self-contained, and a person could survive for seventy-two hours in one if their ship was destroyed. Every feature had weight to it, and the suits had a lot of features.

Dewey moved ahead of them, opening the doors to the training room, and then to the forward loading bay.

"Lt Tyler? Comm from Maj Simmons."

"You have it from here, SSgt Castro?"

"Yes, Lieutenant."

"I'll check in with you before boarding."

Dewey shut the door to the forward loading bay and then jogged back across the training room to the comm on the wall. He tapped the screen awake, and then entered the code for Maj Simmons.

"Lt Tyler, Major."

"Lieutenant. Everyone ready?"

"Yes, Maj Simmons. First squad is prepping the airlock for boarding. Second squad is deployed to the weapons stations."

"Good," Maj Simmons said. Dewey recognized the slight hesitation in the Major's words. Something else was coming. "Lt Tyler, I want you to get permission from the people on that ship to back up their systems. I want logs, navigation, comms, everything. Ask politely, first."

"I understand, Major."

"Be safe, Lieutenant."

The comm clicked off. Dewey ran back through the open airlock to the lockers in the platoon's quarters. He suited up as quickly as he could, listening to the comm detailing the approach. He had his EVA suit sealed but still needed a safety check. From the bottom of the locker, he grabbed his toolbox and hurried forward as quick as the suit allowed.

"Cpl Mitchell?" Dewey had stopped at the entrance to the forward weapons control.

"Lieutenant." Mitchell snapped to attention. The others, by protocol, stayed focused on their duty on the weapons panels.

"I need a safety check."

Cpl Mitchell stepped through the hatch and began the safety check for Dewey. It took fifteen seconds, and then Mitchell tapped the button on the back of Dewey's suit.

"All good, Lieutenant."

"Thank you, Mitchell."

Dewey moved toward the next airlock. On the other side was the forward loading bay.

Once out the airlock, he clumped across the loading bay. There were several storage containers and a half-dozen large crates secured to the deck. Further forward were several pygmy crawlers. Other than that, and the squad at the boarding airlock, the space was relatively empty. The rear loading bay was not so open. Not with four boarding boats, and all the other equipment used by the Response Platoon.

"Hey, Lieutenant. What's going on?"

Dewey stopped next to SSgt Castro and tapped the toolbox he was carrying. "Backing up data."

"Sgt Parks," the staff sergeant said. "We're going to need the long tether for the lieutenant.

Dewey didn't like the idea of dragging the tether through the ship to reach the bridge. He'd rather do without it if he were asked. However, he'd seen several lives saved because of the long tether. He reminded himself that he would insist his team wear them if they had to go any significant distance into the ship during a boarding.

"Contact in five," said one of the crew on the bridge. They counted down. As usual, nothing happened. That meant perfect contact had been made. Outside, unseen by Dewey, several magnetic grapplers had deployed, grabbing the other ship, ensuring it didn't move during the boarding process.

"Deploy," SSgt Castro said.

Sgt Parks acknowledged with a thumbs up, and then punched several buttons on a screen that was generally hidden behind a locked panel.

Again, everything was happening outside. Sgt Parks could see it as there was a small screen on the control box that showed the front of the extending airlock. Dewey only knew from experience that there was a thick rectangle with rounded edges and an accordion extension moving towards the other ship. It would take a minute, depending on the distance, and then it would connect to the other hull. An electromagnet would hold the extension of the airlock in place until a more permanent seal had formed. A seal that wouldn't leak atmo.

"Connection made," Sgt Parks said. Her words were transferred to the bridge so that they could give the other ship a heads up. Not something they would do during a standard offensive entry. Either way, someone would be waiting on the other side.

Now that the connection was made, Dewey waited with the others outside the airlock extension. It had to equalize its atmosphere to that inside the Shnel Shnek before cutting through the other hull. Clamps and pistons would pull the section of hull away, much like a door.

"Breach has begun," said Parks. That was the airlock cutting through.

Another minute and lights on the panel Sgt Parks watched began to flash and change colors.

"We're through."

"Shields," SSgt Castro said.

Pfc Gonzalez and Pvt Foster stepped forward and opened the ballistic shields. The shields would stop most automatic weapons fire, and deflect the explosions from grenades. It would take a high energy round to poke a hole, and even then, it would lose most of its momentum.

With the shields open, SSgt Castro gave Sgt Parks the okay to open the airlock. Everyone else moved so they were either out of the potential field of fire or behind Gonzalez and Foster, ready to give as good as they might get. The airlock hissed, and the mechanisms inside made it sound like the growl of an angry drill instructor who'd been woken too early. Then the hatch swung inward.

The airlock past the hull of the Shnel Shnek extended five meters by Dewey's guess. But that was numbers, and numbers weren't his thing. On the other side, a neatly cut section of the Tunkum Panri's hull had been pulled away, revealing its interior. Standing in the opening were three people in emergency evacuation suits, helmets hanging from a clip on their suit's belts. They had their hands up, palms out.

"I'm Capt Augia Aunztequi," said the man in the center of the small group. He nodded his head to the left, and added, "This is my engineer, Temistokles Aurrano, and this is our medic, Anua Izu."

"Captain. I'm Sgt Parks. "Please remain where you are."

Dewey had taken position behind the other fireteam backing up Gonzalez, and Foster. Sgt Parks turned and looked directly at him as if Dewey's position was to be expected.

"Lieutenant?"

"Cpl Garner, secure the area."

"Yes, Lieutenant," Garner said. He moved forward toward the gap being made between the ballistic shields. "Fireteam, on me."

Dewey waited as Cpl Garner, and his team entered the airlock. Sgt Parks clipped tethers to them as they moved past. Once they crossed to the other end of the airlock, they slipped around the three people on that side. They disappeared for several minutes.

"Lt Tyler?" The voice was on Dewey's EVA internal speaker.

"Maj Simmons?"

"How are things going down there?"

Dewey knew that the major was not in the dark. There were cams in the loading bays that allowed her to keep an eye on her ship. So she could see them standing, and waiting. She had just as likely watched the airlock make contact via the exterior cams. But Maj Simmons liked to hear what was going on as well.

"We've made contact with the captain of the Tunkum Panri, and fireteam two is clearing the other side."

"Good news," the major said. Then, "Soon as the area is secure, we want to get the people from the Tunkum Panri over here quick as a Marine retreat. Don't forget the backups."

"Will do, Major."

The comm went dead and was replaced by another voice that was shared amongst the squad at the airlock. "Cpl Garner here. Area's clear. No weapons visible. No threats currently detected."

"Thank you, Garner," Dewey said. "Have your team hold position."

Dewey moved forward past the ballistic shields. He paused as Sgt

Parks attached the long tether to him. With a nodded thank you, he proceeded forward.

"Greetings, Capt Aunztequi," Dewey said. "We're ready to bring your people over. Do you have wounded that require help?"

"We have wounded, but the others will bring them across, and we have Anua, she's been looking after everyone so far."

Dewey paused and took in Anua, the medic. He gave her a nod, which was returned in kind, before turning back to Capt Aunztequi. "You can give them the orders to start crossing. My team, on the other side, will direct you where to go. We haven't had time to arrange decent bedding and shelter yet. There's a bit of a time crunch."

"You mean the attack ship might come back."

Dewey couldn't miss the anger in the engineer's voice.

"We are concerned that they may return. So it's best to get you over here where there's more protection."

The engineer grinned. "And jump engines."

"And jump engines." Dewey turned back to the captain. "Capt Aunztequi, I'd like permission to backup all of your systems. It's a standard procedure in the Hospitallers fleet. I'll have it all copied on to data disks for you when we're out of the area."

"You're going to go through my data?"

Dewey paused. How honest should he be?

"They are," said the engineer. "We'd do the same thing if we had the chance."

Anua, the medic, added, "If it's the price of being saved, Augia, I'm all for it."

"Besides, they probably already know or suspect we're not a completely-above-board operation," added the engineer.

Capt Aunztequi looked at her. "Well, Temistokles, if they didn't know, they do now."

"We knew," Dewey said. "Now, do I have your permission, Captain?"

"If it's a choice between that, and facing the attack ship, again, then have all the data you want. You know how to reach the bridge?"

Dewey tapped a button on his EVA suit and brought a heads up display online. With his free hand, he manipulated VR controls that only he could see. The captain and his crew might be confused, but every Hospitaller present knew what was going on, and none were phased by Dewey grabbing at empty space and turning it. A 3D overlay of the ship showed Dewey where to go.

"I can find my way, Captain. You see to your people."

"Thank you, Lieutenant," said Capt Aunztequi, "for coming to our rescue."

"It's what we do, Captain, and we enjoy what we do."

03

As Capt Aunztequi started moving his people to the airlock, Dewey followed the map on his HUD. It took him down a short corridor and then up two flights of stairs. Once, someone back down near the airlock snagged Dewey's tether. At the back of his suit, where the tether was latched to him, the connection fed out its own line, braking steadily. This kept Dewey from being jerked to a painful stop.

His comm beeped, and SSgt Castro was on the line. "Sorry, Lt Tyler. Civilians."

The slack returned to the tether. Dewey continued forward to the bridge. If there hadn't been a tether, he wouldn't have to deal with civilians stepping on or grabbing at tethers. But, again, tethers saved lives.

Once on the bridge, Dewey used the info from his helmet to locate the ship's mainframe. It was buried inside the steel of the deck and would require several hours of work to pull panels to reach it. That wasn't what Dewey's toolbox was for. By the captain's station, there was a small access panel. Despite the gloves of the EVA suit, the panel was easy to remove, requiring no tools other than his fingers.

Beneath the panel were several receptacles. Again, the HUD directed Dewey to the correct one. Once located, he opened his toolbox and removed a wide flat cord and a ring of adapters. It took two tries to find the right tab piece for the slot of the receptacle. He clipped the tab to the cord and then inserted it into the receptacle. The toolbox beeped. The download had begun.

Dewey moved over to the navigation station and took a seat. This was going to take a little while. A bigger ship, of course, would take even longer. There was nothing to do but wait. He took out his tablet and synced it to the toolbox. It would let him know how much time it would take and how much was left. It would also allow him, if he were inclined, to sift through data already loaded.

Once he had a reading on his tablet, Dewey contacted Maj Simmons.

"Fifteen minutes, Major."

"That sounds about right. Make sure that navigation gets priority in case we have to bail early."

Dewey made adjustments to the backup process. It paused the engine logs and put processors onto the nav data.

"On it, Major."

"Don't get comfy," said Maj Simmons.

Dewey stood before he was aware of it. He looked around. It was unlikely that the major knew he'd been sitting. She might not even have meant he shouldn't. But people rarely looked busy when they were seated, even if their fingers and eyes were working through terabytes of data.

As he waited, Dewey accessed the downloaded navigation data. Here he had the coordinates of the places visited by the Tunkum Panri. It was ordered backward, working through time to the very first station the ship had been commissioned on. But it started with the last place visited.

And that was odd.

Odd because the coordinates didn't match with any planet that Dewey knew about. He couldn't list every planet by name, but he'd read through the lists several times over the years. Any one of them would have rung a bell. This one did not.

Had the Tunkum Panri discovered one of the planets lost during the Radial War? There had been planets at the beginning of the terraforming process that were supposedly abandoned as the war ramped up. Maybe they'd found one? Was that the reason the Allied Planets sent an attack ship? Didn't seem reason enough to kill a ship of smugglers.

Dewey scrolled to the coordinates prior. A space station. This was under A.P. control. Would the A.P. send an attack ship after someone who skipped on docking and fuel fees? Seemed unlikely as well.

Before that, it was a Dark Worlds planet, and before that another A.P. space station.

A marker on Dewey's tablet informed him that the nav logs were fully backed up to the toolbox. He reached for comm to let the major know the progress. His comm beeped before he could touch it.

He was being contacted.

"This is Lt Tyler."

"Tyler. Maj Simmons. How's the back up going?"

"Navigation is done, Major," Dewey said. "System logs, captain's logs, engine logs, they're coming in now."

"So, almost done?"

"Five minutes," said Dewey. "Maybe a little longer."

"Okay." There was a pause. Someone was speaking to Maj Simmons, but Dewey didn't catch the words. "Soon as you're done, hurry back to the ship. But be prepared to cut and run early. An A.P. attack ship has just appeared in the system."

"Understood, Major."

Dewey checked the time to complete the download. Four minutes, forty-five seconds. He put away his tablet and checked his tether. He moved it around the captain's seat to create a straighter line. The last thing he needed was to snag his tether when there was an emergency. Tether's saved lives. Unless you screwed up.

After organizing the tether, Dewey went and stood over the toolbox. He could see the small panel inside it. Three minutes, thirteen seconds. Almost done. His comm beeped.

"Almost done," he said after tapping the comm active.

"You might want to quickstep the moment you're through." It was Maj Simmons. "Our A.P. friend is coming in hot."

"Yes, Major."

Dewey knelt by the toolbox. His hand hovered over the connection to the smuggler ship. He was going to pull the cord on the toolbox side so he could shut it, and run. The cable was easily replaced. He liked to think that it was not quite the same for him.

Time seemed to slow now that Dewey needed it to go fast. It never ran slowly when he was enjoying a good book. Too soon, the hour he'd carved out for himself was over. Or, too soon, the book was over, and he had to find another one. If only he could trade that kind of time for what he was experiencing now. Two minutes, nineteen seconds.

The ship shuddered. Dewey's hand moved closer to the cord he had to remove from the toolbox. Nothing had struck the ship. It wasn't that kind of shudder. He was isolated from the Shnel Shnek, but it was easy to identify the launching of intercept missiles. If those were being launched, it could only mean one thing.

Dewey tapped his comm. "Maj Simmons? Are we under attack?"

"Sort of," said MSgt Roberson. "We're throwing out counter-measures, but it's not our ship they're trying to hit."

One minute, forty-two seconds. Dewey didn't need to be told. The A.P. ship was shooting at the smuggler ship. The ship that he was currently on.

"You might want to hustle, Lieutenant."

"I know, Master Sergeant, and believe me, I really want to."

One minute twenty-eight seconds.

The shudder of missiles firing from the Shnel Shnek vibrated through the smuggler ship once more.

"Lt Tyler." This time it wasn't the master sergeant.

"I know, Major. I know. Fifty seconds."

Dewey grabbed the cord between finger and thumb. His eyes focused on the timer running down the last seconds.

Without preamble, the ship twisted under Dewey. The vibrations this time were not counter-measures from his ship, but a strike on the smuggler. At least one missile from the A.P. attack ship had made it through.

"Twelve," Dewey said. He watched as the time went from double-digit seconds to single digits. He counted down, his finger and thumb beginning to slowly put tension on the cord. "And five, four, three."

The ship lurched again. Dewey released the cord to keep from pulling it out of the toolbox. He slid more than ten centimeters and quickly crawled back to the toolbox. The countdown had been replaced with a message affirming that the download was complete.

"One," Dewey said as he pulled the cord, and slapped the top of the toolbox closed. He climbed to his feet, staggering as another missile found the ship. The lights winked out and were replaced by red emergency lights.

"Lieutenant!"

"On my way, Major." Dewey ran toward the hatchway, only hindered by the EVA suit he was wearing. Ahead of him, the tether began to take up slack. The system on the other end of the tether was starting to reel it in. There wouldn't be a long trail of it to catch on corners as he retreated to the Shnel Shnek.

He made it to the first stairs as another explosion shook everything around him. A shower of sparks erupted through the hatch to the bridge. The place he'd just been.

"Cutting it a little close, Dewey," he said.

Halfway down the stairs, another strike shook his feet out from under him. He took the remainder of the stairs on his butt. When he landed on the deck, he rolled over and crawled for a meter until he reached a rail and pulled himself up.

"Do we need to send rescue, Tyler?"

"No, Major. Almost there."

He reached the second flight of stairs just as the artificial gravity gave out. Dewey slowly rose into the air. Normally, losing gravity was a problem. He had deck boots on, but they hadn't engaged. A simple correction could fix that, but Dewey had other ideas. He used a carabiner hanging on his suit to secure the toolbox. Then, he began to pull himself down the stairs.

In the EVA suit and gravity on, he had to walk to the bottom of the stairs to get around the railing. Without gravity, halfway down, he was able to slip over the rail, and pull himself down, and forward. It was a short hallway to the airlock they'd cut into the side of the smuggler. A short airlock tunnel, and he'd be home.

The A.P. ship seemed determined to undermine Dewey's plan.

Several explosions rattled the ship as He neared the airlock.

"Lt Tyler." It was SSgt Castro. "We've lost our grapplers. The ship is drifting."

"I'm here," Dewey said as he pulled himself around the edge of the airlock. He could see the accordion corridor and several Hospitallers in EVA suits standing in the opposite airlock. As he reached out to grab the airlock and pull himself into the space between the ships, the smuggler ship zoomed away.

At least, to Dewey's perception, it seemed like the other ship had suddenly pulled away. In fact, as he was able to orient himself, it was clear the Shnel Shnek had been the one pulling away.

Dewey was pulled along by the Hospitaller ship as it put distance between it and the smuggler ship. The Hospitallers in the airlock were guiding Dewey's tether as it drew him closer to them. Behind him, a burst of light threw his shadow across the side of the Shnel Shnek. He could see the different panels of the exterior in stark relief. He didn't need to turn to know that the smuggler ship had exploded.

"Lt Tyler?" asked Maj Simmons. "You with us?"

"Yes, I am," said Dewey as he drifted toward the airlock. Tethers saved lives.

The Hospitallers had been efficient in bringing Dewey into the airlock, then getting all of them into the loading bay. First squad was gathered around as Dewey handed off the toolbox and removed his helmet. Further back in the bay, the crew of the Tunkum Panri were gathered. Dewey counted eleven of them standing, two on stretchers.

"Nice work, SSgt Castro," he said. "You all saved me like I was someone who owes you money."

His comment generated a good-natured laugh from those around him.

"Get all the data, Lieutenant?" The toolbox had been passed along to SSgt Castro. She held it like one might hold a favorite puppy.

"I'm going to say yes," Dewey said. He started to unlatch the rest of his EVA suit but stopped when someone put their hand on his. "Sgt Parks?"

"Might want to leave that on, Lieutenant." With her words, Dewey realized that everyone was still suited up. Sgt Parks added, "The A.P. ship is targeting us now."

It was somewhat like dealing with the marauders that had kept them busy for the last six months. Except the firepower they were dealing with now made the marauders look like kids with marshmallow guns.

"Right. Then let's get ready. Sgt Parks, move the civilians into our dorm. Buckle them down so they don't get hurt when things get messy. Get the two wounded to medical."

"Yes, Lt Tyler." She turned and began pointing at Hospitallers, giving orders in a clipped manner. "Mitchell? Wounded. Go. Garner? Everyone else? Our house. Go."

Both fireteams marched over to the civilians. Cpl Garner's fireteam started directing the standing civilians toward the hatch. Cpl Mitchell's fireteam hoisted the gurneys with the wounded and trotted off. Dewey noticed that the smuggler ship's medic, Izu, stayed with the wounded. There were some words passing between her and Cpl Mitchell.

"Mitchell," Dewey said over the comm. "It's okay to let their medic go along,"

"Roger that, Lieutenant." They left without further conflict.

"Should I store this?" SSgt Castro was holding up the toolbox.

"No, I'll take it to the bridge, Staff Sergeant." Dewey took the toolbox. "I need you in the weapons stage down here. Sgt Parks, you're in charge of the civilians. If you get a chance, inspect those suits for damage. If there's time, we'll change them out for the ones in stores."

One of the small storage trunks on the loading bay floor was filled with rescue supplies. Along with adjustable coveralls, cots, and emergency rations, there were emergency evac suits. Just for scenarios like this.

"Will do, L.T.," Parks said, and then marched off to look after her new wards.

"All right, SSgt Castro, let's go see what all the shooting is about."

04

There wasn't time for Dewey to change from the EVA suit to a combat evac suit. Instead, with the toolbox tucked under one arm, he lumbered up the stairs to the main level and jogged forward to the bridge. As he passed medical, he had a quick glimpse of the medic from the Tunkum Panri, and two of the Hospitaller medics working with the injured smugglers. The medics were in their emergency evac suits, their helmets secured to them with a D-ring at their waist.

That reminded him that he was still wearing his. He released the clips as he walked, pulling it off his head.

On the bridge, Dewey moved to his seat, and buckled in, securing the toolbox at his feet. Around him, everyone else was also suited for emergency evac. Dewey and Cpl Chavez's fireteam were the only ones in EVA gear.

"We taking fire, Maj Simmons?" asked Dewey after pulling his helmet off.

Simmons barked a short laugh. Then, "Not yet, Lt Tyler."

"We've thrown up a lot of countermeasures," said MSgt Roberson. "That was to keep them from blowing up the other ship before you were done."

"We're getting a message request from the A.P. attack ship," said Pfc Edward Boyd, who'd taken over comms while Dewey had been on the other ship. "Capt Reeves of the Azkonarra."

Maj Simmons slapped her hands several times on the armrests of her chair. "Oh, this'll be fun. Open the comm, Boyd."

"Yes, Major." Pfc Boyd turned back to his station. He tapped several places on his monitor screen before looking over his shoulder to nod in the affirmative. The comm was open.

"This is Maj Simmons of the Hospitaller patrol ship, Shnel Shnek. Who am I speaking to?"

She knew, and Dewey knew that she liked to ask, just to give a poke at the person on the other end. She wouldn't have done this to a civilian or other friendly, but the A.P. ship wasn't acting friendly.

"This is Capt Kingston Reeves of the Allied Planets ship, Azkonarra. Why are you in this system?"

The voice of Capt Reeves was accusatory. Dewey knew that Maj Simmons didn't take well to attitude.

"I could ask you the same question," Maj Simmons said. She flashed a smile even though Capt Reeves couldn't see it. "I've checked. This is an open system. Unless the A.P. has laid claim? But I don't have anything in my records that indicate such."

"Were there any survivors on the smuggler ship?"

Maj Simmons tapped a button on her chair that muted the comm on her side. She looked around at the crew present, raising an eyebrow when she reached Dewey.

"I'm thinking that Capt Reeves's ego may be too large for his little attack ship."

There were several nods of agreement, but none of the enlisted laughed out loud. They were used to respecting officers, even those whose egos were too big for their spacesuits.

Maj Simmons tapped the mute button. "We appreciate your concern for the safety of the Tunkum Panri's crew, Captain."

Dewey recognized the emphasis Maj Simmons put on the other commander's rank. It was a less than subtle reminder that she did outrank him, even if they were from different organizations, and on different sides of an encounter.

"So, there were survivors."

The sound of the comm changed. The silence was different this time. Pfc Boyd turned in his seat to face Maj Simmons. "We've been muted, Major."

"Of course we have." She turned in her seat to face Dewey. "Lt

Tyler, have your teams begin plotting for return fire."

"Yes, Major." Dewey rose from his seat and went to the weapons station where Chavez sat with her fireteam. "Chavez, plot for return fire. Send the message down to station two when you're ready."

"Will do, Lieutenant."

Dewey turned back to his chair when Pfc Anderson shouted. "They're firing!"

"Evasive, Cpl Knight," snapped Maj Simmons. "Counters, Boyd."

Several different klaxons sounded off. One, with a long whoop-whoop sound, warned of an imminent attack. The second, a monotone ping ping ping, was the only heads' up the crew was going to get that evasive maneuvers would be occurring.

Dewey jumped for his seat, chased by the klaxons, and slowed by the EVA suit he was still wearing. He flopped into his seat, pulling the harnesses into place as commands were snapped across the bridge.

Despite the gravity plates, Dewey could feel the ship roll to port as it simultaneously powered forward below the plane of contact.

"Return fire, Major?" Dewey asked.

"Hold fire," Maj Simmons said. "Knight? How're we looking?"

"Still have a few torpedoes on our tail."

The ship vibrated. Dewey had enough experience to know that they'd taken a hit.

"Sorry, Major," said Pfc Boyd. "One made it through. The others have been neutralized."

"Damage?" The major turned to look at where MSgt Roberson was sitting.

"Still a hundred percent hull integrity," said Roberson. "It looks like a glancing blow near the engines."

"They're trying to take out the engines." Maj Simmons turned forward. "Lt Tyler, that's what they did to the smuggler, yes?"

"Yes, Major. Engines, and escape pods. Left them sitting."

"Right. Pfc Dunn, fire off a message back to Command. Make it a mayday, under fire."

"Doing it now, Major," Dunn said. Her fingers attacked the keyboard at her station as she complied with Maj Simmons's orders.

"They're firing again," said Pfc Anderson.

"Evasives. Counters." Maj Simmons took a deep breath. "Okay, Tyler, hit back."

"Yes, Major," Dewey said. Then, turning to where Cpl Chavez was watching him, he said, "Fire at will, Corporal."

"On it, Lt Tyler." Cpl Chavez turned and tapped Pfc Cruz on the shoulder.

The Shnel Shnek hiccuped as a round of torpedoes were launched. These were breakaways, four smaller torpedoes packed into a single case. As they passed eighty percent of the distance toward the target, they would unbundle, and spread out. Breakaways weren't unheard of. The U.P. forces had a series of them, as did the Free Worlds. However, the Hospitallers had spent more time perfecting them. So while the other forces used breakaways as an annoying distraction, the Hospitaller forces used them as originally intended, maximum damage on contact.

Of course, contact had to be made.

"They're good, Major," said Cpl Knight. "Their counters and evasions are working. No. Wait. We made contact twice."

"Any chance they're tucking tail and running?" Maj Simmons asked.

"No, Major," said Pfc Anderson. "They've come about, and have fired again."

So now the ship was trying to evade and destroy two salvos of torpedoes. Not impossible, but undoubtedly time-consuming and annoying.

"Cpl Chavez," said Dewey. "Are we ready for another round?"

"Yes, Lieutenant."

"Return fire. Keep firing until ordered otherwise."

"You got it, Lt Tyler." Chavez turned to her fireteam, and said in a loud whisper, "You heard the L.T. Fire when ready. Keep it rolling."

Dewey knew the other team downstairs in station two was watching the action on their screens. They'd be plotting and getting ready should anything happen to the station on the bridge.

The ship shook. This time it was hard. Red lights on the stations lit up, pulsing quickly.

"What did we lose?" asked Maj Simmons.

Dewey knew. He was sure that the major knew, too, but was going through the motions to keep everyone focused.

"We've lost an engine," said Pfc Dunn.

"Hull integrity is ninety-five percent," added MSgt Roberson. We're losing atmo in the aft loading bay."

Dewey tapped his comm. "SSgt Castro. You copy?"

"Copy, Lieutenant."

"We have damage to the aft loading bay. Can you get a visual, and then see if it's something we can patch on the fly?"

"On it." The comm clicked silent.

"We got them!"

Everyone on the bridge turned to Pfc Horton at the weapons station. He had his hands up in celebration.

"Are they out of commission?" asked Maj Simmons. "Boyd? What do you see?"

Seeing didn't mean an actual visual. Even on the monitors, the A.P. ship was nothing more than one more bright dot on the fabric of space. But Boyd was looking at scan data, and not at the spread of stars on the main screen.

"They're damaged for sure, Major. But they still have some power." He paused and then continued. "Yep. They're turning. Well, space rocks. They're firing again."

"How much ammo does that thing have?" Maj Simmons said. She quickly held up her hand. "I know. It's an attack ship. The question was rhetorical. Can we get out of here? Cpl Knight?"

"Not fast enough to avoid everything that's coming at us," said Cpl Knight. "Sorry, Major."

Maj Simmons tapped the comm on her chair. "Sgt Antonio? You're awfully quiet back there in engineering. What's the status on our engines?"

The response was not immediate. Before it came, Dewey could sense the worry in Maj Simmons's posture.

"Major. This is Cpl Lindsey Alexander. Sgt Antonio is down. Chambers is working with him."

Chambers was one of the medtechs. That was enough information for Dewey to know that the sergeant was hurt. If the medtech came to him, it was likely serious.

"Okay, Corporal. That means you're in charge. Tell me about our engines."

"Engine one is out of commission, Major. Two is running at fifty-plus percent. Three is at a hundred. We were working on one when a power bank blew. That's what got Sgt Antonio."

"Incoming," said Pfc Boyd.

"Hang on, and stand by, Cpl Alexander. Incoming."

Before Alexander could respond, everything was jerked sideways. It was like a time in basic training when Dewey had cleared a climbing obstacle. He'd decided to jump down rather than climb. His shirt caught on a corner of a ladder rail as he leaped. The stop had been so sudden, and without warning that he bit his tongue, and banged the back of his head against several ladder rungs. This time, he did not do any personal damage.

"Tell me that's all of it, Boyd."

"Yes, Major. Countermeasures took care of the rest. The A.P. ship took several hits about the same time. They're stationary."

"So are we," said Cpl Knight. "All engines are offline."

"Wonderful." Maj Simmons chewed on the inside of her lip for several seconds before nodding her head, and saying, "Knight, get Cpl Robertson on the comm. I want her back in engineering. Lt Tyler? You go, too. I want – I need – a full report on engine status, and how soon we can get something back online. I'd like to put the planet between us and them."

The planet was Wenshen. The only rocky planet in the system, if one didn't count the burnt rock closest to the system's star.

"On my way," said Dewey in response to the Major's orders. He unbuckled and jogged out off the bridge, and into the corridor that led aft.

As he trundled past medical, Dewey had a quick glance. The two initial injured smugglers had been joined by two more and one Hospitaller. The Hospitaller, Pfc Fox, one of the ship's crew, waved a bandaged hand at Dewey as he passed by. The mess hall was eerily empty, as were the officers' quarters.

At the stairwell that led down to the Response platoon's quarters, Dewey paused to look through the observation window into the loading bay. There was a large tear in the skin of the ship. Debris had been swirling as the bay was vented of atmo. Now it either floated or had settled haphazardly around the open area.

Near the rend in the ship. SSgt Castro, a tether trailing off her back toward the airlock, was standing with a sealant hose in her hands. Sealant was spewing from the hose, splattering against the ship's wound. SSgt Castro was standing just far enough away that the sealant was solidifying nanoseconds after making contact with the ship's hull. She was slowly moving the nozzle back and forth, filling the tear from the bottom up. She was halfway through.

Dewey would have liked to stop and help. Castro was working alone, and that was often a dangerous situation to be in. But she had as much experience as he, and Dewey was operating under a different directive for the moment.

The stairs down were more complicated than going up. When going up, Dewey's deck boots connected to each tread with a toe tip. Easier not to slip that way. However, on the way down, it was his heels that made contact with the stair treads. If he wasn't careful, he risked hitting a tread wrong with his heel and losing his footing. So, the seconds that it took to go up were tripled on the way down. This was exacerbated by the fact that Dewey had to go down one more level to the conduit-walled corridor that led aft as far as was possible.

Dewey stumbled once, stepping on the last tread, righted himself, and began an ungainly lope to the engineering stations.

He arrived winded and then had to go up a complete spiral of stairs before stepping out into the machining room. Everyone was there. Pfc Sutton, Cpl Alexander were at several remote stations, studying the monitors and harassing the keyboards below them. On the deck, Sgt Allen was still being tended to by MedTech Chambers. No one was in the engine rooms, and the airlock was closed.

"What happened?" Dewey walked to the airlock, and looked

through the porthole, though all he could see was the airlock chamber.

"The last explosion tore a hole in the side," said Cpl Alexander. She was still focused on her work at the station.

"Right." Dewey went back to where Chambers was monitoring Sgt Allen's vitals. "How's he looking?"

"Took a solid blow to the head," said MedTech Chambers. "Skull is fractured. I'm worried about swelling around the brain."

"He should be in medical?"

"Yes, Lieutenant." She waved at Cpl Alexander, and Pfc Sutton. "But getting the engines online is priority."

"You're right, Chambers. Stand by." Dewey tapped his comm. "Sgt Parks? You copy?"

"Go, Lt Tyler."

"I need a fireteam to the machine room. On the double."

"You got it, Lieutenant."

Dewey tapped the comm. He smiled briefly at a relieved looking medtech. "Help's coming, Chambers."

"Thank you, Lt Tyler."

Dewey nodded and tromped over to Cpl Alexander. "What do we have, Corporal?"

Cpl Alexander's face was sweating as she leaned in to squint at several graphs and meters on the monitor screen.

"It's not as bad as it could be," Cpl Alexander said. "Though all the engines are offline, one is still operable. We had two ready to go before we got hit. So, two engines, if we can get them back online."

"What's that going to take?"

Cpl Alexander stepped back and looked at Dewey. "Someone's going to have to go outside, and switch some connectors."

"No other way?"

"Not that I can see, Lieutenant."

Dewey tapped his comm to reach the bridge.

"Maj Simmons," said the voice on the comm, identifying herself. "What have you got, Lieutenant?"

"We can get two engines up, and running, Major," said Dewey. "But to make that happen, someone has to go outside and plug them in."

"I'm assuming it's a little more complicated than that." There was a chuckle to the major's voice as she spoke.

"A little," said Dewey. He grinned at Cpl Alexander.

"We need those engines, Lt Tyler."

"Yes, we do, Major. We'll get it done."

"Thank you."

The comm link clicked off.

"You can send the schematics to my HUD?" Dewey asked as he moved, walking back to the airlock.

"Wait, Lieutenant," Cpl Alexander said. "You're going to go out there?"

Dewey looked down at his own body, covered in an EVA suit. "I'm the only one dressed for the occasion."

05

As the outer hatch of the airlock opened, Dewey gave the tether an experimental tug. Now was not the time to float away. There'd been some disagreement about him making the walk to fix the few problems that could only be fixed outside. However, as time was an issue, and he was the only one in engineering already wearing an EVA suit, he won.

Calling it a win was a stretch. Dewey had laughed when Cpl Alexander had said the word as she'd conceded. The winner should be the one who got to stay on their bunk and read a book. Of course, with the enemy rushing to bring their engines back online, and get within targeting range, no one in the Shnel Shnek was kicking back on their bunk. Everyone was alert and ready to do what was needed to ensure they weren't the loser in this altercation.

And that was why Dewey had offered to go outside. It didn't hurt that he'd read a lot about the ship's systems. His tablet had taken a hit during a ship boarding four months ago. While he waited for a replacement, thirsting for something to read, he'd had borrowed the ship's systems tablet. There weren't any biographies, histories, or space adventures in it for Dewey to read. It had only been the ship manuals. Dewey had read them all.

Having read them, he could recall what he needed to help him with the task.

Now, the hatch was open, and Dewey stepped outside. He leveraged himself ninety degrees over the lip of the airlock with the help of the handles on the hatch. As his boots touched the ship's exterior, their magnets engaged. Dewey's right foot was yanked to the ship hull. His left quickly followed. Now he stood on the outside of the ship like the surface of a small planet.

"You all right, Lieutenant?"

"All good, Cpl Alexander. Just orienting myself." Dewey turned left and started a labored diagonal path toward the engine cones and the underside of the hull.

"Back, and down," Cpl Alexander said.

"Thank you." Dewey didn't bother to hide the smile in his voice.

"Right. Sorry, Lt Tyler. Let us know if you need anything."

Dewey continued his walk across the ship. The strange thing was that even though he knew, intellectually, that he was walking upside down in comparison to the ship decks, he didn't feel like he was upside down.

He paused at one point and looked in the direction where the A.P. ship was supposed to be. He couldn't see it, which wasn't a surprise. Distance reduced it to a spot as big as the stars serving as a backdrop. If it were to move, he'd notice it, then. If it did move, he'd know he was in trouble.

Several more steps put Dewey between a stabilizer fin and a cone. Dewey bent at the waist and scanned the surface of the ship. There were dozens of access panels here, and he only needed one, AE-11. Unfortunately, they weren't in order. AE-11 was mixed in with AEE panels, and AO panels. But, with the knowledge pulled from his reading, it took one scan, and he had the panel in his sights.

From a side pocket on his suit, Dewey pulled out a T-shaped tool. It was an oversized key that opened the panels. An easy task. Well, maybe when the ship was newly constructed. But that was longer ago than Dewey had been alive. Rare was the need to come out here and open hatches. Most of those times occurred in Hospitaller shipyards with hydraulic assisted tools. This took a little more work, which Dewey had expected.

"Lt Tyler?"

"Hey, Maj Simmons." Dewey's voice was punctuated with a grunt as he leaned away from the key, both hands on it, trying to get it to turn.

"Need some help?" Fortunately, there was humor in the major's voice, so Dewey knew she wasn't nervous or impatient. Not yet, anyway.

"No, no, Major, I'm doing great." He grunted and pulled harder. He thought he felt the key move a micrometer or two. "Just need a little more pull. Ah!"

The key turned. It turned surprisingly easy after all the initial resistance. The sudden release of tension threw Dewey off balance, and he fell backward. One of his boots disengaged from the deck, and he half-floated parallel to the ship's hull. Fortunately, the key was stuck in the panel it had unlocked, and the panel had its own tether, so they didn't float away, either.

"Lt Tyler?" This time there was concern in Maj Simmons's voice. "Everything okay out there?"

Dewey managed to get his other boot to the hull where it latched on. He did an awkward sit-up, bringing himself to a standing position.

"It is now, Major. Panel's open."

"You see the cables, Lieutenant?" asked Cpl Alexander.

"In my sights, Corporal," Dewey said.

Unfortunately, he didn't have magnetic knee pads. If he knelt, and his feet started to pull away from the metal hull, the boots would register his movement as a step, and disengage the magnets. As the two boots didn't communicate with each other, it was possible that both would disengage, and he could float away until the tether reeled him back in. Not only would it be embarrassing, but it would also be a delay they didn't have time for.

To reach the cables that were behind the hatch, Dewey had to squat. It was not the easiest or most comfortable position in an EVA suit. It could be done, but no one liked doing it for long. So, Dewey quickly uncoupled the orange cable, and moved it over two positions, and connected it to a new socket. He did the same for the green wire, moving it over three positions.

"Cpl Alexander? Check my work?"

"One second, Lt Tyler."

"I'll be here," Dewey said. It raised a chuckle from Alexander as she verified the cable connections. While Dewey waited, he contacted Maj Simmons. "Any news on the A.P. ship, Major?"

"Dead in the water, Lieutenant," said Maj Simmons. "If it weren't for thermal readings, and vibrations on the register, I'd have believed the crew was dead."

"But they're not," said Dewey. "Cpl Alexander?"

"All good, Lt Tyler. We just need to reroute the plasma flow."

Dewey replaced and locked the panel. It went on a lot smoother than it had come off. He stood, and looked around, checking the panels near him. They would serve as guides. "PL-201, where are you?"

"Lieutenant, it's over to your –."

"Right, and about a meter aft," Dewey said. He started the slow march to where the panel waited.

"Sorry, Lt Tyler."

Dewey chuckled. "No apologies necessary, Corporal. We would all do the same thing in your position."

The panel was where Dewey expected to find it. It also came loose with more ease than AE-11 had. Behind the panel was a series of plasma conduits, and valves that changed the flow that served the in-system engines. The valves had to be turned in the correct sequence so as not to block the flow. Not that it would explode right away, but it would explode. At that point, the A.P. attack ship would be the least of their worries.

From memory, from the multiple repetitions uttered by Cpl Alexander, Dewey knew to turn the right green valve, the left red, then the right green again before the right red valve. The light diodes stayed green, which meant that they still had the A.P. attack ship as a priority for worry.

"All done," said Dewey. He placed the panel and turned the key to lock it in place.

"Nice work, Lt Tyler," said Cpl Alexander.

Before Dewey could acknowledge the praise, MSgt Roberson interrupted.

"You might want to hurry inside, Lieutenant," Roberson said. "The

A.P. have an engine online and are moving. We suspect to get into target-lock range while they bring another engine online."

Dewey looked up and out into space. Nope, he still couldn't see the attack ship. "I'm on my way. Maybe we should fire up the engines?"

"You're too close, Lt Tyler," said Cpl Alexander. "The vibrations could shake you loose."

"I'll hurry, and I have a tether," said Dewey. "Now is not the time for niceties."

"Lt Tyler has a point," Maj Simmons said over the comm. "Get the engines online, Alexander. Lieutenant? Get inside."

"Yes, Major," answered Dewey and Cpl Alexander simultaneously.

Dewey turned and started his labored march back to the airlock. Halfway to his goal, he felt the vibration of the in-system engines starting up. They rattled his deck boots with each step until they quickly reached maximum power. At full speed under two engines, they could still reach jump speed.

"Lt Tyler?"

"Yes, Major?" Dewey was five meters from the airlock, walking sideways to the ship's orientation.

"The A.P. have two engines online, now. It's a race, and they have a head start."

"Almost in, Major. Start running."

"Hang on, Lieutenant."

As there wasn't an atmosphere to push back, Dewey didn't feel the acceleration of the ship as it powered forward, trying to at least keep equal space between the two ships. He continued along his path to the waiting hatch. There, he leveraged himself inside, feeling the twist in his gut as he stepped from the vacuum of space onto the gravity plates. The quick slap of the big button started the cycle of hatches closing, air pressure increasing, hatches opening.

Dewey pulled off his helmet as he stepped past the slow swinging hatch.

"How's it looking?" he asked the waiting Cpl Alexander.

"Oh, it's great," she said. Her face had a sour look. "They have two of their engines online, and they've fired missiles. Again."

"You have it under control here?" Dewey asked. He was already moving toward the hatch that would take him under the aft loading bay. It was a long way to the bridge, and he wasn't getting out of his EVA suit anytime soon.

"Pfc Sutton is on his way back from medical," Cpl Alexander said. "Soon as he gets here, we'll have it all under control."

"If I see him, I'll tell him to hurry."

Dewey bounded along the corridor as best as his deck boots would allow. At the stairwell, there was no more bounding. The boots and suit made taking the steps two at a time an impossibility. Dewey settled for quick-stepping his way up, breathing hard to keep from wearing himself out.

Halfway up, he passed Pfc Sutton. "Cpl Alexander needs you A.S.A.P."

"Thank you, Lieutenant."

Over his own heavy breathing and quickstep, he could hear the receding sounds of Sutton doing the same thing but in the lighter emergency evac suit.

At the top of the stairs, just outside the mess hall, Dewey stopped for several quick breaths. He then started walking through the empty space before upping his movements to a labored trot.

He paused once more outside medical, peeking in to check on the status of Sgt Allen. Two medtechs, Chambers, and Phillips were still working with the sergeant. Medic Izu from the smuggler ship was talking to one of her wounded civilians. Dewey gave her a quick nod when she looked up and then finished his trek to the bridge.

"What do we have left for countermeasures?" Maj Simmons was asking the room. She followed that with a tap on her comm. "Engineering? What do we have for power? Can we get more?"

"Eight countermeasures," answered Sgt Parks.

"A.P. is closing the gap, Major."

"Thank you, Cpl Knight." Maj Simmons turned, and acknowledge Dewey with a quick but severe smile. "They fired their latest salvo too soon. But they're gaining now, Lt Tyler. So if you have any suggestions, please feel free to make them."

"Of course, Major." Dewey sat and strapped himself in. "Have we tried a delay on the countermeasures?"

Maj Simmons sat up straighter, though, to Dewey, that seemed like it should have been impossible.

"Star shine, I should have thought of that." She turned to Dewey. "Not the delay on the countermeasures, that's good, Lieutenant. But what about a delay on several missiles?"

"They'd see them," said MSgt Roberson.

"Not if we did both," Dewey said. "We could launch countermeasures on a delay. The moment they go, we drop several missiles with proximity detectors, and delays for insurance."

"They're within range," said Pfc Fox. "And they're firing."

"Do it, Lt Tyler."

"Yes, Major."

Dewey commed weapons station two. "SSgt Castro, you copy?"

"Go, Lieutenant."

"We need a delay timer on the countermeasures, and proximities on two missiles, and we'd like that ten minutes ago."

SSgt Castro laughed. "Only ten minutes? No problem, Lt Tyler."

"Comm me when they're ready."

"We have two missiles inbound right now," said Maj Simmons.

"Sgt Parks," Dewey said. "Launch two counters. Make sure they're not the ones SSgt Castro is playing with."

"Yes, Lieutenant." Parks turned to fireteam one. "Launch from five and six."

"Launching from five, and six," said Pfc Wong.

"Cpl Knight," Maj Simmons said. "Keep us on a straight line."

"Yes, Major."

Less than a minute later, Dewey's comm beeped. "Timers and proximities employed, Lieutenant,"

"Major? We're ready."

Maj Simmons clapped her hands together, rubbing them vigorously before saying, "Launch the delayed countermeasures, Lieutenant."

Dewey turned and nodded to Sgt Parks. She returned the nod before tapping several keys.

"Countermeasures launched,"

"Countermeasures launched, Major. Missiles?"

"Hold, Lt Tyler."

"Not to be a worrywart," MSgt Roberson said. He leaned forward as he spoke. "But we have two missiles inbound, Major."

"One, Master Sergeant," said Pfc Fox. "The counters blew one."

"So, one inbound. All right. We need to be patient." She looked around the room, nodding at anyone who looked her way. "We may have to take a hit, but this isn't about winning every battle. We need to win the war."

This was the sort of time where Dewey missed being an NCO or a regular. If he'd been a Pfc, he'd be at some station, busy with duties and no time for worry. Like Maj Simmons and MSgt Roberson, all he could do now was wait. And worry.

After several long minutes, Maj Simmons turned halfway toward Dewey. "Missiles now."

Again, Dewey relayed the command with a nod. This time, Sgt Parks sent the missiles before returning an affirmative nod.

"They're away, Major."

"Good, now we –."

The entire ship bucked. Dewey grabbed at the armrests of his chair reflexively. He was strapped in and going nowhere. Someone barked in pain.

"Anyone need a medic?" MSgt Roberson asked.

"Hit my head," said Pfc Boyd. "I'm okay. Just hurt a bit."

"Damage?" asked Maj Simmons. "To the ship, Boyd, not you."

"We took it on the side, Major. Knocked us good, but the hull integrity remains the same."

"They overshot the engines," said MSgt Roberson.

"I think they might have been going for the jump drives," said Dewey.

The jump drives, like the bridge, were buried inside the ship to reduce the chances of damage. Without them, it wouldn't matter how many in-system engines they had, they'd be easier to hunt, and then kill.

"Again!" shouted Cpl Knight.

"Again?" Maj Simmons seemed as confused as Dewey was feeling.

Her words were followed by another shaking of the ship. This time the sound seemed to vibrate through the bones of the ship. The lighting took on an orange flashing tinge to it. Red would have been a hull breach and would have appeared near where the breach was located. Orange was a different matter.

Maj Simmons hit her comm, going ship-wide. "Medical, seal up now. Everyone else, helmets, suit systems engaged." She yanked her own helmet down, sealing it with practiced efficiency. "Knight, tell me what happened."

Dewey commed SSgt Castro while setting his own helmet. "Castro, check on the civilians as soon as your helmet is secure."

"They shadowed their missiles, Major," said Cpl Knight. Her voice was hollow, coming from the helmet speakers "We took out one with the counters, but they must have hidden another one behind it."

"Clever," said Dewey. He completed a seal check of his helmet.

"Agreed," Maj Simmons said. She was out of her seat, checking everyone else's helmets.

Behind Dewey, as he was locking his helmet on, he knew that the hatch to the bridge was closing. Hatches throughout the ship were closing, preserving as much atmosphere as they could. Not that it mattered. With the life support systems disabled, they were dead unless they did something soon.

06

Maj Simmons made a quick tour of the bridge, testing everyone's helmet, Dewey's included. She tapped hers to indicate that he should verify that her seal was good, too. He gave her a thumbs up after a thorough check, which she returned before once again taking her seat. She took a few minutes to scan the data on the large, forward screens, and then the one next to her seat.

On the big screens, the view of open space had been replaced with a schematic of the ship. The one breach that SSgt Castro had been sealing was marked with a large yellow dot. Life systems, which was just forward of the loading bay, and under the medical section, was a larger red dot. The rear section of engineering was also red. The rest of the ship had green dots marking each section, indicating that they still had atmo in those areas.

"MSgt Roberson," said Maj Simmons. "Gather up Cpl Robertson and Pfc Dunn. Take them with you down to life systems, and see what kind of repairs we're going to need."

Roberson started unbuckling himself. "Yes, Major."

Dewey could see him tap the comm on his chest and then began speaking. He couldn't hear because the master sergeant had set a direct link to Robertson and Dunn. Dewey did the same thing, comming Sgt Perry down in the weapons station two.

"This is Sgt Perry."

"Perry, Lt Tyler here," Dewey said. "What's the status on the civilians in the platoon's barracks?"

To Dewey's side, MSgt Roberson had punched a code and was

waiting for the hatch to open. When it did, it was only because there was an equilibrium between the bridge and the corridor beyond.

"I'm there now," Sgt Perry answered. "SSgt Castro and I are checking the suits. They'd be better off in our evac suits, but I don't know if we have time."

The comm clicked, and Pfc Fox's voice overrode all other communications. "Incoming."

"Stand by for further orders," Dewey said to Sgt Perry. He switched comms to speak to the bridge. "What about our countermeasures?"

"We have the one set deployed," Sgt Parks answered from her position at the weapons station.

"Good. Once they go, launch what countermeasures we have left. Do it in stages in case they try the same trick again."

"And fire everything else at them, too," added Maj Simmons. Keep them distracted.

"You heard the major."

"Yes, Lieutenant. Yes, Maj Simmons." Sgt Parks turned back to her fireteams and began passing orders to them.

"Cpl Alexander," said Maj Simmons. "You copy?"

"I copy, Major."

"How soon can we get to jump speed?"

The answer did not come back immediately. Dewey knew that was never a good sign.

"Corporal?"

"Sorry, Major." Again a pause. But then came the bad news. "We aren't going to make jump speed. That last explosion rattled something. We're at eighty percent at best."

"Thank you, Cpl Alexander. Keep me apprised of any changes." Maj Simmons tapped her comm, and then looked in Dewey's general direction, best as the helmet would allow. "No jump. No life support systems. Just another day, eh, Lt Tyler?"

"Must be a Monday, Major."

The comm beeped again. "Maj Simmons? MSgt Roberson here."

"Go, Roberson."

"No go, actually, Major. The Life systems are busted like Marines on shore leave. It'll cycle, but it won't renew, and there's structural damage to the hull. We had to install a portable airlock just to get in."

"So we're just moving the same air around, but it'll slowly get more poisonous. That right, Master Sergeant?"

"Sums it up, Maj Simmons." A muffled cheer whispered through the bridge.

"Stand by, Roberson."

"It worked," Cpl Knight said through the comm. She turned, her grin apparent even through the glass of two helmets. "The A.P. Ship drove right over both missiles. They're down to one engine, and they're venting atmo. We tore a hole in their mid-section."

"So they aren't going anywhere," said Maj Simmons.

"And neither are we," added Dewey. "Plus –."

"No life support," said the major. "Roger that, Lt Tyler. Okay, Knight, push us as far away from the A.P. ship as you can."

"Where to, Major?" asked Cpl Knight.

"Towards the planet," said the major. "What's it called? Wenshen? Make for Wenshen."

"Major?"

"Secure comm, Lt Tyler," said Maj Simmons in response to his query.

Dewey tapped the comm, engaging secure communications.

"Yes, I understand the atmosphere will kill us," Maj Simmons said. There was a slight whistle to her words, a side effect of the security measures. "And if you didn't notice, staying put will also kill us."

"We've fired off a request for aid. We should only have to wait a bit until help shows up. The suit systems can recycle for thirty-six hours, and we still have additional scrubbers for the suits down in the holds."

"Yes, Lieutenant, we do. But I'm not going to sit here and wait. We don't know what messages the A.P. ship might have sent, too. The next ship that comes off of jump might be an A.P. ship. A bigger ship with lots more power for destruction."

"We don't have enough shuttles and emergency pods to get us all down to the surface in one go. Especially if we have to bring supplies."

Dewey could see Maj Simmon's helmet nod. "We won't have to.

Now, you said there was a research facility on Wenshen?"

"Three hundred plus years ago, Maj Simmons. Who knows what kind of corrosion it has undergone since then. There could be nothing but building stumps."

"Or," said the major. She tapped on her seat-side monitor. "Or this."

She ended her short sentence with another tap that pushed a scan of Wenshen onto the screen. Dewey studied it for several moments before he realized what he was seeing. Amongst low shrubbery was a relatively new series of buildings. They were, based on the readings, exactly where the old First Expansion research facility had been. These had a little bit of wear to them, but not three hundred plus year's worth.

"Cpl Robertson ran scans right before you told us about the planet," said Maj Simmons. She was tapping her screen, causing the image on the main screens to zoom in. "As a precaution. What if the A.P. had some sort of base here? Then you said it was uninhabitable."

"And then I was proven wrong," Dewey said. He was still watching the screens. There were four buildings. All of them were low, barely three meters tall. He had a feeling they were just the tips of icebergs.

"Space is uninhabitable, too, Lt Tyler. But we manage out here. And now it looks like someone has been managing down there."

"We've run life scans? Infrared?" Dewey would be surprised if they hadn't.

"Nothing," said Maj Simmons. "There's some indication that there's a power source, but it's either weak or somewhere below the surface."

"The original research buildings had been like silos, buried in the ground, and then connected via a series of tunnels." Dewey accessed the map and overlaid an image of the original structures. They were both covered by the larger of the new buildings. "If they've expanded the surface structures, they've likely done the same below. Do we have evidence of tailings?"

Maj Simmons pulled out on the image. "There are low hills nearby. They're covered with ground foliage that is similar to the surrounding landscape."

"Implies it's been like this for a while."

Maj Simmons nodded as Dewey spoke. She tapped her comm and then said, "Pfc Boyd, tell the lieutenant what else we've found."

Boyd, in his evac suit, had to turn halfway around to see and be seen by Dewey. "There's a breathable atmosphere inside the buildings. Slightly elevated O-two levels, but that could be because no one is there to exhale carbon dioxide."

"So, we have shelter," said Maj Simmons. "And we have breathable air."

"Is it defensible?" Dewey asked.

"Maybe not," admitted the major. "But if it does go deep, then we at least have shelter from an air bombardment."

"If they come by ground, there's no windows," said Dewey, feeling better about the Major's idea. "Just the airlocks, which would create a bottleneck."

"So we'll be able to survive a whole lot longer there than here," said Maj Simmons.

"We can eject an escape pod with a transponder," added Dewey. "It would allow for a relay and a beacon."

"Won't the A.P. just knock it out?" asked Sgt Parks from her position at the weapons station.

"We can move it, send it around the planet," said Cpl Knight. "I can program it to go, and return to stationary after it starts to receive data from us or from another Hospitaller ship."

"Great idea," said Maj Simmons. She tapped her comm. "Pfc Dunn, to the bridge."

"On my way, Major."

Speaking to Cpl Knight again, Maj Simmons said, "Soon as Dunn gets here, put her on nav, and you get to work on the pod. The rest of us will stay alive and away from the A.P. ship until then.

In the hours it took to reach Wenshen, the hull breach in life systems had been plugged. Air had been cycled through to occupied areas. Other areas, like the loading bays, and officers' quarters, had been sealed off, and the air pulled from there. Dewey now had his helmet off, but hanging by a lanyard. The helmet banged against his thigh as he made his way down the stairs to the Response Platoon quarters.

SSgt Castro was waiting when he arrived.

"Everyone's alive down here, Lieutenant." She saluted as she spoke.

Dewey returned the salute and looked around. Most of the civilians were still strapped in. A few of them, like SSgt Castro and one of the fireteams from second squad, were moving around, passing out emergency rations and water pouches.

"What news, Lieutenant?"

Dewey located the voice. It was Capt Augias Aunztequi. He was huddled near a group of three other members of his crew.

"We've taken some damage," Dewey said as he approached. "So has the A.P. ship. No one's going anywhere anytime soon."

"We're derelict?" This was the engineer, Aurrano.

"We have some power. So do the A.P."

"We going to chase each other around the system?" asked SSgt Castro. She had a grin on her face as if to imply she thought that would be great fun.

"That might have been possible before we lost our life systems. We're running on fumes, literally. So, no. No playing cat and mouse out here. We're going down to the surface of Wenshen."

In the pause that followed the information, Dewey couldn't miss the looks that passed between Capt Aunztequi, Engineer Aurrano, and the other two smugglers. He couldn't determine what it meant, but he couldn't miss that they were passing some sort of message in those looks.

"If you're worried about the atmosphere," Dewey said, doubting that was their concern but playing as if that would be the most natural worry, "we've got a solution."

"What kind of solution?" asked one of the other smugglers near Capt Aunztequi. "That atmosphere is supposed to be corrosive."

"Been there?" Dewey asked. He was used to mastering his emotions as an officer and as a Hospitaller. Keeping calm was always effective when dealing with the innocent battered by war.

"What? No," said the same person. "But we do – did – have a

database on our ship, too."

Dewey chose not to mention that their database didn't have that information. He had provided it at the request of Maj Simmons. It might have been there, but finding it would have taken longer than the few minutes it took Dewey to recall. A legal civilian database would have just said uninhabitable, and left it for smart people to stay away.

"There are some old buildings on the surface," said Dewey, feeding them a sliver of information. "They have sublevels. We believe they may still hold breathable air."

"And if they don't?"

"We'll improvise," said SSgt Castro.

"So, we still have a couple more hours of approach," Dewey said, cutting off any chance for further conversation. He had a lot to think about. More than when he'd come down the stairs. "We'll let you know so you can buckle in and re-secure your helmets. SSgt Castro? I need you upstairs."

Dewey left after a quick check on second squad at weapons station two. There were no more missiles or countermeasures to fire, but they could monitor the A.P. ship from here until there were more important things for them to do. SSgt Castro followed him up the stairs. She was experienced enough to know not to say anything until in the mess hall, and even then, she kept it to a whisper.

"Something going on, Lieutenant?"

"Not sure, Castro," Dewey said. "There's something about that smuggler crew. Keep them together, but keep an eye on them at all times. If you can arm yourself without drawing attention, do that, too."

"Will do, Lt Tyler. Anything else?"

"Cross your fingers?"

Castro laughed, saluted, did an about-face, and went back down to the platoon's quarters. Dewey waited for a second, letting his thoughts percolate before continuing forward to the bridge. He stopped at medical along the way. They'd unsealed their hatch, but everyone inside was still dressed in emergency evac suits.

"MedTech Phillips? How are things in here?"

"Good, and bad, Lieutenant," Phillips said. "Sgt Allen will be fine. He has a concussion and a stubborn attitude. I've had to give him some meds just to keep him from trying to kill himself getting back to engineering. He's sleeping. We're monitoring him."

"Is that the good or bad?"

"The good." MedTech Phillips pointed to where the civilian medic, Añua Izu, was taking vitals of one of the smugglers injured when their ship was attacked. The other injured smuggler was missing. "The other smuggler died. Internal injuries, probably a brain hemorrhage based on the location of the wounds. We put him in the cooler for now."

"Right," said Dewey. He moved closer to Phillips, lowering his voice as he spoke. "Keep a close eye on them. Something's not lining up right with them."

MedTech Phillips looked to the smugglers, and back to Dewey. He gave a shallow nod of understanding. "I'll let you know if I learn anything, Lt Tyler."

"Keep us apprised of Sgt Allen, too. Let me know if I have to come back here and order him to get better."

Dewey left and made his way to the bridge. On the main screens, they'd put up the exterior view. Most of it was filled with the curvature of Wenshen, slowly rotating as they moved in orbit around it. Their position was indicated on the far left screen. One hundred twenty kilometers above the surface and getting closer with each second.

"How's everyone?" Maj Simmons asked.

"We lost one of the injured Smugglers. Sgt Allen thinks he's got super regenerative powers."

The major laughed. "Of course he does."

"Also, Major, I think there's something not quite right with the smugglers."

"They're smugglers," said Maj Simmons.

Dewey nodded agreement. "However," he said, "I think it's more than just about them being smugglers. They seem to know a few things about Wenshen."

"Do they?" Maj Simmons pursed her lips and nodded. "Well, this adventure just keeps getting more interesting."

"It's about to get even more interesting," said Pfc Dunn at navigation.

"It's not time to enter atmo," said Maj Simmons. "So, what else is it?"

"The A.P. ship, Major. They have power, and they are on an intercept with our trajectory." Dunn pointed up at the main screen. A green dotted line and a red dotted line appeared on the screen. They intersected at a point just above the outer layers of Wenshen's atmosphere.

"I think they're going to try and ram us," said PFC Dunn.

07

Both ships were moving slow, relative to their capabilities. Each was powered by a single in-system engine operating at less than a hundred percent thrust. Dewey examined both trajectories. They had time. Now the only question was –.

"How much time, Dunn?" asked Maj Simmons.

"They're picking up speed, Major. I think they might be getting power from a second engine. So, twenty-two to thirty minutes, depending on how their engines hold up."

"And our engines?" Maj Simmons tapped the comm. "Cpl Alexander? How's the propulsion situation going?"

Cpl Alexander commed back immediately. Almost as if she'd been expecting the call. "One engine, eighty-seven percent. Sorry, Major."

"No sorry needed, Corporal. Keep doing your best." The major tapped the comm, closing it. "Dunn, plot as direct a course as possible to those buildings. Update it every minute, and prepare to execute on my command."

"Yes, Major." Dunn hunched over the nav station, her hands moving quickly between keyboard, monitor screen, and several hardwired buttons along the top edge of the station.

"We're taking the entire ship into atmo?" asked Dewey. He knew it could be done. It had been done on more than one occasion. But it was a one-way trip. There'd be no getting the ship off the planet once down, even on one with a friendly atmosphere, and all in-system engines at a hundred percent. Dewey half-smiled at the thought of tilting the ship up on its backend. Maybe then it would launch.

"Something amusing, Lt Tyler? We could all use something to cheer us up."

"No, Major. Just considering options to get us back off the planet."

The major smiled and nodded. "Right. I was thinking a trébuchet."

Dewey laughed. It was short. "I didn't have anything that elaborate in mind, Maj Simmons."

"That's why I'm in charge." She barked a short laugh at her own joke and turned forward. "Dunn? You got it worked out?"

"Yes, Major," said Dunn as she sat back in her seat. The palms of her hands were pressed against the edge of the station. "Though, the longer we wait, the steeper the descent. We'll be off-target more, too."

"Noted." Again, Maj Simmons tapped the comm. This time it was ship-wide. "Attention Hospitallers, and passengers. Very soon, we'll be taking the Shnel Shnek into the atmosphere of the planet Wenshen. So if you haven't gone to the bathroom, you're about out of time. Fifteen minutes, and you need to be suited and secured. This will be a bumpy ride."

As she ended the comm, Cpl Knight returned to the bridge. "Escape pod is ready, Major."

"Good, take your position at Nav. Pfc Dunn will fill you in."

Cpl Knight joined Dunn, their heads tilted toward each other while Dunn quickly explained the situation.

"How long do you think we'll have in our suits?" Maj Simmons asked Dewey. "Once we're on the surface. How long?"

"I can't say, exactly, Major," said Dewey. "The information about the atmo wasn't detailed. The metal may oxidize. The helmet plex may start to corrode, limiting vision. As to how it will affect the suit gaskets and the material? Time will tell."

"So, first we have to get there. Then we have to just wait and see."

"Sounds about right, Major."

"Sounds like another day in the Orphan Corps."

Ten minutes passed, and Cpl Knight turned to Maj Simmons with an update.

"The A.P. have found a way to get more power to their second engine, Major. Intercept is five to seven minutes."

"Thank you, Corporal. Lock in the course for seven minutes from now." Maj Simmons tapped the ship-wide comm. "Change of plans people. You need to be suited and secured immediately. No more trips to the potty."

"Six minutes," said Cpl Knight.

"The suspense is killing me, Major."

Dewey looked over his shoulder. MSgt Roberson had entered the bridge, and moving quickly, even for someone in an emergency evac suit.

"Oh, it won't be the suspense that kills you, Master Sergeant," said the major.

While they waited down the next five minutes, Dewey did a comm check-in with SSgt Castro and Sgt Perry. The smugglers, though nervous, and a bit freaked out by the actions of the Hospitaller C.O., were tucked in and ready for the show. Like the major, SSgt Castro seemed to be taking all of it with great calm, and a little bit of humor.

"I've been in an emergency ship landing before, Lieutenant," Castro had said just as Cpl Knight marked one minute to insertion. "A light cruiser, though. So this'll be like eating cake on Founders' day."

Dewey had his doubts it would be that easy.

"Time, Major."

"Launch the evac pod, Cpl Knight."

There was a pause, and then Knight said, "Pod away."

"Very good, Cpl Knight. Takes us down. Try not to break anything."

There wasn't much to feel, with everything oriented on the ship's gravity. The only evidence of a sudden and sharp change in angle was on the view screens. Where the planet had been a curve of greenish-yellow at the bottom, it suddenly welled up, filling the view, sometimes tilting to either side before coming back on an even plane.

"A.P. have changed course, too," said Pfc Dunn. She snorted a laugh. "Nope, not enough."

"And?" asked Maj Simmons.

"They missed, Major," said Pfc Dunn. "They're altering course, but it'll take too long to come around and try for us again."

"Strange that they would sacrifice themselves to stop us," said MSgt Roberson. "They have to know our chances of survival on the planet are slim."

The ship began to vibrate noticeably.

"Unless what they don't want is for us to even reach the surface," said Dewey. The actions of the A.P. had seemed extreme to him from the beginning.

Even though the conversation was taking place through the helmet comms, Maj Simmons leaned in Dewey's direction as if listening to him without helmets. "So, you think the goal was to keep us from reaching the planet?"

The vibration of the ship began to rattle the interior more. The helmets dampened exterior sounds. The vibrations could be seen and felt more than they were heard.

"I think that's the goal now," Dewey said. He realized he was clenching the arms of his seat and forced himself to relax. "Before, I would have suspected that they just didn't want anyone to know anyone was here in the system. Now I wonder if the A.P. ship even followed the smugglers here. Maybe they were already here when the smugglers arrived and didn't want them to leave once they were."

"Sounds kind of paranoid," said MSgt Roberson.

Dewey could see beads of sweat on the master sergeant's forehead. He was nervous, too, but not comming that energy to the ship's crew.

"A bit of paranoia has kept the Hospitallers safe for centuries," said Maj Simmons. "Cpl Knight, how we looking?"

"Heating up, Major," said the corporal. "But the angle is good, and nothing's fallen off."

"Yet," said Pfc Dunn. Apparently, she hadn't realized she was on the comm, too, because she followed up with, "Sorry, Maj Simmons."

"No harm, Dunn. It was my feeling, too."

The ship continued to rattle. Dewey watched the world rolling toward them as they pushed further into the atmosphere, reaching for the surface. A glance to the far right screen showed their trajectory. They were coming down in an arc that ended with their path grazing the planet.

"Um, Major?"

"Yes, Lt Tyler?" The major had a sturdy grip on her seat's armrests.

"How do we stop? We don't have reverse thrusters strong enough to stop us. Not on a planet."

"Friction, Lieutenant. Friction."

"Yes, Major." So they would be skidding to a stop. Hopefully, Dunn had found a nice flat place to put the ship down. And hopefully, it didn't have a precipice at the end. That would certainly put the wrong end of the ship facing up.

For the next fifteen minutes, minus updates from Pfc Dunn, and Cpl Knight, the bridge was quiet. The ship itself vibrated a little more than Dewey was used to, and there were occasional drops that happened suddenly, and without warning. They were always followed by Dunn or Knight quietly saying, 'Sorry, Major.' Dewey was glad the Major had insisted everyone was buckled in for the ride.

On the screen, what had been just a ball of greenish-yellow had begun to reveal details. Dewey was surprised to see what looked like forests and bodies of water. Though, based on the atmosphere's high pH, he wouldn't recommend swimming or even climbing a tree. Nothing on the planet was going to be safe to make contact with. Hopefully, they would have better luck underground. If not, if help didn't arrive, the end was going to be incredibly uncomfortable.

Another ten minutes, and Cpl Knight spoke, but with more than just an apology for hitting an air pocket. "On approach, Major."

"Ship still holding together?"

"Nothing's fallen off, yet," said MSgt Roberson. "Ship integrity is down to eighty-five percent, Maj Simmons. If we don't land soon, something might fall off."

Maj Simmons laughed. "I have a feeling when we land, a whole bunch is going to fall off. Don't forget, not only do we not have reverse thrusters capable of slowing us down, we don't wheels, either. Gravity, friction, we're going to have a smooth bottom by the time we're done."

As if to confirm the major's proclamation, the ship began to rattle a little harder. Somewhere, something clattered to the deck and slid for several seconds.

Dewey's comm pinged. He tapped it. "Lt Tyler."

"Lieutenant. Castro here. How are things on the bridge?"

"Shakey," said Dewey. "How are the civilians?"

"Nervous. I've had to clean out a couple helmets."

"Wait. Are you unbuckled, Staff Sergeant?"

"Yes, Lieutenant," said SSgt Castro. "But I overrode the controls on my deck boots. I might dislocate a knee, but I won't be bouncing off the ceiling or walls."

Vomit in an evac helmet wasn't anything pleasant. Very few people knew Dewey spoke from experience, and there wasn't any way he was going to admit that to anyone. The worst part was that if the bile got into the suit's recycling system, it could clog water and air filters. Then, if help wasn't obtained quickly, a person got to asphyxiate on their own refuse. A painful and smelly way to go.

"Right, SSgt Castro. But let's keep that to a minimum. Buckle up every chance you get."

"Will do, Lt Tyler. Will do." The comm clicked and went silent.

Dewey took the opportunity to check on medical. Sgt Allen was holding up okay. MedTech Phillips had to threaten the civilian medic because she'd refused to buckle in while attending her living patient. After the first air pocket, the medic had thanked Phillips for demanding she buckle in.

So, everyone in medical was holding on. The civilians, and Response Platoon, except for a few puke-painted helmets, were doing okay. Dewey commed engineering.

"Cpl Alexander? You two okay back there?"

"Doing okay, Lieutenant. We're watching the engines. The second we get the command, we'll shut them down. Not that there's a lot of thrust to shut down."

The conversation was interrupted by Maj Simmons on general comm.

"Minutes, people. We're coming in hot, and a little faster than expected. Cpl Alexander, cut engines. Everyone else, clench up, it's going to be rough."

Dewey double-checked his restraints. He looked across the bridge to the squad at the weapons station. Sgt Parks flashed a thumbs up. They were ready. On the screens, the landscape was flashing by. It was just like a simulator. Something that Dewey had hundreds of hours of training in. Likely Dunn and Knight had the same, if not more.

Greenery flashed by on the screen. A narrow river undulated along before disappearing from view. Dewey thought he saw the buildings they were going to attempt to retreat to, but his attention was interrupted.

"Contact!" Cpl Knight's voice was sharp as it came through the helmet speakers.

Not a nano-second after the warning, the ship slammed down. Dewey felt himself float inside his restraints before he was then shoved back into his seat. The process repeated several times and then settled. On the center screen, there was a spray of debris flowing up. The other screens had switched to data, which likely meant that they had lost the exterior cams on the forward port and starboard sides.

Back on the center screen, the world began to pan left. The ship was starting to turn even as it continued sliding forward. Dewey had a momentary thought that the ship might flip. Though, with its size, and weight, if it did, that was likely the end of everyone on board.

"Knight?"

"Slowing, Major," Knight said. "Slowing."

Everyone was thrown sideways, held in place by their restraints. Then, they were all rocked halfway back the other way. When the motions stopped, they were all sitting at a slight angle.

"And stopped, Maj Simmons."

"Thank you, Cpl Knight. Pfc Dunn." Maj Simmons looked around. "Anyone want to do that again?"

MSgt Roberson laughed. He sounded relieved to still be alive. "I'll pass, Major."

"Pity, Master Sergeant. I think Knight and Dunn were just getting the hang of it. What's the ship's status?"

MSgt Roberson began tapping the screen at his seat.

"I know we could do better with one more go," said Pfc Dunn.

Her comment earned a general round of laughter from the bridge.

"Thank you, Dunn, but I think MSgt Roberson is right. Once is probably enough."

"Seventy percent integrity," MSgt Roberson said. "The aft loading bay is damaged and losing atmo. Forward seems to be in about the same condition."

"Living quarters?"

A quick pause, and then the master sergeant responded. "Except for Life Systems, which seems to have taken more abuse, all other areas are at ninety-five to ninety-nine percent."

"Thank you, Master Sergeant." Maj Simmons tapped the comm to open a connection to the entire ship. "Hospitallers. Guests. Welcome to Wenshen."

08

"Lt Tyler," Maj Simmons said. "You want to do a visual, please? See how everyone's doing?"

"On it, Major." Dewey freed himself from his chair and stood. Even though he could see them from where he stood, Dewey commed Sgt Parks.

Sgt Parks looked in Dewey's direction as she answered. "We're all good here, Lieutenant. All the controls went offline with first contact on the planet. I'd say all the ship's weapons systems aren't just down, but gone."

Dewey chuckled. "It'd be a shame, except we don't have any more missiles to fire."

"Almost like we planned it that way, Lt Tyler."

"Almost." Dewey ended the call and started off the bridge. He had to stop and open each hatch, shutting them once through before proceeding.

Medical was first. The space looked a bit like someone had thrown a wild party. Drawers, despite the safety locks, had burst open, unloading their contents across the room. Sgt Allen was still secured to his bunk, his helmet on. A noise attracted Dewey's attention, and he followed it to find MedTechs Phillips, and Chambers, picking up the debris, and collecting it in a collapsible tote.

"Inspection all ready?" MedTech Phillips said after tapping his suit comm. He was smiling despite the disaster around them.

"A Hospitaller is always ready for inspection," Dewey said. It was a joke because it was the Marines that were obsessed with inspections.

"I knew I'd joined the wrong space force," MedTech Chambers added, after joining in on the comm.

"Too late now. Besides failing inspection, how are we doing here?"

"We're alive," said Phillips. He'd handed the tote to Chambers, and then stood. He looked over at Sgt Allen. "Allen's holding up. He may still be on bed rest by the time we leave, so I'm not sure about that. The smugglers are fine. The one injured still alive is awake but groggy. Probably also will need to remain prone for as long as possible."

Dewey scanned the room. Medic Izu was talking to the civilian on one of the other bunks. Their comms were separate from the Hospitallers'. Dewey was curious if he could override their comm, and listen in, but decided to hold off until it seemed necessary. Finally, he returned to MedTech Phillips.

"If we can get the crawlers out of the loading bays," Dewey said, "We can set up a med station on one of them. I'm not sure how far the crawlers will go, but as long as they work, Sgt Allen and anyone else injured will have a ride."

"Good to know, Lieutenant."

Dewey nodded and then tapped the comm to close the call. He gave a shallow wave to the medic as she looked up, and then he left Medical.

The only things in the mess hall were the tables and seats. All of them were bolted down with the seats having lap straps for when gravity was a problem. So, despite everything that had happened, standing in the middle of the mess hall, it looked like nothing had happened. It was a bit eerie and raised a shudder in Dewey's shoulders. The benign silence and lack of disturbance seemed more alien than the world outside as viewed on the monitors.

The solution was to leave. Dewey passed the rest of the way through the mess hall to the stairwell. Pausing and looking through the observation window, Dewey nodded in appreciation. The view looked exactly like what he would have expected after crashing on an alien planet.

Loading bays, despite their reinforced walls, were a weak point. They were like storage drums that, with enough force provided, could be crushed. There were no cross supports like floors, and interior bulkheads to resist external forces, like missiles, and rockets. And if it weren't for the keels that ran lengthwise across the top and bottom of the ship, the Shnel Shnek would have been severed. The starboard wall of the loading bay was torn open, leaving just the ribs, and exposing the bay to the outside atmosphere. By pressing his helmet against the window, and leaning to the side, Dewey could see a small slice of the landscape.

The other side of the loading bay had fared better. There were a couple tears, and one of the ribs had buckled. It was the kind of damage the ship's crew could have repaired. But no amount of sealant was going to plug the damage to starboard.

Dewey took the stairs slowly, wary of losing his footing. He was concerned about his own safety, but his thoughts were also drifting elsewhere. Two of the crawlers were in the aft loading bay. They were currently being exposed to the acidic atmosphere. It was still not known what kind of damage would be done to the machinery, but sooner than later, they were going to find out. He hoped that the forward bay had been treated more gently.

On the Response Platoon deck, Dewey found most everyone still seated and buckled. SSgt Castro was moving with enough dexterity that Dewey knew her deck boots had their magnets turned off. She and MedTech Moreno were checking civilian suits. One of the other Hospitallers was helping a civilian into a new suit. It looked like it was the smuggler captain, Aunztequi.

Dewey commed SSgt Castro. "What's going on with Capt Aunztequi?"

Castro looked around and nodded when she was looking in Dewey's direction. "Malfunction with his recycler. Same with one of the other smugglers. Crew member Honorata. Her heating element went bonkers, and she about melted."

A suit could cook a person if the systems ran away like that. It could cause a variety of malfunctions, including making it difficult to remove the suit.

"Everyone's okay now?"

"We're finding that out as we speak, Lt Tyler," SSgt Castro said. "We're about halfway through."

"Good," said Dewey. "We'll want to make sure everyone's suit is in top shape. We won't have any room for errors once we're outside."

"We'll have them sealed in tight, Lieutenant."

They exchanged a salute, and Dewey went back to the stairs. He started down to the next level and stopped. Halfway down, the stairwell was crushed.

"MSgt Roberson?" Dewey asked over the comm. "Are we sure about the atmo inside the living quarters? The lower level looks like it took extensive damage."

"Stand by, Lt Tyler."

Dewey waited. While he did, he went down the stairs as far as he could and examined the damage. It looked like some giant had punched the lower level from below, compacting it into a single layer. He wondered if the damage was like this the entire way across the bottom of the ship.

"Lt Tyler," said MSgt Roberson. "I've run the reads and scans three times. There is an atmo leak, but it's small. We're losing about a thousandth of a percent every hour."

"So, we have time?" Dewey didn't bother hiding the amusement in his voice.

"Plenty, Lieutenant. We'll likely die of carbon dioxide poisoning long before we run out of atmo."

The master sergeant's voice was deadpan. Perhaps Dewey should take the situation a little more seriously, but finding humor in bad situations was a Hospitaller trademark. If you can laugh at it, you can deal with it. However, for the moment, maybe MSgt Roberson was right. They had a lot of other things to deal with. Dewey would find the humor later.

He tapped the comm for the major.

"Lt Tyler? How's my ship? Rough landing?"

"Yes, Major, pretty rough. The lower section is crushed. I can't take the tunnel to engineering. Any chance we've heard from them?"

"Nothing," said Maj Simmons. "So you know what that means."

"I do, Major. I do. I'll let you know what I find." Dewey tapped the comm to close the call and then reconnected with SSgt Castro. "Castro, I need a companion. We need to do an EVA to engineering."

The comm clicked. That meant someone else had been brought into the conversation.

"Sgt Perry," said SSgt Castro. "L.T. needs a second for a quick mission to engineering."

"Cpl Mitchell's in EVA gear. I'll send him to you, Lieutenant."

"Thank you, Perry, Castro." Dewey went back up the steps to the Response Platoon quarters. Just next to the stairs was an airlock leading to the aft loading bay. He punched in the code for a systems check. His comm pinged, and he tapped the switch in response.

"Cpl Mitchell reporting, Lieutenant."

The airlock systems check flashed green. Dewey hit the button to open the hatch.

"We have to do a visual on engineering, Mitchell. No one's responding. How do you feel about being the first Hospitaller to walk on the surface of a planet?"

"Can't say it's on my bucket list," said Cpl Mitchell.

"Pencil it in, because here we go." He waved for Mitchell to proceed, and then followed, hitting the cycle button as he crossed the threshold.

The hatch shut, and the system cycled through, removing the good air, and letting in the bad. Dewey wondered if the acidic air was going to play havoc with other ship systems. It would be very inconvenient if the airlock systems were ruined while he was still outside. For now, things worked as designed, and in a short period, the lights winked green. The cycle was complete, and the door to the loading bay opened.

"Do you want me to go first, Lt Tyler?"

Dewey couldn't imagine there was anything to defend against, and Cpl Mitchell wasn't even armed at the moment.

"Do you want to go first?" Dewey asked. "First Hospitaller on a new world?"

Cpl Mitchell laughed. It was short, and a surprise even to Mitchell.

"Sorry, Lieutenant. No, it doesn't matter to me who goes first. I wasn't even thinking about being the first to do something."

"Of course you weren't," Dewey said. "But you can take point. We need to see if the engineering airlock on the other side is working."

"On point. You got it, Lieutenant."

Cpl Mitchell pulled the airlock hatch open and stepped over the threshold lip, stepping into the loading bay. Dewey followed. Crates, containers, and other equipment had been whipped up in a blender of destruction. They had to push several plastic crates aside to clear the beginning of the path. From there, it was a matter of winding through a maze of debris.

At one point, Dewey called Cpl Mitchell to a halt. One of the crawlers was on its side. That meant Dewey could access its systems panels without having to climb up on top. He opened the hatch, and punched in the code to bring systems online, and then set it to perform a system maintenance routine. He shut the hatch and indicated with a pointing finger for Cpl Mitchell to proceed.

In less than a minute, they'd reached the other airlock. Cpl Mitchell was already punching the keypad for access.

"Nothing, Lt Tyler."

Dewey could have double-checked, but there wasn't any reason. There was a dent on the edge of the hatch and the hatch frame of the airlock. Something in the bay had slammed against the wall hard enough that the two were pinched together. They might be able to override the controls, and then pry the hatch open. To do that, they'd have to search for the tools they needed in a bay full of tossed equipment. If Cpl Alexander and Pfc Sutton required medical attention, then enough time was already being wasted.

"We go around," Dewey said. "We can use the aft exterior airlock, assuming it's working. Lead on, Mitchell."

"Yes, Lieutenant."

They wound their way through the disarray, this time working towards the gash in the side of the ship. It was wide enough that they could slip through with little effort or concern about catching their suits on ragged edges. It was also wide enough that they'd never be able to patch it with sealant.

Dewey blinked in the bright yellow-green light of a Wenshen day. It was still a surprise to see that plants thrived here. Even the ground, which Dewey would have expected to be sand, he found loose rock and dirt. Dirt that looked healthy, clearly capable of sustaining life. As he followed Cpl Mitchell toward the back of the ship, Dewey ran an atmospheric check with his suit's systems. If would be funny if the data had been wrong, and this was actually a habitable planet.

While the suit checked atmo, Dewey looked around. Mostly, he watched the ground so as not to trip over something he hadn't paid attention to. But he also scanned the side of the ship. The damage was clear enough to see. But what kept drawing his attention was the ship itself. Dewey had seen many ships from space, observing them from space station observation windows, and ship screens. He'd even walked on them while in space. He'd done that very thing on the Shnel Shnek what seemed like a lifetime ago but was really only just hours.

The size of the ship, even though just a patrol boat, seemed to be magnified now that it had been plopped down on a planet. There was so much shielding, and redundancy that the outer layer was almost as thick as Dewey was tall, and he was of average height. He'd walked to, and boarded atmo ships, and they never felt this large.

"Lieutenant?"

Dewey stopped. "Mitchell?"

"Your head, Lieutenant."

Dewey looked around and then chuckled. He'd almost walked into one of the stubby stabilizer fins. "Thank you, Corporal. Carry on."

"Little bit further, Lt Tyler."

Dewey continued, being more mindful of his situation, something he already thought he was doing. They passed the engine cones, which distracted him for a few steps before he recalled himself to the task of reaching the airlock without falling on his face. He'd dropped behind Cpl Mitchell by several meters. The corporal already had the airlock open by the time he arrived.

"Good work, Cpl Mitchell."

"Punching buttons, Lieutenant," Mitchell said. "So easy a U.P.

Marine could do it."

Dewey laughed and gave the corporal a good-natured push to move him into the airlock. He climbed in after Mitchell and punched the button to start the cycle.

"Cpl Alexander? You copy?" Dewey asked.

The airlock cycled to green.

"Alexander?" Dewey stepped back while Cpl Mitchell pulled the hatch open.

This time, Dewey stepped through first. He looked around, turning with his whole body until he saw Cpl Alexander, and Pfc Sutton, strapped in their chairs, slumped over. There was some debris across the floor, and Dewey was mindful of it as he clumped as quickly as he could to where the two Hospitallers were.

He started with Cpl Alexander, easing her into a sitting position. He tapped the screen on the front of her evac suit and waited for vitals to appear. They came up green. She was alive, just unconscious. No bleeding, likely nothing broken. Dewey assumed she'd been shaken hard enough in the landing that it did a job on her.

"Lt Tyler," Cpl Mitchell said.

Dewey looked over to see that Mitchell had eased Sutton up, too. Pfc Sutton's vitals were red. Blood had seeped from Sutton's nose and dripped onto the face shield of his evac suit. Dewey tapped his comm and waited.

"MSgt Roberson, Lt Tyler."

"Master Sergeant," Dewey said. "We got into engineering. Cpl Alexander looks like she's going to be okay, but we lost Pfc Sutton."

09

Dewey waited for a response from MSgt Roberson and was reaching to check his comm when someone else spoke.

"Tyler? Maj Simmons."

"Yes, Major?"

"I'm sorry to hear about Pfc Sutton."

"Never forgotten," Dewey said.

"Always remembered," said Maj Simmons, and MSgt Roberson. The Major continued, "We'll want to get Cpl Alexander back here to medical. But I need you to run diagnostics. How much power do we have? Can we reroute life systems from engineering up to quarters? Then, we need inventory. What's still usable in the loading bays. And we might want to hurry."

"Is there a problem, Major?"

"Might be," said Maj Simmons. "Cpl Knight believes that the A.P. ship is going to try and land, too. I believe Knight, and considering their willingness to ram us in space, I wouldn't put it past them to try the same thing here. At the moment, we're sitting ducks."

"Understand, Major. We're moving now." Dewey tapped the comm, closing the connection. "Cpl Mitchell, move Sutton into the rear airlock and seal him in. He'll be safe there until we figure out what we're going to do next."

Cpl Mitchell removed the restraints that kept Sutton in his seat. Sutton's body started to fall sideways. Mitchell leaned to grab the escaping body, almost losing his own balance. Dewey helped Mitchell get control of Sutton's body before turning to the control stations, and his duties. He flipped through several windows on a monitor screen until he had the diagnostics and control menu. Once he had it open, he directed the systems to run diagnostics of all systems. He wasn't sure if life systems could be rerouted through all the damage. He started looking through the other systems to see what might be possible.

Dewey was at if for several minutes. He was aware that Cpl Mitchell was hovering on the periphery, waiting for orders.

"There's a stretcher in the med-locker," Dewey said. "Assuming that it wasn't destroyed or the contents thrown about. You know where it's at?"

"I know where it's supposed to be, Lieutenant."

"Start there, then." Dewey returned his focus to the schematics he was looking at. They were active schematics. A touch on a valve could turn off or on the flow of whatever was controlled in those pipes. Breakers could be reset. Temperatures could be controlled.

The engineering life systems were hemorrhaging. Fortunately, Dewey and Cpl Mitchell had not removed their EVA helmets. If they had, they might have accidentally asphyxiated themselves on the oxygen-depleted air. Dewey tapped several valves on the screen, rerouting the flow of oxygen, and controlling access to the scrubbers. He made several attempts to get the air flowing past the loading bay but was ultimately beaten by the damage to the undercarriage, and the loading bay.

After tapping the comm, and contacting Maj Simmons, Dewey brought the bad news. "Sorry, Major. The damage is too much to bypass. If we had a couple days, we might be able to cobble something together."

"I'm not sure we'll have that much time. The trajectory for the A.P. ship is established. They will either hit our ship or come close enough to prove themselves poor neighbors."

"Roger that, Major. We'll bring Cpl Alexander back to medical."

"Soon as you get back inside," Maj Simmons said, "have one of your people help Mitchell. We need to get supplies loaded and start getting people off the ship. Then, if possible, put some distance between us, and whatever it is that the U.P. folk have in mind."

"Right away, Major." The comm ended. Dewey turned to the sounds and vibrations of Cpl Mitchell, coming back into view with the stretcher. "Let's get Cpl Alexander loaded and into the airlock. We've got a lot of work ahead of us."

"On it, Lt Tyler."

It took them ten minutes to get Cpl Alexander into and through the airlock. Her vitals, according to the screen on her suit, indicated that she was holding steady. Breathing regularly. Steady heartbeat. Blood pressure a little low but within norms. Cpl Mitchell lost his footing once during the short trip back around to the opening in the loading bay.

"Sorry, Lieutenant."

"No problem," Dewey said as they prepared to lift the stretcher once more.

"It's just that I thought I saw something move."

Dewey paused and looked in the direction Mitchell had indicated with a helmet nod. There were some low shrubs, several stubby trees, and a waving sea of grass-like plants between everything. The A.P. hadn't landed yet. The buildings were miles away, and they were supposed to be deserted despite their structural upgrades.

"Could have been a tree branch falling," Dewey suggested. Or just your imagination."

"Probably, Lt Tyler."

Dewey didn't think Mitchell sounded like he believed either of the suggested hypotheses. He would pass the observation on to Maj Simmons when he got a chance. Nothing in the books, and papers Dewey had read ever suggested that there was life on Wenshen. That didn't mean there wasn't. It just meant that no one knew or bothered to write it down if they did.

The remainder of the trip was uneventful. Dewey and Mitchell had to lift the stretcher higher several times rather than moving boxes or crates. They were both sweating by the time they got into the airlock.

"Soon as we're through, Cpl Mitchell, grab the rest of your fireteam and get Cpl Alexander to medical. Then hustle back down. We've got a lot of work to do."

The airlock cycled, and the door swung open. Dewey pulled it aside as Cpl Mitchell was speaking over the comm on a closed channel. Within moments, three Hospitallers trotted over to where Cpl Mitchell waited. One of them was in an EVA suit. The other two were in combat evac suits, a step below EVA but ten times better than emergency evac.

"Pardon us, Lt Tyler," said one of the Hospitallers. They'd spoken over a general-local channel that automatically broadcast to anyone within several meters.

"Not a problem, Wallace," Dewey said. He'd recognized the voice as the Hospitaller spoke.

Dewey left them to take care of Cpl Alexander. He found SSgt Castro.

"SSgt Castro," Dewey said over a closed comm. "We need to abandon ship as quickly as possible but take supplies with us."

"Crawlers?" asked SSgt Castro.

"Yes. As many as we can salvage." Dewey poked a thumb over his shoulder. "I put one of the aft loading bay crawlers on diagnostics. We'll want to be alert for any corrosion damage to the crawlers from the start. So, load everything we'll need to survive but spread it out among the crawlers so that if we lose one, or two, we don't have to waste time redistributing equipment."

"There's only one emergency med structure, Lieutenant."

SSgt Castro was referring to an inflatable building that also had an airlock built in. Typically the airlock was there to secure against airborne contaminants. But it could also work here, keeping the poisonous atmosphere out.

"Load it last," said Dewey. "Just in case."

SSgt Castro gave a nod and a salute before turning away. She tapped on her comm plate, and even though Dewey wasn't part of the conversation, he could just hear the muffled bark of her orders through the helmets. Someone tapped him on the shoulder. He turned.

"Captain?"

The smuggler captain was now in one of the ship's emergency evac suit. "What are you planning to do, Lieutenant? We've mostly been kept in the dark here."

"We're trying to keep everyone alive," Dewey said.

"Thank you, I gathered that." The captain's annoyance was clear to Dewey. The captain added, "However, there must be something we can do. To help?"

Dewey smiled. It was short, quick, meant to convey understanding. "Right now, Captain, staying out of the way, though frustrating for those not working, is the best thing you can do. Once we have the gear loaded, your cooperation will be the most helpful thing you can offer."

"You are aware that the atmosphere out there is poisonous? Acidic?"

"I am," Dewey said.

"Then why go out there? Wouldn't it be better to remain here, inside the ship?"

Dewey paused to look around. The rest of the Hospitallers were still tending to the smuggler ship crew. He'd have to pull another fireteam to help with the aft loading bay. Probably pull Sgt Parks, and the fireteam down from the weapons station. Likely they were twiddling their thumbs, and eager to get moving.

"We can't stay here," Dewey finally said. He brought his full attention back to the smuggler captain. "The A.P. ship is looking for us. They tried to ram us in space. They'll likely do the same thing if they see our ship here. Not sure about you, but I don't want to be inside it when they do come."

"So, you're going to head for the old research buildings?"

Dewey didn't miss the quick glance the captain made to his left. Having already looked around, Dewey was aware that several of the captain's crew were sitting there, watching the conversation.

"That was our intention. Unless you have a better idea?"

Too quickly, the captain responded. "No, no. That's probably the best idea. I'll just get out of your way now. Thank you, Lieutenant."

Dewey watched as the captain removed himself, walking with restrained speed to where the other crew waited, leaning forward in an action of anticipation. As he walked away, Dewey tapped his comm.

"Cpl Garnier, where are you?"

"Over here, Lt Tyler."

Dewey scanned, and then saw a waving figure in a combat evac suit. "Got you. Can you see the smuggler captain from where you are? He's at five o'clock to my position."

The figure that had waved stood taller, looking past Dewey. "I have eyes on him, Lieutenant. There a problem?"

"Not sure. But if you can just keep a casual eye on him. Let me know if he does anything that might be a concern down the road."

"You got it, Lieutenant."

Dewey switched comm connections. "Maj Simmons?"

"Go ahead, Lt Tyler."

Dewey tapped the button to open the airlock to the forward loading bay.

"We're loading crawlers now, Major."

"Thank you," the Major said. "Any idea when we can close shop and move out?"

Dewey pressed the big button to cycle the air so he could enter the loading bay. "I'll know for certain in a few minutes, but I would say CSMO in fifty minutes. Longer if the damage is extensive. What's the A.P. up to?"

"They entered atmo about five minutes ago. If they plan on ramming us, they're going to have to hold their glide position for a long time. Cpl Knight thinks they'll fall short by about eight kilometers."

The lights for the completed cycle blinked several times. Dewey tapped the unlock button and gave the opening hatch an assist.

"Cpl Knight's pretty reliable," said Dewey. He stepped through the hatchway into the forward loading bay.

"Yes, she is. So I think we'll have time."

"Unless they're prepared for this kind of situation," said Dewey. He paused to take in the disaster that was the forward loading bay.

Maj Simmons laughed. "You sound as paranoid as I feel."

"I'll take that as a compliment, Major."

"You should. Keep me updated, Lt Tyler." The comm clicked as the connection closed. Dewey looked around until he located SSgt Castro. He made a direct comm connection to her. "SSgt Castro. How are things looking in here?"

As far as the entirety of the loading bay, things looked like a disaster. A storage container had broken free of its deck locks and punched a hole through the starboard side bulkhead just behind the airlock, and loading hatch. Another container that had also lost its grip on the deck had t-boned a third container.

Smaller containers had stayed mostly in place except where one of the crawlers had slid across the bay, cutting a swath like a plow through a field. A few of the plastic crates had burst open, liberally distributing their contents across the open space. It was enough of a mess to give a dorm mother a panic attack if this were an orphan squad dorm room.

"Lt Tyler," SSgt Castro said over the comm. "One of the crawlers rolled, and damaged its electronics, and pierced a battery. It's not going anywhere. Soon as we get the one on its side back on its tracks, we'll have three good crawlers here."

"What about the aft bay?"

The conversation was stalled by the groaning of metal. The one crawler on its side was slowly reaching the tipping point, helped along by Hospitallers, chains, and ratchet binders. Once past the tipping point, all of the Hospitallers stepped back, giving the crawler space as it slammed down onto its tracks, sending a vibration through the deck.

"Aft bay? Both crawlers are good. We just need to get that one back on its feet. Clearly, we have the experience."

"Sounds good." Dewey paused and took a breath. "Maj Simmons wants us to close shop on the double, Staff Sergeant. How quickly can we get everything loaded that we need? I told the major fifty minutes, about ten minutes ago."

"If we're not too picky, Lieutenant, we can be loaded in thirty. We might not get all the supplies, but we'll have most. If we do a detailed job, it'd take more like ninety minutes."

"Let's not be picky," Dewey said. "I'm going to send Sgt Parks down with her team. She can start in the aft bay. I also want to put the civilians to work. But, we need to keep an eye on them, just to be safe."

"You don't trust them?" SSgt Castro asked. Though, to Dewey, it sounded more like a statement of fact.

"I don't know them," said Dewey. "So I don't trust them. Doesn't help their case that they act a little shifty."

SSgt Castro laughed. "They are smugglers, Lt Tyler."

"Are they?" Dewey asked. "Are we sure about that?"

10

Dewey closed the comm, and with a final visual inspection of the bay, he reentered the airlock. Once the cycle started, he commed Sgt Parks and directed her to the rear loading bay. He gave her the same orders as he'd given SSgt Castro. They'd both been in the Orphan Corps the same number of years, their experience being nearly identical. Parks knew how to handle herself in emergencies. She'd have the aft bay ready to go on time.

The conversation with Sgt Parks lasted longer than the cycling of the airlock. Dewey emerged to find Cpl Garnier near the hatch as it opened. He'd made a direct link comm request.

"Everything okay?"

"Yes, Lieutenant. Saw you were cycling through, so I thought I'd pop over here. The four of them, the smuggler captain, and those crew members have been having a heated discussion. Lots of hand waving and stomping. Actually kind of funny when you can't hear a thing they're saying."

"Thank you, Cpl Garnier." Dewey still had a squad of Hospitallers and all of the civilians to worry about. "Everyone's suited? No more problems with leaks or puke?"

"Far as we can tell," Garnier said. When Dewey looked at him quizzically, he went on. "Some of the civilians don't want us touching their suits. So we had them do their own diagnostic, and then recharge oxygen and water through our suit stations."

"It's almost like they're hiding something," Dewey said. He'd said it with a humorous tone. Still, there was no denying that the civilians, smugglers or not, weren't exactly being open with the Hospitallers. Most smugglers were aware that the Orphan Corps wasn't a policing or military organization. Not in a typical way. Yes, the Orphan Corps was probably the fourth largest military force in the second radial arm of the galaxy. Still, they didn't put military might as their focus. They had at least two other primary responsibilities. Those were to aid and comfort people harmed by war and/or natural disasters. The third responsibility, to protect, was where the guns came into play. Unfortunately, there was more protecting to be done than there used to be.

The thoughts flashed quickly through Dewey's mind, even as he determined what to do next.

"Okay, Cpl Garnier. I'm going to put the civilians to work. We'll let Capt Aunztequi divvy up his people. But wherever he goes, you go. I'll let Perry, and Castro know about your super-secret mission."

"Sounds fun," Cpl Garnier said. He popped a salute and marched away. Dewey assumed it was to position himself in just the right place to keep an eye on the captain and his crew.

Dewey made his way to where Capt Aunztequi was making a lot of hand motions. One of the crew, facing in Dewey's direction, reached out, grabbed the captain's arm, and pointed. The captain said something in their closed comm. Dewey saw his mouth move but heard nothing until the captain tapped his chest plate. Dewey accepted the comm request.

"Everything okay, Captain?" he asked.

"Yes, yes," the captain said. He added a chuckle before adding, "We were just talking about our current adventure."

"Of course. It's about to get more interesting. You said you wanted to help. I believe you said that earlier?"

"Of course." The captain clapped his gloved hands together, rubbing the palms before tapping on his comm once more. The link clicked, informing Dewey that the comm was now shared with others. "What would you like us to do, Lieutenant?"

"We need to load our crawlers, and we need to do it quickly. If you'll split your crew into two groups, send one to the forward bay, one to the aft bay. The NCOs will start putting you to work."

"We'll do that right now."

The smuggler captain turned, but Dewey wasn't finished. "Captain. We are tight for time, so make sure your crew knows to stay on task. If they can't, then they need to step out of the way."

"I'll make sure they know," Capt Aunztequi said. He nodded, and tapped his comm, cutting Dewey out of the rest of the conversation.

Dewey had no idea what was being said now, but the smuggler crew was up and moving, separating into two groups. It did not slip past him that the three people Capt Aunztequi had been having the animated conversation with, joined him in the group moving toward the aft bay. Behind them, Cpl Garnier followed.

Orders were passed to the remaining Hospitallers who also hurried to enter the loading bays. Dewey wasn't worried that things would get done on time. Not with Castro, and Sgt Perry overseeing the task. Now they had to work out how to handle the people in medical. And the A.P. ship, there was no forgetting the A.P. ship.

On the top level, an emergency airlock had been installed between the mess hall and the rest of the spaces forward. It was narrow, and the doors opened outward. Privacy comm booths on space stations were about as roomy. Dewey stepped in and punched the cycle button. He had enough room to turn around as the air was filtered. It was a precautionary set-up, to make sure that the atmosphere here wasn't slowly contaminated with the acidic air that was slowly leaking into the lower areas. Soon enough, they'd have everyone on the other side of the airlocks, outside the ship. Then things would get interesting.

In medical, Sgt Allen was sitting, the bed back lifted to provide support. He looked a little disorientated. Likely, he was surprised to wake up and find himself not only in medical but in a combat evac suit.

"Sgt Allen," Dewey said. He looked past Allen, catching MedTech Phillips's attention. The medtech gave Dewey the okay sign.

"Lt Tyler. Sorry about being out of commission."

"We won't hold it against you. But you may owe Cpl Alexander a few beers."

Sgt Allen looked over to where Cpl Alexander lay on her own med bed, in her evac suit, unconscious. "Pfc Sutton, too, I would imagine," he said.

"Unfortunately, we'll all be denied Pfc Sutton's company in the future."

Sgt Allen paused, his lips pursed. "Never forgotten, Lt Tyler."

"Always remembered. You rest, Sergeant. I'm going to check in with Phillips."

"There might be some brain swelling with Cpl Alexander," MedTech Phillips said once he had a closed comm with Dewey. "Sgt Allen has a mild concussion. I've got him resting, and I've only had to threaten him four times about staying still. He's going to need to ride on a crawler along with Alexander. Even then, the jostling might be too much, especially for Alexander."

"We'll try to take it easy on Cpl Alexander, Phillips."

Dewey spared a quick moment to check in with the other medtechs, assuring himself they were packing the things they thought were most important. Fortunately, there was also a full emergency med crate that came with the med tent.

The medic for the smugglers had her patient stabilized. They wouldn't be walking in the near term, either.

"We'll put all three of the wounded on the same crawler," Dewey told her. "Then you, and MedTech Phillips will ride along to monitor their vitals."

Dewey reported in with Maj Simmons about the same time he received a comm request from SSgt Castro.

"We're all ready, Lt Tyler," the staff sergeant said. "We have the crawlers lined up in both bays, ready to depart. MedTech Phillips has already sent a request for help with the stretchers."

After Dewey confirmed the update with SSgt Castro, he entered the bridge and passed the information on to Maj Simmons.

Simmons stood, stretching left and right, her hands against the small of her back.

"Okay, Cpl Knight," the major said. Let's shut down Shnel Shnek, and button it up. Set the locks. Prepare the party favors."

Several people on the bridge chuckled. The party favors the major referred to had nothing to do with an actual party. Though, it would be a surprise to anyone who tried to force their way into the ship without the proper access codes. It would be a big, explosive surprise with no survivors.

"Starting shutdown procedures now, Major," Cpl Knight said. "Party favors will be active once you enter your code on the way out."

"All right then, people." Maj Simmons set her comm to general broadcast. "Listen up, everyone. We're in a bit of a bind here. There's no getting away from the fact that we are marooned on a planet whose atmosphere will kill us if given a chance. Add to that the A.P. ship still eager to do the same. Add to that a long walk to a series of buildings we know very little about. Things can go wrong, and some likely will. But you're all Hospitallers, and you all know how to handle bad situations. Things didn't go as planned, which we always plan for. I'm going to get as many of us through this as I can. I'd very much like to not have any more names etched on the wall of my office when this is over. That's assuming I'm given an office after this."

"Never forgotten, Hospitallers."

The comm echoed back the words spoken by thirty-one voices. "Always remembered."

"CSMO, people." Maj Simmons turned to Dewey. "See you outside."

"Yes, Major." Dewey left the bridge. He paused at the airlock as three Hospitallers fell out of it. He laughed, as did they. But they were getting through the lock faster. Cpl Mitchell was with them. "Bypass the lock controls on the way out, Corporal. You'll never get the stretcher through otherwise, and there's no need to keep the air pure, now"

When all the Hospitallers who'd come to assist with the injured were through, Dewey used the airlock and passed into the mess hall. It was still ghostly empty. When he reached the Response Teams quarters, they were devoid of life, too, and made more ghostly by the slowly dimming lights. The lumens would be at a quarter of full until the major punched in her code. Then they would go off completely.

One more airlock and Dewey was in the forward loading bay. The three crawlers were lined up, the tops of two of them were blunt-tipped pyramids of equipment. The third one had less than half a load, all of it piled fore and aft with space in the middle for the injured.

"Ready to move out, Staff Sergeant?" Dewey asked.

"Looking forward to stretching my legs, Lieutenant."

"All right, then. Drop the outer hatch, and let's get ready. The wounded will be here in a few minutes."

"On it," SSgt Castro said. She turned, tapping her comm. "Burke, Gonzalez, drop it."

Dewey felt the vibration in the deck as the mechanics that controlled the door began to move. The port side hatch split horizontally in the middle. Part of it went up and back. The bottom part lowered to become a ramp. Except the ramp wasn't moving.

"Pfc Gonzalez?" SSgt Castro asked.

Over by the port side of the bay, a Hospitaller threw their arms upward to identify their location. "I don't know, Staff Sergeant. The retractor cogs might be damaged."

"Pull the pin, Gonzalez. Not like we have to worry about damaging anything."

"You got it."

The figure turned and tapped the Hospitaller next to them and gave a signal. There was a pause, and then the lower section of the door seemed to disappear. The disappearance of the door was immediately followed by a thunderous boom that vibrated up Dewey's legs and rattled his helmet.

"Ready to roll, Lieutenant." SSgt Castro had a face-splitting grin.

"Stand by." Dewey pinged Sgt Parks. "Ready to roll, Sergeant?"

"Ready, Lt Tyler."

Dewey switched to general comm. "Move out."

In his comm, he heard his orders echoed by SSgt Castro and Sgt Parks. He watched as the first two crawlers, bracketed by Hospitallers, and civilians, rolled out of the ship, and onto alien soil. A movement to his right drew his attention away from the mini-exodus. He saw the three stretchers accompanied by laden medtechs and the Hospitallers from the bridge.

"Lt Tyler. Wait for the injured to be loaded. Let me know when you've all disembarked. I'll be over at the forward bay."

"Yes, Major. FYI, we won't be able to close the loading hatch here. We had to pull the pin to get it down."

"Understood. We'll seal this airlock with thermite, and use the code on the other side."

The major spoke directly to MSgt Roberson, who then went back to the airlock as he dug through a pocket on the hip of his evac suit.

Dewey knew that Roberson was pulling out a cylinder that could be pressed into the seal of the airlock as it closed. A remote, broken off the end of the cylinder would cause the thermite to ignite. It would melt the plastic, and metal, fusing the door in place. The airlock would be permanently damaged. Not that it mattered anymore.

Leaving the master sergeant to his duties, Dewey moved to the last crawler to observe, and help if required, the loading and securing of the three injured. MedTech Phillips had a closed comm with the Hospitallers helping to load the three stretchers, so Dewey wasn't able to hear what was happening. But, knowing Phillips, he was being extremely concise in his directions and placement of the stretchers.

It felt to Dewey as if the job was taking longer than necessary. He resisted tapping the comm to inquire. If the injured weren't laid out and secured to MedTech Phillips liking, the concerns and complaints would go for hours.

"Lt Tyler." It was Phillips.

"Ready to go?"

"Yes, Lieutenant."

Dewey tapped the comm, connecting with Pvt Ramirez Foster, who was in charge of the crawler. "Foster? Move out."

"Aye, aye, Lieutenant."

Within seconds of the command and response, the crawler moved forward as smoothly as butter sliding down a warm serving dish. Foster was a genius at crawler controls. That was why he was given charge of the one with the injured.

Commonly, all of the crawlers could be electronically linked to each other, with only one driver needed. The crawlers would follow the exact same path of the crawler in front of them. But, as they might lose some of the crawlers from corrosion, it made more sense to keep them independent with separate drives. If they lost control of the lead crawler, stopping the others would be difficult and dangerous.

The drivers didn't ride on the crawlers either. There wasn't space for a cab. The drivers either used VR and access virtual controls, or, as they were doing here, or they had remotes at the ends of straps hanging around their necks, manipulating manual controls in that manner.

Dewey held back as the medical crawler rolled down the ramp. He turned to verify that everyone was out of the bay. MSgt Roberson had left just as the crawler began moving and touched Wenshen soil. Smoke still snaked up from where the thermite had been ignited in the airlock door. Not seeing anyone, Dewey turned and followed the crawlers as they began the parade toward the buildings hidden over the distant rise.

11

Dewey paused at twenty meters from the ship. He turned to look at it, still impressed by the size of the hull. It always looked smaller in space. Now, sitting in a shallow trench, stunted trees still standing in its vicinity, it looked substantially larger. So many things seemed to combine to generate illusions of size.

"Lt Tyler?"

"Major?"

"Nine o'clock, high," the major said. "You might want to get moving a bit faster if you want to see how this day ends."

Dewey looked left and then scanned up into the sky. A distant dot, trailing smoke, was growing steadily larger. It was the A.P. ship, now in atmo, and on a laser line to where Dewey, or to be more precise, where the Shnel Shnek rested.

"Would running help?" Dewey asked as he turned and began to trot. Wenshen had a gravity one percent greater than standard, which was the setting on the ship's gravity plates. Even if he'd had a lighter gravity, moving would still be slightly cumbersome in the EVA suit. The combat evac suit would have provided a bit more movement, but there hadn't been time to change since the adventure began.

Over the general comm, Dewey heard the major. "Double time, everyone. Quick as you can. We don't want to be near the impact zone."

Ahead of Dewey, the crawler kicked up a brief rooster tail of dirt and rock as it surged forward. He couldn't hear it, but Dewey could well imagine MedTech Phillips growling at Pvt Foster to watch what he was doing with the controls.

Dewey continued his own mobility-challenged trot, keeping up with the crawlers as they hastened away from the scene of imminent destruction. Several times he looked over his right shoulder to catch a quick glimpse of the A.P. ship. Each time he looked, it seemed to double in size. After a third glance, he slowed down and tapped his comm.

"Maj Simmons," he said when the comm connected. "I think it's going to miss."

"Stand by, Lieutenant."

Dewey kept walking, looking over his shoulder more frequently. His observation seemed to be holding up. The A.P. ship didn't have the necessary angle to strike the Shnel Shnek. It was going to miss and miss by a lot.

"Good eye, Lt Tyler," said the major. "Cpl Knight says it's leveling off. Thoughts?"

He had many thoughts but kept it to one for now. "If they were trying to ram our ship to keep us from leaving, they're likely aware we have already left."

"We're not hiding," said Maj Simmons.

"No, Major, we aren't. So they may have revised their plans. If they survive their own landing, they may come looking for us."

The major laughed. "Talk about dedication to a job."

"They act like a bunch of Hospitallers," Dewey said.

"I was thinking they were acting more like Marines," Maj Simmons said. "But I get your point. Keep moving, then, we need to open the distance between them and us, and close the distance between us and the research buildings."

Over general comm, the major made the same suggestion to everyone else. Dewey had gained on the medical crawler. One of the medtechs was standing, braced against the stacks of supplies, watching in the direction behind Dewey.

Dewey didn't have to turn around to know what was going on. The A.P. ship was low enough that it was making its presence known in volume. Even through the helmet, Dewey could hear the deep roar as it passed behind him. He looked left and watched it speed past. He stopped and followed its progress with his eyes. It was on a slow convergence with the ground, much like the Shnel Shnek had done.

In a few more seconds, the ground rumbled and vibrated. Hidden beyond the stunted trees, and rise of the land, the ship had made contact. A billowing cloud of debris shot upwards and then arched out on all sides, showering the ground in the immediate vicinity.

Dewey gave it a few more seconds of observation before he tapped his comm, looking for Cpl Knight.

"Lt Tyler?"

"Hey, Knight. Any chance we have a distance for that A.P. ship?"

"Sort of," Cpl Knight said. "My tablet's acting up, but I have it at eleven point three kliks."

They still had to get out of their ship before they could head off in pursuit. That was assuming the A.P. survived their landing.

"Thanks, Knight." Dewey started to close the comm line and stopped. "Wait, Cpl Knight. You said your tablet is acting up. You have it out? Exposed to planetary atmo?"

"Yes, Lieutenant. Maj Simmons has already pointed that out."

"Do you know how long it's been exposed to the Wenshen environment?"

"Twenty-three minutes. Since I stepped out of the airlock."

"Mark the time when it dies," Dewey said. "And then let me know."

Most of their equipment was either encased in plastic or under a layer of oil. The metal connectors on the outside of Dewey's EVA suit already had visible pitting. Not a lot, but enough to remind him that the atmosphere here wasn't friendly. Knight's tablet, like all the tablets, would work in zero atmosphere. None of them had been designed to stand up to an acidic environment because there'd never been a reason to be in an acidic atmosphere, let alone bring a tablet into one.

Knowing how long the tablet lasted might give them some idea of how long other equipment would last. Equipment like the crawlers.

They continued moving in the direction of the research buildings. Several hours passed before Maj Simmons called for a break. Dewey had walked over to the medical crawler. He was talking to MedTech

Phillips and Sgt Allen when someone started shouting on the emergency comm channel.

"Medic! We need a medic! Hurry, please!"

The civilian medic started to climb off the crawler.

"Hold, Medic Izu," Dewey said. He moved to block her access to the ground.

"That's one of my people!"

"We're aware. Phillips and Chambers are combat trained. They'll go."

Medic Izu stepped back onto the flat top of the crawler. "This isn't combat, Lieutenant. This is an alien world."

"You are half correct," Dewey said. "With the A.P. ship on the ground, it's only a matter of time before this does become a combat situation."

Next to him, Phillips and Chambers had dropped off the side of the crawler and started hustling forward, looking for the emergency. Dewey would have liked to follow, but he realized it was just him, MedTech Moreno, and Izu at the rear of the convoy.

Dewey tapped a direct comm to Moreno. "Keep an eye on Izu," he said. "Make sure she stays on the crawler."

After that, Dewey walked to the back of the crawler and looked around. He did not expect to see the A.P. crew trotting up, prepared to kill. What Dewey was looking at was the lay of the land. The stunted trees all had an umbrella spread of branches and leaves, their trunks barely ten centimeters wide. The bushes were low and flat for the most part. There were orangish fern-like clumps that were the only thing tall enough to hide behind.

Currently, there wasn't a breeze. So, nothing Dewey looked at was moving. Did the place even have wildlife? Seemed unlikely. Not with this kind of atmosphere. Still, better to be over-prepared than not prepared at all. He turned and tapped his comm, looking for SSgt Castro.

"Hey, Lieutenant. Enjoying the stroll?" asked SSgt Castro.

Dewey paused in his response. Phillips and Chambers were hurrying back to the medical crawler. Between them, they were helping a limping civilian. They had a hand width band of emergency suit tape around the left thigh.

"Good day for it," said Dewey as he hurried to meet up with the medtechs, and their patient. "I could use a fireteam for company back here."

"I'll send them."

Dewey tapped the comm, shifting it to connect with MedTech Phillips. "What happened? What do you need?"

Phillips pointed up at the gear on the crawler. "Gray crate, Lieutenant. Need an atmo isolation box."

"Coming right up." Dewey clumped his way up the side of the crawler, his eyes already searching for the gray crate.

On the ground, now joined by the civilian medic, Phillips, and Chambers were helping their patient lie down.

"Should be near the middle," MedTech Phillips said on the comm. "You can open the crate where it is, and slide one out."

"See it. Working on it." Dewey turned the latches and dropped the front of the crate. Stacked neatly inside were four of the isolation boxes, collapsed for storage. He pulled one out and then closed and locked the crate. At the edge of the crawler, he was met by the civilian medic, Izu.

"I can take that." She held one hand out, wiggling her fingers. Her other hand still gripped the ladder rung.

"Phillips?"

MedTech Phillips looked up. His face was barely viewable through the reflection coming off the helmet shield. He nodded. "That's fine, Lt Tyler. I'll let you know if we need anything else."

Dewey passed the flattened box to medic Izu. She took it, and with a quick look behind, she jumped, stumbling to a stop next to Phillips, and Chambers. Her leap hadn't been the best idea. No Hospitaller would have risked falling back and onto the other patient, and medics. Rather than just mark it up to Izu being a civilian, he chose to believe she was hurrying because she was concerned for the safety of her crewmate.

From the top of the crawler, Dewey observed Phillips snapping the isolation box open. Phillips worked with Chambers, and Izu to cut a slit on opposite sides of the box. They slid the patient's leg through, and then pressed the edges of the slits together. The material was self-sealing and also adhered to the patient's evac suit. Small remaining gaps were filled with sealant. A connection was made between the suit and box, allowing the box to be equalized with the atmo and pressure inside the emergency evac suit.

On the other two sides, some gloves currently stuck out, wiggling like arms of an oddly shaped toy. Phillips and Chambers pushed their gloved hands into the box's gloves. They moved forward until they could look down through the clear top. A top that was visible to Dewey from where he stood.

"Lt Tyler? Cpl Chavez reporting with my fireteam."

Dewey reached for his comm as he watched Phillips cut away the suit tape. "Chavez, move your team to the rear. Stay close, but keep a watch. Anything moves or seems odder than odd, let me and SSgt Castro know."

"This whole planet's odd. Will do, Lieutenant."

Dewey switched the comm back to the scene below him. Izu had one hand on the top of the patient's helmet.

"Zeledon? How are you doing?" she asked.

"Okay, I guess." He patted his thigh, just outside of the isolation box. "Burns real bad. Itches like crazy."

"It's a burn," Chambers said. He'd started cutting away the suit material, removing the frayed edging of the tear. "Like a second-degree sunburn from the looks of it."

"How did it happen?" Izu asked.

Zeledon laughed. "I tripped, and as I fell, my leg brushed up against one of the tall plants. The plant, its leaf, did that."

"Wait, you're saying a plant leaf did that? You're sure?"

"That the officer?" Zeledon looked around and seemed to finally focus on Dewey. "Yes, it's true. It took me a few seconds to realize what was happening with the air in my suit, and the burning because I was just looking at the plant. How could a plant do that?"

"We've been flushing his suit's atmo, Lt Tyler, from the moment we slapped the seal on." Phillips talked as he opened a small tube of salve, and squeezed some of it onto the cherry-red burn mark. "But he's likely got a first-degree burn over most of his leg and may have inhaled some of the local atmo. We'll have to monitor him for a while."

"Another guest for the medical crawler," said Maj Simmons

Dewey looked around and spotted Maj Simmons approaching.

"Yes, Major," MedTech Phillips said. "Not a good idea for him to exert himself, and do more damage to his lungs."

They'd now put a patch over the burn, and started on a larger piece for the suit. Chambers had brushed an adhesive around the edges of the enlarged hole. The adhesive would change color in a minute. It was an indicator that the patch could successfully be applied.

"Lieutenant," Maj Simmons said. "Besides the increase in patients, how is everything else looking back here?"

"Quiet, Major. I've brought a fireteam back here as a rear guard. Just in case."

"Right, just in case." The major paused, and appeared to be scanning the area around them. "Good. Let me know when Mr. Zeledon is tucked in for the ride, and we'll get moving again. The closer we get to the buildings when the A.P. strike, the better I'll feel."

"Will do," Dewey said.

"Good work Phillips, Chambers," Maj Simmons said as she turned and marched back to the middle of the convoy. She gave one more command over the general comm as she walked. "Everyone, don't touch the local plant life. Not unless you want to get cut and get a painful burn. You'll walk either way. No more free rides."

Dewey caught several Hospitallers chuckling just before the comm clicked off. Down below, Chamber and Phillips had the suit patch on and were tracing its edge with a UV penlight that would cure the glue and create an impervious seal. After that, it was just a matter of removing the isolation box from around Zeledon's leg and helping him to stand.

"How's it feel?" Izu asked.

"Much better, but I feel itchy all over."

"A mild antihistamine should help with that." MedTech Phillips opened a small case and pulled out a metal vial. He opened a panel on Zeledon's evac suit. There were several slots, and Phillips tucked the vial into the first one. He shut the panel and tapped a permission code into the panel's screen.

Dewey had received a painkiller like that when he was still enlisted. A ship-to-ship boarding where he'd been shot in the leg. The round had gone completely through, in one side, out the other. He'd had a combat suit on at the time. They were self-healing for minor tears, like bullet holes. But that didn't stop the pain. The medic on his team had slapped a vial into the panel on Dewey's chest. An aerosolized painkiller briefly flooded the suit's atmo, and the pain had quickly receded. It was likely that the civilian, Zeledon, was having a similar experience.

"Can you climb up?" Izu was asking Zeledon. Her hand on his arm was directing him to the crawler.

"Yeah, I can climb," said Zeledon. Then, turning to Phillips, "Wow, thanks. That's much better."

"No problem. Just remember that I can only do that a few times, so try and hold off as long as you can before asking for more."

Zeledon climbed the ladder. Dewey waited at the top, just in case he needed help, which he didn't. As the others made their way to the top of the crawler, Dewey crossed to the other side and climbed down. The discussion on the comm turned to getting Zeledon comfortable, so Dewey cut himself out of the conversation.

He walked to the back of the crawler and stood next to Cpl Chavez. Her fireteam, Cruz, Horton, and Hart had marked three equidistant points of a half-circle. They stood facing outward, their assault rifles on their chests, one hand resting on the pistol grip.

"Nothing?" Dewey asked Cpl Chavez.

"So far, L.T."

Dewey tapped the comm and connected with Maj Simmons. "We're ready to move out, Major."

"Let's get going, then."

12

Two more hours of walking, and Dewey began to wonder if the A.P. ship's crew had survived their landing. Of course, Dewey also knew that if he were in charge of the A.P. crew, he would be making a laser line to the research buildings. Rather than chase Maj Simmons, and her people, it would make more sense to cut them off and reduce the chances of them getting into the buildings. But maybe the A.P. thought differently.

Dewey put his musings on pause when something slapped the side of the crawler, and ricocheted away. He hadn't heard anything, though, with the EVA gear on, it was difficult to hear anything. He looked around and started running when he saw Cpl Chavez and another Hospitaller converging on a third Hospitaller who was on the ground, limbs splayed in unintentional angles.

"We're taking fire," Dewey said after hitting the general comm on his chest plate.

"It's Cruz," said Cpl Chavez. She'd rolled Cruz onto her back. Dewey could see the dimple in Cruz's suit, where the sealant had already closed the hole. It was just above the comm plate in Cruz's suit.

Something grazed Dewey's helmet shield, scratching it. Dirt kicked up just past where he and the other Hospitallers were. At least now he had an idea where the firing was coming from.

"Chavez, Horton, bring Cruz around the other side. Hart, pull back. Shoot at anything that even thinks it might move." Over the general comm, Dewey said, "We're taking fire! Port side of the convoy.

MedTech Phillips, deploy ballistic shields to port, and send a medic to the ground, starboard side."

Down the line of crawlers, Dewey saw the rest of the Hospitallers moving for cover.

"I'm sending Moreno down, now," said MedTech Phillips.

Dewey was on the corner of the crawler, just next to Pvt Hart. "See anything, Hart?"

"No, Lieutenant. They might have pulled back." A round smacked the crawler near the corner where Hart was looking. She jerked back. "Nevermind. They're still there."

"Keep a sharp watch. But don't make yourself a target," Dewey said. He gave Hart a clap on the back before turning back to where MedTech Moreno was kneeling next to an unmoving Pfc Cruz.

"Lt Tyler?" The major's voice cut into the comm. "What's your status down there?"

"Taking fire, Major." He paused as Moreno looked up and slowly shook her head, and helmet. "We've lost Pfc Cruz. Everyone else seems okay. Haven't made contact with the enemy."

"Understood," said Maj Simmons. "Taking shots here, too. Not sure if they're trying their best or just stalling. We need a better look at the situation."

"I'll see what I can do, Major." Dewey tapped the comm so he was one-on-one with SSgt Castro. "Castro, did we bring eyes with us?"

Eyes were specialized spheres, developed by the R&D at Hospitaller HQ. They provided visuals from the most basic image up to interactive VR. The more eyes in a situation, the more details were available.

"One case, Lieutenant."

One case was four rows of eight. So, not very many. Ideally, Dewey would have had his teams load the eyes into grenade launchers and fire six to eight of them over the enemy, capturing data to analyze in VR. That was a lot of eyes when they had so few. True, they were retrievable and reusable, but only if they weren't damaged, and they had a chance to gather them back up. None of those options were risks Dewey wanted to take. But there was always another way.

"SSgt Castro," Dewey said. He was moving to the forward end of the crawler. "Did you say you once modified an eye with a flare parachute?"

After a brief laugh, Castro said, "I didn't think anyone remembered my war stories, Lt Tyler. But yes, I did. Want me to show you how it's done?"

"I want you to show two Hospitallers how it's done." Dewey didn't bother to keep the grin suppressed. Castro was one of the most good-natured Hospitallers he'd ever worked with. It didn't hurt that she was good in a firefight. "Set the eyes for full spectrum, and thermal. When they're ready, send one back here, and one to the front. We want a crossfire over the area on the other side of the convoy."

"I'll need fifteen minutes," said SSgt Castro. "Twenty if I can't locate the crates I need."

"You don't fool me, Staff Sergeant. You know where everything is."

"I'll have them ready in twelve, then."

Dewey tapped the comm and closed the line. He turned back to where Pfc Cruz still lay on the ground. Cpl Chavez was sitting next to Cruz's body. Dewey knew what she was going through. This was Chavez's first leadership role. Her first fireteam. She was responsible for them. Cruz was her first loss. If Chavez stayed in the corps after her first six, she'd likely see more. As she moved up, like Dewey had moved up, the numbers seemed to get larger with each increase in rank.

There'd been a time when Dewey wondered if he'd stayed a staff sergeant would there have been fewer deaths? It was a foolish thought, but that was the way of foolish thoughts. They cropped up and never seemed to ever go away.

"Cpl Chavez?" He finally said.

Chavez jumped to her feet. "Yes, Lieutenant?"

"You still have two Hospitallers that require you to lead. Get back to Hart, and make sure she gets the support she needs. Take Pfc Horton with you."

"Yes, Lt Tyler." Chavez turned and looked around. "Pfc Horton? Let's go."

"On your six, Corporal."

They both trotted the short distance to where Hart was watching the corner of the crawler. Several centimeters away, rounds smacked the ground, spitting up puffs of dirt.

"You're not going to give them time to grieve?"

Dewey looked at medic Izu. He tapped his comm so that only she could hear him, and vice-versa. "We're being shot at, Ms. Izu. The enemy isn't going to give pause so we can mourn our dead."

"I was told that Hospitallers don't care about their dead." She sounded defiant and disbelieving all in one roll.

There wasn't time to explain to Izu about Hospitaller tradition, about Orphan Corps tradition. She'd likely never seen the inside of a commanding officer's office. Never seen the one wall they always faced. A wall etched with the names of the tens to thousands who'd died. They reminded every leader in the Hospitallers of the price of their orders.

It was also unlikely that she'd ever been to Denhaag, where the Hospitallers' headquarters stood. Dewey had never been there. But he'd seen the images in history texts of the walkway leading to the main doors. A slab for each year that the Orphan Corps existed lined the walkway. The dead for each year was etched into the slabs. There were only three years where no Hospitaller had died. Instead of slabs engraved with names, benches had been set for those years. The supreme commander of the Hospitaller Orphan Corps walked that path every morning and every evening.

The price paid was never forgotten.

"We mourn in our own ways," Dewey said.

He gave Izu a brief nod, and turned away, unwilling to continue the conversation. Fortunately, a Hospitaller was approaching. In his arms, he carried his weapon with the barrel changed out for grenade launches. One of the significant advances in Hospitaller armaments was the multi-use weapon, the MUW. Barrels could be changed out, receivers and stocks could be changed. All of it focused around the pistol grip and trigger mechanism.

"Pfc Wong," Dewey said. He returned the quick salute offered by

Wong. "You're here with SSgt Castro's magic trick?"

"Yes, I am, Lt Tyler. Where do you want me?"

"See Cpl Chavez. She'll position you."

"On it." Wong dashed around Dewey, and over to where Cpl Chavez turned to acknowledge his presence. Dewey didn't fail to notice the strained look on Chavez's face. However, she greeted Pfc Wong professionally and gave him directions. Dewey felt sure she'd learn to accept the cost of responsibility.

He moved back toward the front edge of the crawler. Several times, in the space between the medical crawler, and the one ahead, dirt kicked up from several A.P. rounds. Through the helmet, he heard the whisper of ricocheted rounds striking the crawlers. At the back edge of the other crawler, another Hospitaller kept watch, taking occasional quick glimpses around the corner.

"Wallace. How you holding up?"

Pfc Eduardo Wallace looked over at Dewey. The grin on the Hospitaller's face was evident. "Been caught in the open a few times, Lt Tyler. Never had the luxury of a thirty-five-ton ballistic shield for cover."

"Keep using it. I'd like to keep as many of us alive as possible."

The grin faltered on Wallace's face. "I got you, Lieutenant. I liked Cruz. She was good people."

Dewey liked to think that all of his people were good people, but understood that they were all individuals, and were each drawn to certain personalities. He kept his philosophical ponderings to himself, saying only, "She was."

Further conversation was interrupted by the comm buzzing for a connection. Dewey tapped it.

"SSgt Castro here, Lieutenant. We're ready to go."

Dewey turned around to see that Wong was several meters back from the crawler but still within its defensive shadow. He was adjusting his aim. Dewey knew that inside his helmet, Wong was receiving data that would put his eye up with the other eye to provide the best coverage of the area.

"When you're ready," Dewey said. He knew he could jump into VR right now. Some people did like the rush of riding the eye as it flew upward. Dewey was okay without it.

"Making it happen," said SSgt Castro.

There was a pause as if the world held its breath, and then Wong rocked back several centimeters as the eye shot out of the barrel. It flew up and over the crawler. Dewey followed blindly, unable to see the actual eye. Seconds later, he shifted his focus several degrees to the right where a small parachute had opened. In his peripheral vision, he saw the second chute.

"Nice work, Staff Sergeant."

"Thank you, Lieutenant. Collecting data now."

Dewey caught Wong's attention and waved him over.

"I'm going into VR, Wong. Make sure I don't fall over or walk into the line of fire."

"Got your back, Lt Tyler."

With a smile of appreciation, Dewey tapped on his chest plate. Controls appeared, glowing in bright colors. In real time, he reached out. In VR, he saw his hands, too, but they were able to manipulate the controls only he could see. He pulled up the data from the two eyes and loaded it.

He was now standing in the air, looking down. The eyes recorded in three hundred sixty degrees. If Dewey looked up, he'd see the parachute. Down, he could see the crawler convoy. He could even see himself, Pfc Wong close behind.

On the other side of the convoy, Dewey looked down on the near-perfect circles of the trees, and the patches of bushes. There were plenty of the ones with razor-sharp leaves. He took a quick look in the direction they were heading. There was a shallow draw between two hills, and then the buildings were just visible. He captured an image and forwarded it to Maj Simmons before turning back to look for the A.P. forces.

In visible light, they were impossible to see. Dewey switched to thermal and found them quickly enough.

"SSgt Castro, you with me in here?"

"Piggybacking, Lt Tyler."

That meant that Dewey had the controls, and Castro was along for the ride.

"How many do you see?" Dewey asked.

"Three, four, and just four. Yep. That's weird."

It was weird because they were taking fire from more than four points. Dewey zoomed in, looking for a signal that would solve the mystery. Smaller thermal signatures. Not humans, but warm rifle barrels.

"You see it?"

"I will, Lieutenant," said SSgt Castro. "Soon as I catch my balance."

The problem with piggybacking was more than just a lack of controls. The person controlling the view knew when the scene was going to shift, turn, or zoom. Anyone else, it was like riding a rollercoaster in a dense fog. It also didn't help that they were working with a shifting image as the eyes slowly fell to the ground.

"Sorry, Castro."

"It's all good. I see they're using remotes."

Dewey nodded, even though no one could see it. "And they left four people here to reload as necessary."

"Left? You think there are more of them," SSgt Castro asked.

He did. But he wanted to be sure.

"Hang on, zooming out, and panning." Dewey pulled back and turned the view forty-five degrees. He changed the settings on the thermal readings.

Anyone on the planet surface would have a suit on. The suits were a lot cooler than a human body. Dewey found the four A.P. bodies because they'd been close to the weapons. And since they'd had to move from one rifle to another, they'd been exerting themselves. It had only been a few degrees above the surrounding temperature, but it had been enough.

Someone walking might not warm their suit by several degrees. But the suit would show some warmth. The eyes were sophisticated enough to show differences in tenths of degrees.

That was all Dewey needed.

"There they are."

"See them." SSgt Castro's voice trailed off for a second and then bounced back. "I count nine, Lieutenant."

Dewey did his own count. "Agreed."

The nine were moving in the same direction as the convoy, but off to port. They'd likely be making for the hills to set up an ambush.

"Moving," Dewey said. He switched the view back to where the four bodies. One of them was moving, stopping at one of the thermal markers for a warm barrel. Dewey reached out and tapped all eight spots. They were now marked with red circles. "SSgt Castro, sixteen grenades. Two to each target. When you're ready."

"On it."

The comm went silent. A moment later, while Dewey kept his eyes on the targets, he felt a hand on his shoulder.

"Wong?"

"Yes, Lieutenant. SSgt Castro wants me to lock and load."

"I'll be fine for now, Pfc Wong. Go blow something up."

The hand left his shoulder, and Dewey was alone. He scanned the view below him, ready to change targets if one of the four A.P. bodies suddenly went somewhere else.

"We're firing, Lieutenant," SSgt Castro's voice said over the comm.

A second later, Dewey felt the light concussion of Wong's grenade launcher next to him. The feel reminded him, and he dimmed the view of the VR. Seven seconds later, poppies of explosions bloomed where the red circles were. The distant sounds of exploding grenades whispered through Dewey's helmet.

When the blooms faded, Dewey brought the VR back to full brightness and zoomed in on the areas still marked with the circles. Everything was colored red but slowly fading as the ground cooled. Dewey was able to identify the rifle barrels, all of them had been knocked out of their original position. Then, he found the bodies.

Dewey counted them twice.

"Three down," he said.

"Maybe the fourth one got spread out," said SSgt Castro.

The grenades were high-powered, but not so much that they could tear a body apart, and fling the pieces everywhere. No, in Dewey's opinion, someone got lucky. He pulled back on the image, catching SSgt Castro by surprise. He scanned right, along the path the other nine A.P. bodies had been moving.

"Found them," Dewey said. He zoomed in, again surprising SSgt Castro. He'd apologize in a few minutes. The thermal image not only showed a body moving slowly, but they were leaving quickly cooling dots on the ground. "Sorry about the movement, Castro. Hopefully, you can see the image? Number four is wounded. I doubt they'll make it to the rest of their people."

Then, as Dewey continued to watch, the thermal image of the body disintegrated. It flew apart in a way similar to what SSgt Castro suggested earlier. Was there other movement? Dewey reached out to adjust the thermal controls. All the imagery went black before he could fine-tune the readings.

"What happened?"

"Eyes failed," SSgt Castro said. "Maybe something to do with the atmosphere."

"All of the other eyes are still sealed?" Dewey didn't want to lose any to the acidic air before he had a chance to use them.

"Safe, and sound, Lieutenant."

"Good. I need to check in with the Major. Get everyone ready to move out." Dewey tapped the comm and raised Maj Simmons. "The attack has been suppressed, Major. Four A.P. dead. Nine others are on the move out ahead of us."

"There's a pass up ahead," Maj Simmons said. "Seem like a good place to set up an ambush?"

"Possible," Dewey said. "Or wait on the other side. Box us in."

"Anything to keep us from reaching the buildings."

"Seems that way, Major."

There was a pause. Dewey imagined that Maj Simmons was doing what he was doing, planning, and calculating their next moves.

"All right. Good work, Lieutenant," the major said. "Let's close the distance to the hills, and then circle up for the night. Tomorrow we'll plan on how to deal with the rest of the A.P. forces."

13

Another two hours and the convoy was stopping. Less because they were in an area large enough and clear enough to circle the crawlers, and more because the civilians were starting to complain. Granted, since the attack by the A.P. ship it had been twelve or so hours filled with adrenaline-pumping situations. The Hospitallers could have continued until it was was dark blue across the sky to where the sun was setting. Maj Simmons chose to find a positive in the moment.

"It's our best guess, but we're halfway to the pass. Depending on resistance, we should be at the buildings in six hours, give or take an hour."

"Best guess, Major?" Dewey asked. It seemed like a vague proclamation.

"Cpl Knight's tablet gave up the flag," Maj Simmons said.

By which she meant it had stopped working. She used the metaphor from the popular capture-the-flag game that all of them grew up playing at the orphanages. Something they played even now when they were stationed at one of the hundreds of Hospitaller bases in the second radial arm of the galaxy.

"That was less than six hours," Dewey said. He'd also checked people's suits. The emergency evac suits were showing signs of pitting, and some of the exposed gaskets looked like they were developing cracks. He'd had his Hospitallers begin spraying the gaskets with a lubricant that he thought might slow the damage from the Wenshen environment.

"It was. We definitely don't want to expose more of our equipment to the atmosphere than we have to."

After the crawlers had been moved to create a protective hexagon, Dewey had the Hospitallers pass out food and water to the civilians before eating their meal. Calling it a meal was an exaggeration as they were nothing more than a paste in a pouch that connected to a tube. A person then squeezed the pouch, forcing the food paste through. Most Hospitallers agreed the flavors weren't bad. When the food pouch was empty, the water pouch was put in its place. This did double duty of washing down the thick paste and cleaning the tube. That way it didn't clog as it dried.

MedTech Phillips insisted the injured remain on the crawler.

"I'll stay with them," he said. "I'll stand guard, too, I just don't want to move them more than necessary."

"Understood," Maj Simmons said. She turned to Dewey. "Can you post a guard close to the medical crawler?"

"I'll make sure there's always someone nearby," said Dewey. Most Hospitallers seemed to be happy being in motion, a stationary position tended to dull the mind.

By the time the sky was dark and dotted with stars, Dewey and SSgt Castro had the watch schedule worked out. Dewey stayed up for the first shift.

One squad was on the perimeter. Cpl Garner's squad. Dewey caught the occasional glimpse of one of them passing the gap between the crawlers. Maj Simmons was talking to MSgt Roberson. Many of the civilians were lying still.

It was unlikely that most of them would sleep right away, if at all. It was an awkward feeling, trying to sleep in an evac suit. No position was comfortable because of the different attachments like the comm plate and oxygen cycler. A person never knew how many hard spots there were on a suit until they tried to lie down in one. There was also the understandable fear that they might suffocate. Some would likely hyperventilate. A small alarm would go off on their suit, usually snapping them out of the fearful moment. If not, a medtech would come and talk and maybe snap a cartridge into the chest plate that would relax the person inside.

Every Hospitaller had gone through evac suit training without even knowing it was happening. At the orphanage where Dewey grew up, they'd taken an excursion to one of the small moons that circled the planet. They'd stayed the night, sleeping out under the stars. It had been fun, and even though the suits were uncomfortable, they'd been young and slept anyway. Children from other orphanages had done variations of the same thing. Some did tethered spacewalks, others toured the outside of space stations. All of it was to teach teamwork and trust. And though no one said it out loud, it was to prepare them should they decide to join the Orphan Corps.

While the civilians struggled to find sleep, Dewey stepped out of the circle of crawlers and made contact with Cpl Garner.

"You think the A.P. folks might try and sneak up on us?" Garner asked. They stood side-by-side, watching outwards.

"Hard to say," said Dewey. "Would depend on how many of them are left."

The memory of the A.P. soldier's heat signature suddenly disintegrating popped up unbidden. He'd forgotten about that. He needed to talk to Maj Simmons about that. The only time he'd seen a signature even close to similar was several years ago. He'd been on a night patrol and was scanning an open meadow. An enemy patrol was passing through when one of them stepped on a landmine. The heat signature of one of the other soldiers had evaporated like mist. A second one had flown apart, three signatures in three directions.

"So we'll just keep watching, and if they do, they'll wish they didn't," Garner said.

Dewey agreed. He was just about to say so when the general comm came on. A gurgling scream pierced Dewey's ears. From his quick observation of Cpl Garner, he'd reacted the same.

"Who's hurt? Who's hurt?" Dewey asked after slapping the comm with his palm. "Medic, rendezvous on the injured."

"Med station!" Dewey recognized MedTech Chambers's voice in spite of the fear it was projecting. "They're attacking the med station!"

Through the comm and the as a whisper through the helmet of his EVA suit, Dewey heard several rifles firing on full automatic.

"Cpl Garner, hold your people in position." Dewey started running as best his EVA suit would allow, around the perimeter toward the medical crawler. Across the general comm, he gave quick orders. "Cpl D. Mitchell. Cpl Fleming. Fireteams to the med crawler. Move now."

Dewey passed Pfc Burke, who was at the ready, the butt of his rifle's stock pressed to his shoulder. He dipped the weapon, pointing the barrel to the ground as Dewey lumbered past. He nodded a quick nod to Burke and continued along the length of the crawler before stumbling to a complete stop. He brought his weapon up into position and pulled the trigger, unloading the entire magazine.

A nightmare had crawled out of the darkness.

One of the creatures turned, appearing to look over the mass of the one Dewey had just shredded with a full magazine. The imagery was akin to an Earth ant if ants were three meters long with a platypus tail. And if the tail was ringed with gleaming white triangles that looked like they would shred anything they brushed against.

Dewey took a step back and pushed the button that released the empty magazine. Somewhere nearby, he could feel more than hear several other weapons also firing on automatic. He didn't look to see who was firing or where. The giant ant, with its tail swinging, was stepping across the one Dewey had already killed. Dewey took another step back and pulled a magazine out of the thigh pocket of his suit. He'd removed the safety cap earlier when they'd been attacked by the A.P. That meant he only had to slip it into the receiver and set the first round. He aimed for the creature's head and pulled the trigger.

Three rounds fired piercing the head of the creature. Then, the rifle jammed.

Without looking away from the stunned ant, Dewey felt along the side of his rifle. He found and pulled the manual set for the rifle. It ejected the jammed round and set the next. Dewey aimed and fired once more. This time, one round and the weapon jammed.

The giant ant had crossed over the dead ant and was moving toward Dewey. He pulled on the manual set again, but he was beginning to wonder if he was going to have to use the rifle as a club. He pulled the trigger. This time he didn't get a single shot. Yes, he was going to have to make a club of it. He detached the strap supports and flipped the rifle, so he had the barrel in his hands.

"I'm on your six, Lt Tyler. Don't hit me."

Dewey moved sideways, toward the crawler. MSgt Roberson stepped past, his rifle braced to his shoulder. He pulled the trigger and held it, unloading the full magazine and disintegrating the creature's head.

"You okay, Lieutenant?"

"I am now. Thank you, Master Sergeant."

"My pleasure." The master sergeant ejected the magazine and loaded another one after removing the safety cap. "I've seen a few strange things through the radial arm, Lt Tyler, but I've never seen the likes of that."

"Neither have I," Dewey said. He ejected the partially used cartridge and inserted a third one. This one still had the safety cap when he pulled it out of his pocket.

"Up here, Lt Tyler, MSgt Roberson." Dewey looked up to see Maj Simmons on the crawler. "You need to see this."

Dewey followed MSgt Roberson to the ladder on the side of the crawler. He gave the dead ant monsters one more look before climbing up to join the other Hospitallers and Civilians. One of the monster ants was dead. It was sprawled out in the middle of the space marked out for those too injured to walk. Around it, there was death. Too much death.

Medic Izu and the civilian who'd suffered the tear in his suit, Zeledon Ayo, were alive. As were MedTech Chambers and Moreno. The other civilian, Sgt Allen, and MedTech Phillips were all dead. Dewey assumed they were all dead. If one of them had escaped, he wouldn't have been able to tell until all the body parts were pieced together.

"Chambers," Maj Simmons said. She was on local comm. Most of the other Hospitallers and every civilian would not hear the conversation. "Tell it again."

"Yes, Major." MedTech Chambers looked across the small massacre and nodded. "Lieutenant, Master Sergeant. We heard a noise. Well,

Phillips said he heard a noise, and he looked over the edge of the crawler. He shouted for us to get back. Then, he started firing down toward the ground. That thing came up over the edge and started swinging its tail. It sliced through Phillips and Sgt Allen before we realized what was happening."

"They saved us," said Medic Izu. "They managed to pull me and Zeledon back before that thing could get us. We would've...."

Her voice trailed off. Even through the helmet face shields, Dewey could see she was pale, and her eyes red-rimmed. Dewey had seen some horrible things during his fourteen years in the Hospitallers. As a private, they used to make him angry. But he adapted, as all Hospitallers did.

"We killed it," Chambers said. "Maybe if we'd figured out sooner what was happening, we could have saved others."

"Chambers, you weren't listening," Maj Simmons said. She pointed at medic Izu. "You save them. That's better than losing everyone. Keep a hold of that."

"Something's approaching!" It was Private Becker from Cpl Garner's fireteam. "Starboard side."

Dewey instinctively looked to the right of forward. There, several Hospitallers were rushing across the open ground in that direction. The civilians were shifting away, guided by Cpl Chavez.

"Fire on sight," ordered Maj Simmons. "Do not let them get near you."

As soon as the major was done, Dewey jumped on the comm. "SSgt Castro? We're going to need more ammo. Everyone on perimeter, hold your ground. Reinforcements will be coming to support your position."

Gunfire vibrated the air as Dewey tapped the comm to close the line. He tapped it again to raise Cpl D. Mitchell. "Mitchell, Take your fireteam to port. Grab ammo on the way."

"Company at nine o'clock!" It was Pfc Shultz on the left side of the convoy circle.

"You need to hurry," Dewey said to Cpl D. Mitchell.

"On it, Lieutenant."

Dewey had a quick glimpse of four Hospitallers running in the direction of Pfc Shultz's location. He looked around at the mess.

"Moreno," Dewey said as he stepped across part of a dismembered body, "help me get this thing over the side."

MedTech Moreno stepped over to where Dewey already had the giant ant by one limb. He was pulling on it and getting very little progress for his efforts until Moreno grabbed a limb on the other side. Together, they dragged the carcass to the edge of the crawler and dumped it to the ground. Dewey paused for a moment. There were a lot of the ant bodies piled across each other. How many more of them were they going to have to deal with? And what else was out there?

"Lieutenant?"

Dewey blinked and stepped back from the edge. "Yes, Moreno?"

"There's more." She pointed past Dewey to where some movement could be seen, pushing past plants that sliced evac suits but did nothing to the giant ants' skin.

"Get ready," Dewey said. He turned and looked for MedTech Chambers. "Chambers. Over here."

"Yes, Lieutenant." Chambers worked her way around the mess that they still had to deal with.

They would get to that, Dewey knew. But first, they would have to respond to the attack that seemed to be slowly surrounding them. Dewey stepped back to the edge, flipping the safety of his rifle off. He aimed, sighting on the head of a giant ant now free from the surrounding bushes and plants. He pulled the trigger and held it until the magazine was empty.

The next several hours were more of the same. There seemed to be an inexhaustible supply of giant ants. As Maj Simmons noted over the comm, they weren't resistant to bullets but seemed unaware of that fact. They were piled three and four high and just deep before they finally stopped attacking. Through the assault, several civilians had offered to help. Three had been given weapons taken from the dead. Others helped by running ammunition to the Hospitallers.

It was the eighth time that Dewey had gone to the inside edge of the crawler to grab and pocket several more cartridges when he realized the air was no longer vibrating with the sound of near-continuous rifle fire. He looked around and noticed that most of the Hospitallers were standing still, rifles hanging from their support straps.

"All clear?" he asked across the general comm. "Fireteams report."

It took several minutes to get all the information. The ants had stopped coming. No one had seen them retreat or wander off. Rather, it felt more like there just hadn't been any more of them to come.

"Everyone, hold your positions," said Maj Simmons. Then, "Lt Tyler, MSsgt Roberson, SSgt Castro. My position, A.S.A.P."

Dewey used local comm to give orders to the Hospitallers on the medical crawler. "Stay sharp. Half at rest, half on watch."

Maj Simmons was waiting for them in the middle of the open space surrounded by the crawlers. The civilians who had huddled in fear had moved away. The other civilians, who'd run ammo through the attack, were sprawled on their backs.

"Everyone still standing?" Maj Simmons asked.

"I don't think a single one of those things made it topside," said MSgt Roberson.

"Agreed," said SSgt Castro. "No further casualties."

"Should we rest or go?"

"I don't think it'll matter, Maj Simmons," Dewey said. "I'd say that they either finally caught on or there aren't anymore."

"So if we move, we might move into a new area with more of these things," Maj Simmons said. "That's a good point. All right, we'll do this. Put the civilians on the crawlers. Those that didn't help, they'll keep guard with two Hospitallers for support. They see something, they sound off. Everyone else, get a bite to eat, recharge your oxygen, then rest. Six standard hours and we're on the move."

"The A.P. force?" MSgt Roberson asked.

"We'll deal with them soon enough."

14

Dewey woke with a start. He thought he'd heard a noise. We're there more monster ants? He scrambled backward, patting the ground next to him. He stopped when his hand touched the barrel guard of his rifle. At that moment, he realized he wasn't alone, and it wasn't an enormous ant about to slice him in half with its platypus tail.

"Sorry, Lt Tyler." It was SSgt Castro. She was smiling through the shield of her helmet. "If it's of any help, just about everyone woke up the same way."

"So, I'm in good company." Dewey dispelled his rush of adrenaline with a chuckle. He held out a hand, which SSgt Castro gripped and pulled. Dewey rose to his feet in one smooth motion. "How's everyone?"

Dewey had taken command of the first watch. MSgt Roberson had taken command of the second. If he had to bet creds, Dewey would bet that Maj Simmons was awake for most of both shifts.

"They're good. A couple of the smugglers had a bit of a breakdown. MedTech Chambers popped a little something in their air lines to calm them down. Pvt Foster almost puked in his helmet while cleaning up the mess on the medical crawler. They talked him down."

"Good." No one needed vomit trapped in their evac suit. Not at this moment. "You eat anything? The day's going to be long."

"Went back for seconds," said the staff sergeant.

They shared the laugh because no one went back for seconds on evac suit rations, except Marines, and even they might hesitate.

Dewey left SSgt Castro to continue rousing those who slept through anything and made his way to where Maj Simmons and MSgt Roberson were standing. He saluted as he said, "Major. Master Sergeant. Been a dull six hours?"

"Yes, and I hope it stays that way, Lieutenant," said the major. "Now, we need to determine what the A.P. are going to try and do to us."

"Can't be anything like what these bugs did," said MSgt Roberson.

"Agreed," Maj Simmons said. "But unlike these creatures, the A.P. shoot back."

"We can put a crawler on point, to provide cover for a fireteam. If we make it to that pass in the image I shared, we can pop several eyes up with SSgt Castro's little adaption."

"And if we encounter resistance before the pass?" asked MSgt Roberson.

"We can still put up an eye," Dewey said. "And SSgt Castro packed a little of everything from the armory. So we have several shoulder-fired rockets."

The didn't have mortars, which Dewey would have preferred. Mortars were useless in ship-to-ship combat. But let a Hospitaller outside a ship, with a shoulder rocket at close quarters, well, the only thing crazier would be seconds of suit rations.

"Do we put anyone on top of the crawlers?" asked Maj Simmons. "To watch for more of the creatures?"

"Risk being hit by A.P. snipers," said the master sergeant.

"We can rig an eye on top of several crawlers, then have a couple people keep a watch from the ground. They can ride on the backs of the crawlers, so they aren't a visible target."

Maj Simmons's nod was barely visible through the evac suit. "All right. Sounds like we got part of a plan. Let's get everyone up and the crawlers back in line. Lt Tyler, arrange for the eyes and the crawler on point. When we've got it all ready, I want a company formation for roll call. One hour."

"Yes, Major." Dewey saluted and walked away.

Roll call wasn't what it sounded like. They didn't need to make sure they had everyone, that no one had wandered off in the night. No, roll call was where the names of the dead were read off so that everyone knew who had paid the ultimate price.

The hour deadline passed. Dewey, with the help of the staff NCOs, we're still working on getting everything and everyone lined up. One of the crawlers wasn't functioning. A panel had been torn open during the attack of the giant ants, and several critical electric relays and switches had corroded through the night. Not everything on the crawler could be shifted to the remaining five. SSgt Castro led a work party to unload all the supplies and then picked the most important to distribute among the remaining crawlers.

While SSgt Castro worked to reload the equipment and supplies, Dewey had to deal with the civilians.

"You can't just leave them there." Capt Aunztequi jabbed a finger in the direction of the bodies. Fortunately, the bodies were bagged, so no one had to look at the dismembered parts.

The plan had been to just leave them there. In typical combat situations, bodies or remains were recovered after the action was completed or when it was safe to do so. They were then cremated at a facility on the ground or transported to a Hospitaller ship that was capable of doing the same. The cremated remains were then sent to Headquarters placed in the communal urn for that Standard year.

"It makes no sense to bring them along," Dewey said. He knew it would sound cold to the captain and his crew based on medic Izu's reactions earlier. "If we get a chance, we'll come back and reclaim them."

"Scavengers," said one of the other civilians, Juvenal Mecolaeta, the smuggler ship's executive officer. "You'll be lucky to find a single bone by the time we get back."

Dewey would have liked to explain that the body bags the Hospitallers used were incredibly tricky to get into because they were designed for such contingencies. However, he was aware that their emotions were going to be impossible to debate with. His first thought was to store the remains under the broken crawler. But he could see the holes in that argument and didn't bother to mention the idea. They could put the bodies on top of the crawler, but the same problem existed.

He finally accepted that they would have to do this in an old-fashioned way. Putting the civilians to work, and cautioning them to be aware of the local foliage, Dewey had them collect large rocks. They covered each body bag with the largest rocks the civilians could carry, creating a series of meter tall cairns. At one point, Dewey almost mentioned that scavengers could just as likely dig up from below. He quickly tamped down that idea as they'd been halfway done stacking rocks at that point.

When everything was ready, Maj Simmons called everyone into formation. The civilians, looking unsure, clumped together while the Hospitallers stood in straight rows, equidistant from each other, just as they'd done since their first years in the orphanages. The major then read the names of each of the Hospitallers who had died while landing and since then. The names were pronounced, and then the rest of the Hospitallers would repeat the name.

Major Simmons included the civilians who had died, which was not standard procedure. Still, the Hospitallers responded to their names with equal solemnity. After the last response was made, Maj Simmons gave the command, and the convoy commenced once more.

Dewey had Cpl Fleming and her fireteam up with the point crawler. An eye, set on a pole and strapped to the front of the crawler, allowed the corporal to watch the way ahead for any large obstacles.

"How's it look, Mitchell?" Dewey asked. They were on local comm as he had quick marched to join them up at the front.

"Boring, Lieutenant," Cpl Fleming said. "On the good side, the bushes with the razor blades don't look as numerous. But the small trees are a different matter. There are more of them here than back where we started."

Dewey hadn't noticed the reduction in the number of plants with razor-sharp leaves. He had noticed the increasing numbers of the stubby trees. Their umbrella-like foliage would make it difficult to search for the A.P. fighters from above.

"Keep a sharp eye out," Dewey said. "I want a heads-up before things stop being boring."

There was still another kilometer to go until they reached the shallow pass. The trees on the slopes would be good places to hide in preparation for an ambush. It's what Dewey expected to happen. Maj Simmons and the staff NCOs were in agreement. So when the comm exploded with warnings and commands, Dewey was surprised and momentarily confused.

"Taking fire on the port side!" someone shouted into the general comm.

"Starboard side! Starboard side! Cpl Garner's been hit!"

"Lieutenant," said Cpl Fleming. "You getting this?"

"I am." Dewey tapped the comm, so he had the corporal and her fireteam isolated. "Everyone, hunker down. Mitchell, start looking."

He backed up to the crawler. As he brought his rifle to his shoulder, he knelt, making his target size smaller. Tapping into the general comm was like opening a door to chaos. Several more people had been hit. At least one civilian was injured.

"Lt Tyler? How are you all holding up?" It was the major.

"We're fine, Major. No one's firing on our position."

"They set their trap in the low areas," said Maj Simmons. "I hate to admit that someone in the A.P. military outsmarted us."

"Humility 101," Dewey said in response.

"Hey, Lieutenant," Cpl Fleming said into the comm.

"Pardon me, Major." Dewey tapped the comm to communicate with Cpl Fleming. He scanned the area as he spoke. "Go ahead."

"I don't see anyone in front of us or to our sides. So, I threw on the thermal. There's a hot mass to either side of the rest of the convoy. Five to eight people in each group. The tree trunks are in the way, but it looks like they're dug in."

"Got it, Corporal. Climb down, we're about to have some action."

"Finally."

Dewey connected with Maj Simmons, again. "Major, I have a plan."

"I'm all ears until someone shoots one off, Lieutenant."

Dewey explained the plan. It didn't involve shoulder-fired rockets, which he was sure would disappoint SSgt Castro. But Dewey wanted to hold onto those for a desperate situation. This was more of a nuisance. The major liked the plan and gave him the go-ahead. He switched comm to explain the idea to Cpl Fleming and the rest of the fireteam.

"Remember," Dewey said. "You want to avoid the plants, especially the one with sword-shaped leaves. Use them for cover, just don't dive into them. Cpl Mitchell, let's get going."

"You got it, Lt Tyler." Cpl Fleming turned and spoke to the Hospitaller closest to her. "Ramirez, you're on point. Two hundred fifty meters. Go."

Pfc Ramirez started moving. Mitchell waved for Pvt Wells to follow and then indicated Dewey should go next. She followed, leaving Pfc Wallace to guard the rear.

Dewey left five meters between him and Pvt Wells. He followed as Wells weaved through the bushes, shying away from the ones they knew would cut through an evac suit. Further ahead, Dewey caught the occasional glimpse of Ramirez another fifteen meters ahead. To the left, Dewey could just hear the sounds of gunfire.

"On target." Pfc Ramirez's voice was a whisper as if she was worried the A.P. fighters might hear her. "All clear."

The rest of the team moved forward until they marked Ramirez's position. They gathered but still left space between them. Dewey used the heads up display in his helmet to verify they'd gone the right distance. They were now parallel with the A.P. shooters on this side of the convoy.

"We're closing the gap," Dewey said after connecting with Maj Simmons.

"We'll be ready."

"Okay, Cpl Mitchell, let's spread out and see if we can create a distraction."

Mitchell signaled to her fireteam. They spread out on a line, and when she gave the next signal to move, they moved as one. Dewey was on the line with them. He watched the plants ahead, looking for a glimpse of the A.P. forces despite them being dug in.

They moved slow, closing the space between them and the A.P. fighters. At twenty meters, Cpl M. Mitchel signaled for everyone to stop. She knelt and took aim. The rest of the team mimicked her actions.

Now she used the comm. "On three. Short bursts. Move sideways, don't stay in one location."

She counted down. At zero, the fireteam began firing short bursts. The response was initially hesitant, then it took on more ferocity.

"Down!" Mitchell shouted in the comm.

Everyone went prone. Dewey rolled on his side as he contacted Maj Simmons. "Your turn, Major."

"On it."

Dewey rolled onto his stomach and started firing again. He didn't bother with the sights as he couldn't see the enemy through the plant life. Though, with the amount of ammo chewing at the greenery, that was likely to change very soon.

"Watch the razor plants!" someone shouted.

Dewey paused and looked around. He was right next to one. Looking up, he saw several half-meter-long sections of the leaves torn nearly free from their lower half. They were listing in Dewey's direction. He rolled away and started firing again.

There was more firing, but this time it wasn't directed at Cpl Fleming's fireteam. The sound didn't carry well through the helmets, but Dewey was pretty sure that the increased sound meant that Maj Simmon's team had charged forward as planned.

"Move them forward, Cpl Mitchell," Dewey said.

Mitchell gave the command, and everyone was up and moving forward, firing a path through the bushes and trees. Ten slow meters of progress and the return firing had suddenly stopped. Dewey caught Mitchell's attention and gave her the signal to stop. She passed it on to her team. Everyone went to one knee, still watching forward.

"Maj Simmons?"

"Hey, Lt Tyler," said Maj Simmons. Her voice sounded pained.

"You hit, Major?"

"No, not hit, but thank you for asking. However, we did rout the enemy on this side, and the other squad's reverse ambush was also successful. Threat's neutralized. Now, can you zero in on my position without telling anyone what I'm up to?"

Only now did Dewey realize that the major had put them on a private comm. He checked the HUD and marked the location for Maj Simmons. It wasn't an exact location as they weren't relying on satellite data.

"I'm on my way, Major." Dewey switched the comm. "Cpl Mitchell, mission success. We've routed the enemy."

"Do we pursue, Lieutenant?"

"No, I think we'll have enough time to reach the research buildings before they can put any more surprises together. Bring your team back to the crawler and standby."

"Understood."

Mitchell pulled her team together. They started a winding path out of the bushes, back to the crawlers. Several meters along, Dewey turned to his left.

"Lt Tyler?" Cpl Fleming asked.

"It's okay, Corporal. Just get your team to the crawlers. I'll be along."

"Yes, Lieutenant. See you there."

Dewey continued a meandering path, his eyes flicking between the ground and the small dot on his HUD. His green dot was slowly approaching the orange dot that was supposed to be Maj Simmons. He almost tripped over her.

15

Dewey took a step back. Maj Simmons was on her side, one arm was draped back over her hip. Her weapon was wedged between her and the ground but still secured to her with the sling straps. She wasn't moving. He'd been talking to her before. Was she dead already?

"Maj Simmons?" He knelt and reached to check the vital readings on the major's suit.

"Don't move me, Tyler." Dewey pulled his hand back as she spoke. "Not yet. You have suit wrap?"

"Suit wrap? Yes, Major, I do." Dewey dug out the small packet. He was in an EVA suit, and a wrap was part of the inventory. "You tear your suit?"

"In a manner of speaking." She rolled further on to her front and patted the back of her hip. "We'll joke about this later if I live."

If they hadn't been fighting for their lives on an unfriendly planet with an unfriendly atmosphere, Dewey definitely would have laughed. A long, narrow leaf, like a rapier, was embedded in Maj Simmons's right butt cheek.

"I didn't want to pull it out," the major said. "The suit's system isn't detecting a leak, so I think this pain in my butt is keeping everything airtight."

"But it has to come out," Dewey said. Who knew what kind of toxins it might be releasing.

"Right. So this," Maj Simmons said as she held out a small canister, "and then the suit wrap."

The canister was liquid bandage. A sealant for the body. Dewey would have to pull out the rapier leaf and then seal the major's wound before sealing the suit.

Dewey took the canister and popped the cap off. "I need to move quick, Major. The less you move, the easier this will be."

"It hurt going in," said Maj Simmons. "I expect that it'll hurt as bad or worse as it comes out."

"If I could send for MedTech Chambers, she'd have some anesthetic. I don't think she'll tell anyone about the location of your wound."

"It's more than that, Lt Tyler. I'm worried about morale. That's why I charged with the squad. We're not in the best position on the planet. And it's looking like a dead end. So I need to keep everyone optimistic. Getting a leaf jammed in my butt, kind of deflates that goal."

Dewey didn't exactly agree, but he understood the argument. "Understood, Major. Any chance you can tell me how this happened?"

"Ducked return fire. When I came back up, I tripped over my foot," the major said. Dewey broke the seal on the suit wrap and shook the canister of liquid bandage while he listened. "Almost stumbled straight into the razor blade plant. Dodged left, tripped again. This time, on a rock. Then I fell backward on this plant."

Maj Simmons waved in the general direction of a plant that looked like an Earth sea anemone but with flattened quills.

"Rotten luck," Dewey said. He grabbed the quill after testing it for sharpness and finding it thick edged rather than honed. "Here it comes."

The major's response to the narrow leaf being yanked from her flesh was a hiss of surprise and pain. Dewey paid it little attention. He had already tossed the leaf aside and had the liquid bandage in his hand. He pressed the suit down and open with one hand before pushing the canister into the space and depressing the small button on the bottom.

Another hiss escaped the major. "Okay, that hurt more than expected. Also, my skin is starting to itch."

Dewey dropped the canister and picked up the suit wrap. "It's the atmosphere of the planet," he said. "The civilian described it the same way."

As the wound was on the buttock and not the thigh, Dewey couldn't go with fast wrap several times around the opening. He needed to lay strips across the cut and then press everything together to generate the seal. The pocket knife he was given when he turned fifteen was inside his suit. He wouldn't be using that. Instead, there was a knife for zero atmosphere work. When Dewey pulled it out, he could see that the rusting on it from the acidic air was already advanced.

He stuck it tip down in the dirt and stretched the suit wrap across the major's butt. He pressed it in place and then used the rusting knife to cut it. With the knife back in the dirt, he ran another strip of the wrap over the first. He cut and repeated the process five times, overlapping the wrap so that it would seal with the underlying wrap and the surface of the suit.

"Okay, Major, I'm going to have to push. Hard."

"Well, hurry up. I'm already getting commed by MSgt Roberson. He's like having a dorm mother around all the time. And I'll ship you off to the tip of the arm if you repeat that."

The arm meant the second radial arm of the galaxy. The tip was an ice planet orbiting a red dwarf star. There was nothing there but the threat of being sent to it. Dewey had heard it from many a drill instructor in basic training.

"My lips are sealed," he said. "Pressing now."

Dewey rose up on his knees. He placed one hand over the other and then pressed down against the suit wrap. He needed to push and hold. If he'd been able to wrap it around instead of cutting it into strips, it would have sealed with less external pressure. They didn't have that luxury. So, despite the major's obvious discomfort, Dewey pushed hard and held the pressure. At the same time, he counted to a hundred twenty in his mind.

When he eased off, sitting back, Maj Simmons responded with a groan of relief.

"I never want a massage from anyone with that technique," she said and then laughed. "That hurt."

"Sorry, Major." Dewey climbed to his feet. "Can you stand?"

Maj Simmons held out her hand. "Let's find out."

She came up easily. Dewey noticed only the slightest limp as she took two steps. He reached out and tapped the screen on her suit to call up the vitals readings.

"You have a slight temperature and elevated heart rate."

"That's between you and me," said Maj Simmons. She moved Dewey's hand aside and tapped the screen, hiding the readings. "You and I both know this will probably get worse. But that's also between you and me."

"The medtechs can help," Dewey said.

"Maybe." Maj Simmons checked her weapon and then started walking, waving Dewey to come along. "When we get inside those buildings, and we have some modicum of safety, I'll let them look at it. Until then, I need to lead."

Back at the convoy, Dewey was relieved to find that there were no further injuries, no more dead to have their names read the next morning. The A.P. were less fortunate.

Dewey's idea had been a ruse. After he'd attacked the A.P. position on the port side of the convoy, the major pulled everyone to the same side and took half with her on a frontal assault. As hoped, the A.P. on the starboard side had attempted to attack the unguarded crawlers. Except, the crawlers weren't without a guard. The third squad, with the ship's crew, had moved to the front and rear of the convoy. They caught the A.P. fighters in a crossfire. It was over quickly. Likely, it was that defeat that sent the remaining A.P. running from the fight.

Cpl Garner had been grazed in the side. He now sported a broad band of suit wrap around his waist that he repeatedly attempted to scratch with his gloved fingers. Pfc Boyd had been shot in the arm. The bullet remained. The medtechs had chosen to leave it until they could either set up the med tent or get inside the buildings with their promise of a normal atmosphere. Two civilians, Ms. Barricarte and Mr. Arluzea, had been grazed as well. Barricarte had a wrap around her leg, and Arluzea had one around his leg and opposite forearm.

Dewey was glad that no one had died. They wouldn't have to lose another hour building more cairns.

Maj Simmons seemed equally as glad. As soon as everyone was patched up, she had the A.P. fighters pulled out of the way and their weapons and ammo stripped before she put the convoy in motion once more.

They proceeded at the same pace as before. Sgt Shelley Perry and Cpl Chavez's abbreviated fireteam took the point position. Dewey remained back with the rest of the platoon to observe Maj Simmons and Pfc Boyd. MedTech Chambers had confided in Dewey. She was worried that Boyd was bleeding in his suit, despite his insistence that he was fine. Currently, Dewey couldn't order Boyd to remove his glove, which would have easily shown if the wound was bleeding freely.

"But maybe the bleeding is a good thing," Chambers said after several thoughtful seconds. "Maybe it'll keep the wound from becoming infected by whatever is in the atmosphere."

Dewey's private thought was a concern for Boyd running out of blood before they reached the buildings. Infection or no infection, there'd be nothing to cure if Boyd was dead from blood loss when they arrived.

The nearing pass was a good distraction from the worry over Boyd and Maj Simmons. SSgt Castro had taken two more eyes with the adapted parachutes up to Sgt Perry. As the forward crawler entered the pass, Castro had two of Cpl Chavez's team launch them skyward, one to port, the other to starboard.

"You want to look?" SSgt Castro asked Dewey.

"I'll tag along," Dewey said. "You can have the controls."

Dewey called up the VR as he put one hand on the side of the crawler he was walking next to. A quick wave of nausea washed over him. Suddenly, standing in the sky, looking down at the convoy and the hills on either side. He could feel himself walking and the solid presence of the crawler. But that wasn't what he saw, and his mind did not appreciate the quandary it was put into. Dewey had grown to find his reaction humorous. This wasn't the first time he'd been in the situation with the VR. He hadn't kept count, but to say he'd done it thousands of times wouldn't be much of an exaggeration.

"Ready, Lieutenant?" SSgt Castro asked.

"As much as I'm going to be. Let's get looking."

The view shifted, zooming toward the ground. Dewey stumbled for several steps in real life until he regained his balance. Castro had taken them down, close to the treetops. The view was limited to two data sets. Some of the VR image was nothing more than black squares and rectangles. However, there was enough that they could peek under most of the trees from the position of the pass.

"I'm not seeing anything," SSgt Castro said.

"Agreed." Dewey had seen nothing that was cause for concern. Not even a self-contained machine gun nest that could be operated remotely. Though, if the A.P. had been in possession of that much firepower, they wouldn't have risked their lives the way they had. "I'll let the major know."

Dewey pulled out of the VR. He took several steadying breaths, letting the crawler slide past under his hand. When he was sure he wouldn't fall over, he stepped aside and waited for Maj Simmons and the next crawler to approach. She was walking with one of her hands on the crawler. She had not been in the VR with Dewey and SSgt Castro. Dewey was pretty sure that she was using the crawler for support.

"Major?" Dewey queried over the comm.

Maj Simmons looked up and then waved Dewey over to where she was walking past.

"How's the pass look?" she asked as he fell into step beside her.

"Looks clear," Dewey said. "How are you feeling, Major?"

"Like someone set fire to my butt cheek." She laughed, but Dewey was sure it was more forced than unintentional. "Temperature is up. Blood pressure is down. What's left? Two kliks to the buildings?"

"Two point three as of this position, Major."

"Oh, well, point three," she said. "Could it be any easier? Don't answer that."

"Of course, Major. But as we seem to have a clear run to the buildings, maybe you'd agree to ride the rest of the way?"

Dewey barely saw the shake of her head inside her evac suit's helmet. "No. I'll walk. Boyd. I put him on the med crawler a few minutes ago. They need to get that bullet out and clean that wound the moment we can get him out of his suit."

"And you, Maj Simmons?"

"Of course." She paused. Dewey wasn't sure if it was from exhaustion or thought. But then, she said, "Go forward. Take the first crawler and push ahead to the buildings. Find the entrance and prep it so we can roll in rather than wait."

"That's a good idea, Major." Dewey threw her a salute that she didn't return. Likely focused on staying upright, Dewey surmised.

Leaving the Major, Dewey trotted forward until he reached the point crawler, halfway through the pass.

16

The point crawler approached the largest of the buildings at a quick march that ate up the last kilometers of distance and left the rest of the Hospitallers and civilians far behind. The last fifty meters of approach was at a much slower pace. Everyone was on alert for a possible A.P. attack. Cpl Chavez and Pfc Horton watched from the port side of the crawler. Dewey and Pvt Hart maintained a watch from the starboard side. In the rear, Sgt Perry watched with Pfc Dunn, who had been conscripted from the ship's crew to fill in for Pfc Cruz.

The plant life around the buildings was sparser, stunted. There were smaller, scrubbier version of the razor-leafed plants, the rapier-leafed plants, and several that looked like crabgrass transplanted from the fields near the orphanage Dewey grew up in. The crawler could move in a straight line and rarely touch one of the plants.

The final ten meters of ground leading up to the wide access door of the main building were crushed rock and gravel, pressed into the ground. Dewey didn't think it was human-made. He was sure of it.

"Horton," Dewey said through the comm. "Stop the crawler."

The crawler stopped with a crunching sound as its weight settled on the rock and gravel.

"Anything we should be worried about, Sgt Perry?" Dewey asked.

"I haven't seen an A.P. uniform nor a giant ant monster. Maybe both have retreated to lick their wounds?"

"Maybe. Or maybe they're just waiting for a better opportunity to attack."

"Hey, Lt Tyler," Cpl Chavez said. "I thought you were the fountain of optimism."

"This is optimism, Corporal." Dewey's comment got a few laughs from those listening on the comm. It kept them busy while Dewey approached the doors. Doors large enough that they could get the crawlers inside. The only questions were, how many could they get inside, and how would they get them inside?

There wasn't a visible control box that he could open and push the big green button that started things in motion. There might not even be any power. If the people who built the buildings never intended to return, they may have just taken the power source and mothballs and left.

Dewey tapped the comm to make sure he still had everyone connected. "Stay in pairs. See if there's another entrance or a button that says, 'push to open.' Hart, stay here with me."

Chavez and Horton went clockwise around the building. Sgt Perry and Dunn went counterclockwise. Both teams quickly disappeared around the corners. From the images of the buildings, Dewey knew that there were wings on both sides. It was shaped like a stubby T with the cross part being deeper than the base of the T. If they had no luck here, they'd move on to the other buildings. They were smaller, and none of them had doors large enough to accommodate vehicles. They'd have to leave the crawlers outside, prey to the acidic atmosphere.

"Hey, Lt Tyler?"

"Hart? You see something?" Dewey looked around for the private, finding him six meters away, squatting and looking toward the ground. Dewey joined him. "What've you got?"

"I'm sure it's just random, but doesn't that look like a footprint?"

"Not one of ours?" Dewey asked. He scanned the area. Possibly, the A.P. had made it here ahead of the Hospitallers.

"Not unless one of us was walking around barefoot, Lieutenant. And the impression I've gotten is that it would be too painful to do so."

"'Footprint,'" Dewey said. He'd naturally assumed Hart meant a booted footprint. He bent over, hands on his knees, to look where

Hart pointed.

As Hart had said. There on the ground was what looked like a human footprint. Dewey looked around the footprint and saw a few more. He stood and looked beyond the couple meters he'd already studied. There were dozens more. Some of them were faded with time and wind. Some looked fresh.

"I find it hard to believe that these are made by a human," Hart said. She'd stood as she spoke, looking around her. "Could there be a suit with footprint soles?"

"Only as a practical joke," said Dewey. And if it was a practical joke, it was wasted. He didn't believe the A.P. had done it. Why would they? Would someone come here, see the prints and think it was okay to remove their suit? That didn't seem likely. "Maybe it just looks like footprints. Maybe it's some creature that's native to Wenshen that we haven't yet seen, and its paws just happen to have some similar characteristics to human feet."

"You think so, Lieutenant?" Hart sounded relieved by the idea.

Unfortunately, Dewey couldn't provide the relief that Pvt Hart seemed to need. "I don't know what to think. Nor do we have the time to investigate. We need to get inside the buildings. Another half-hour and Maj Simmons and the others will be here. And I want to get them inside, A.S.A.P."

Dewey returned to examine the doors to the building. Things not being what they seemed, had given him an idea. The doors, rather than being seamless and smooth, looked like they'd been constructed of numerous smaller panels. A quick count across and up, multiplied by two made for twenty-seven hundred panels. Taken as a whole, they all looked identical. A more patient examination of panel sections about shoulder high revealed one with scratch marks along its left side. The kind of scratch marks a person might make if they were trying to pry a panel up.

At any other time, Dewey would have pulled out his pocket knife top pop the small door open. Hard to do when inside an EVA suit. However, the suit, in addition to having numerous pockets, also had a few tools. One of them was the type used to pry panels up if someone needed to access what was behind it while outside a ship. The outside of the building was much the same. Dewey stuck the flat edge of the tool under the panel next to the scratches. It slipped in easily. When Dewey pushed the handle of the tool toward the door, the panel popped open, swinging on a long hinge.

"Everyone return to the crawler," said Dewey. He pocketed the tool as he examined the board that had been hidden behind the panel.

It was apparent that whoever had constructed the building must have never believed anyone else would come here. Or if they had, they could be stopped from getting this far. The panel was rubberized and had two raised buttons with embossed letters. Dewey pushed the one that had the word OPEN on it.

As Sgt Perry and the others returned to the crawler, the doors parted and began to swing inwards while also bending in the middle like simple accordion doors.

"Was there a magic word?" asked Sgt Perry. She'd stop to watch as the doors continued to part, and the yellowish daylight flooded the space beyond.

"'Please,'" said Dewey. Then, "Actually, it turns out there was a hidden panel."

"Helpful."

"Agreed. You want to clear the space?"

Sgt Perry saluted. "My pleasure, Lieutenant."

Though the interior space was large, it was quick to clear. The interior was similar to one of the loading bays of the Shnel Shnek, except it was empty, and larger. Sgt Perry did manage to identify the control buttons on the other side of the space, not hidden on the opposite doors but off to one side. Apparently, there wasn't a need to keep it a secret once someone made it this far.

While Sgt Perry and the fireteam moved the crawler inside, Dewey contacted Maj Simmons.

"We have access," he said once the major had confirmed the connection. "And I have eyes on the convoy. So you're almost here."

"Good." The major's voice sounded weak, exhausted. She must have realized it because she added, "Chambers and MSgt Roberson forced me to ride on the medical crawler. I would have fought them, but I don't have the energy."

"And the wound?"

"I still feel like my buttcheek is on fire. The medtechs don't get to look until we're inside, assuming the air is breathable. Last thing I need is my naked butt in an emergency med box."

"There's the med tent, too," Dewey said. "Worst case, they can put you and the others in there."

The med tent, once inflated, would hold ten wounded and space for a small surgical theater and front clinic.

"I'd like out of this suit."

"We'll do what we can, Major." Dewey would like out of the suit, too. As much as he'd like a shower, he'd be okay with a box of body wipes to clear away the sweat and odor.

"I know you will, Lt Tyler."

The conversation ended. Dewey went into the cavernous space. The crawler was back and to the left. They could easily get all the crawlers inside with room to spare.

Cpl Chavez had located small observation windows embedded in the interior doors. Unfortunately, the room beyond was dark. They'd been trying to shine task lights through other windows while looking through one. They'd also tried night vision on the helmet face masks, which yielded the same response.

"Hey, Lieutenant." Sgt Perry was waving his hand. It wasn't empty. "This worked. We did infrared with an eye pressed to one of the windows. Space is about twice the size of this with an overlook at the far end. Doors on all the walls. Most of them are double doors with some height. And there's a section in the middle of the floor that looks like it lowers into the ground."

They knew from earlier scans that there was open space below the buildings. Some had been there before the newer buildings had been constructed over the original. What they didn't know was what was beyond the doors. Was there anything? Was it all empty space? Was there oxygen? There was one answer for all of them and only one way to find that answer.

That would happen just as soon as they could get the rest of the convoy inside and the doors shut.

Standing at the end of the trail and watching the convoy crawl closer was almost physically painful. SSgt Castro had informed Dewey that MSgt Roberson wasn't willing to max the speed of the crawlers. It might jostle the wounded. And as Maj Simmons was one of the wounded, he was especially cautious.

However, like all journeys, this one drew to an end. MSgt Roberson saluted as he approached. The first of the convoy crawlers passing him and entering the interior space under Sgt Perry's guidance.

"Lieutenant," Roberson said.

Dewey returned the salute. "Almost sent out a search party."

"Unlikely, you could see us the entire time." He passed by, following the crawler.

The next crawler entered, bringing with it SSgt Castro. She saluted as well, but she also had a rueful grin on her face.

"I tried to convince the master sergeant that major would be okay if we sped up a little bit." She dropped her salute as Dewey returned it with his own. "Please tell me, Lieutenant, that I won't be like that when I become a master sergeant."

"It's a painless surgical procedure," Dewey said. It was a common joke among the Hospitallers, like generals having their sense of humor removed the day they were promoted. "You'll never know it happened."

"In that case, I'll just stay a staff sergeant forever."

The third crawler moved past.

"Not if I can help it." Dewey's expectation was that as long as Castro was a staff NCO and renewed her contract, he was going to drag her up the ladder with him as he obtained his next promotion.

"Heck, Lt Tyler, I thought you liked me." She laughed, threw a salute, and followed the third crawler inside the airlock.

Inside, Sgt Perry and Chavez's fireteam were directing the positioning of the crawlers. Already, civilians and Hospitallers were climbing onto the loads to keep out of the way. The medical crawler was the last. There was plenty of room for it inside.

When it groaned to a stop, Dewey climbed up the side.

MedTech Chambers was waiting for him. Her voice was a scratchy growl through the comm. "You could have told me the major was injured, Lieutenant." She saluted at the end.

Dewey stood and returned the salute. "I had orders, Chambers."

"You still could have told me." She turned away and walked to one of the temporary beds for the wounded. Dewey followed.

The major didn't look good. Her face was splotchy and shiny with sweat that beaded on her forehead. Her eyes were closed. Her jaw was tightly clenched.

"Major?" Dewey asked on a closed channel.

"Hey, Lieutenant." She opened her eyes and gave him a brief nod.

"We're all inside the airlock." He looked up and around. He couldn't see the panel that Sgt Perry had to use to shut the doors, but he did see that they'd begun to move. "Hopefully, we'll be in good atmo, and Chambers can get a look at that wound."

"She's very angry," said Maj Simmons. She smiled as she spoke. "I didn't know I had so many people concerned about my well being."

"You have the keys to the ship, Major."

The major chuckled and said, "Ah, that must be it."

Her comment was punctuated by an explosion. It knocked Dewey into MedTech Chambers and both of them to the crawler deck.

Over the comm, someone shouted, "Rocket fire."

"Sorry, Chambers." Dewey rolled off the medtech and rushed to the end of the crawler.

A quick peek over the supplies on the back end showed the doors were two-thirds shut and still moving. Out on the open space from which they'd come, six people were approaching. One of them had an empty shoulder-fired rocket launcher. Another person was unwrapping a second rocket.

Dewey lifted his weapon and rested the barrel across a box of surgical kits. He tracked the person with the rocket and pulled the trigger before they could load it. They dropped with the impact of the bullet Dewey had released. The rocket bounced on the ground and rolled away. Someone else scrambled for it, and Dewey quickly shot in their direction. He'd been aiming for the rocket but missed the smaller target by millimeters. Dirt kicked up where the bullet hit, and the person reaching for the rocket jerked back.

The doors were almost closed. Five meters to go. Dewey aimed again, looking for the person with the launcher. Something rattled the surgical kit box, and splinters knocked against Dewey's EVA helmet. He dropped down as more return fire chewed at the boxes protecting him. He looked up.

Two meters to go.

The back of the crawler exploded, tossing Dewey forward to slam against the supplies stacked there. He fell, landing on someone. Someone else was helping him to his feet.

Dewey shook them off, turning to look at the doors just as they touched, bathing the entire space into darkness. There was another explosion that vibrated the doors, but they held. His comm pinged, and he tapped it while stepping over supplies that had been dislodged by the rocket explosion.

"You okay, Lieutenant?"

"Yes, Major," Dewey said. He leaned over the broken rear of the crawler and turned on his task light. The seal between the doors was unbroken from the ground up. "I think we just made it."

17

Dewey climbed down from the crawler to find SSgt Castro waiting for him.

"That may have been my fault."

"You're fault, Castro? What was?" Dewey went around to take another look at the damage from ground level.

"The rockets, Lt Tyler. I think they're my fault."

"You fired on us?" Dewey grinned. "Or do you mean you left some rockets with the abandoned crawler?"

With a rueful grin, Castro said, "Yeah, I think that's what happened."

"Right. Next time, initiate the self-destruct." Dewey clapped her on the shoulder. He wasn't mad at her. They were all under pressure. And it never occurred to Dewey that the A.P. would dig through the gear they'd abandoned. "Now, let's see about cycling the air in the chamber. I don't know about anyone else, but I could use a real bathroom break."

"I think Sgt Perry has found the controls," said SSgt Castro.

Dewey tapped his comm for Perry while he wove his way through the crawlers, Hospitallers, and civilians. After Perry chimed in, Dewey asked him, "You get the cycler moving?"

"System's old," Sgt Perry said. "It's still booting up, but everything looks green. We should be able to start in a few more minutes."

"And how long after until we can open the inner doors? Two hours?"

There was a lot of air to cycle through, removing the tainted, acidic air and replacing it with breathable air that wouldn't burn the lungs.

"Hopefully," said Perry. "But if it takes a bit longer, don't hold it against me."

Several minutes later, while Dewey helped the medtechs with Maj Simmons, a sound vibrated the air. It began low, like a windy whisper, and very quickly built up to an ocean roar. Fortunately, the EVA and evac helmets only transferred a fraction of the noise. Though, Dewey found that his helmet took on an annoying buzzing during this time.

Along with the sound came wind. It blew across the interior space, slowing and switching directions several times. Then things became a little more interesting.

Dewey held out one hand as he tapped the comm with the other. "MSgt Roberson? Castro? You seeing this?"

"You mean the snow?" asked MSgt Roberson."

"Well, good," said Dewey. "I'm glad to know I'm not hallucinating."

"I don't think it's snow," said SSgt Castro. "I think it's borax. It'll help neutralize the acidic molecules in the air and whatever has taken up residence on our equipment or on us."

"Interesting," Dewey said. It had a few other names, based on his readings. And it made sense that they would use it here. Likely, they had a ready source of it on the planet or were able to recycle it for repeated use. He tapped the comm for general broadcast. "If you're wondering about the snow, it's sodium borate, also known as borax. It might look like snow, but I wouldn't stick my tongue out to catch it. It's part of the cycling process of the system. Sgt Perry, how much longer?"

A short pause filled the comm before Perry responded. "Another hour, looks like, Lieutenant."

The borax snow fell for a few more minutes, layering everything that wasn't moving. The wind began again. The force of it stirred up the borax flakes, creating miniature hurricanes that were then sucked in through a dozen vents in the ceiling high above.

As it turned out, it only took an hour and thirty-seven minutes, standard time, for the cycling process to complete. While they'd been waiting, Dewey had the Hospitallers shuffle the crawlers around and then used one of them to pull the damaged medical crawler as far forward as they could. They unloaded all of the medical equipment in preparation. There was plenty to be done, and Dewey, with Maj Simmons's suggestion, put some of the civilians to work.

Capt Aunztequi was nowhere to be seen during the work.

"Cpl Garner?" Dewey said through the comm on a direct line.

"Hey, Lieutenant," Garner said in response.

"I know you're injured, but any chance you know where the civilian captain, Aunztequi, is?"

"I'm not that badly injured," said Garner. "Though, the itch seems to have gotten worse. However, I have eyes on the captain. He's huddled with two of his people on the other side of the crawler behind you."

Dewey turned around. Sitting on top of the crawler mentioned, sat Cpl Garnier. He waved, his big smile visible even through the helmet shield and distance. He pointed across his body and down. In the shadows between the crawler and the interior doors, Capt Aunztequi was barely visible. It was only his emergency evac suit that gave him away. His movements made it clear that he was having a heated discussion with someone. It brought to mind the memory Dewey had of the captain's discussion aboard the Shnel Shnek with several of his people.

He would have wandered in the captain's direction, but the interior doors to the airlock clicked several times as locks were released. Then, the doors began to grind their way open. Dewey noticed some of the civilians clapping. No doubt they were anxious to get the evac suits off.

"SSgt Castro," Dewey said.

The staff sergeant responded as if she'd been waiting for the call. "I've checked, Lieutenant. All the levels are good. Safe to remove helmets and take a deep breath."

"You first, Staff Sergeant." Dewey laughed, but he was already turning the latches to separate his helmet from his suit. Before he removed it, he tapped the comm for general communication. "Okay, everyone, SSgt Castro says atmo is green. Make sure you blame her if your lungs start burning."

Dewey made sure to quickly pull his helmet off so that others could see him without it. Several civilians looked his way. He gave them a thumbs up. Their grins shined through their helmets as they helped each other with their helmet locks. Over where the doors were halfway open, Capt Aunztequi was pulling his helmet over his head. There was a whispered conversation going on between him and the other civilians now visible.

"MSgt Roberson," Dewey said after tapping his comm. "Can we keep everyone inside the airlock for now? Especially the civilians?"

"Especially that captain," MSgt Roberson responded. "He seems mighty keen to get moving."

"Call up Cpl Mitchell's fireteam and post them as guards until we've had a chance to clear the area."

"Sounds good, Lieutenant."

MSgt Roberson's bellow filled the air as he called for Cpl Mitchell.

Cpl Garner's voice was heard as well. He'd come down from the crawler and placed himself between Capt Aunztequi and the rest of the building, saying, "Hold up there, Captain. We might want to wait until the CO has given the all-clear."

While Roberson and Garner dealt with securing the civilians, Dewey continued forward to where the medtechs and all their gear were stationed.

"Chambers, how do you want to handle this?" Dewey asked. "Wait to see if we can find an appropriate room for the wounded and injured? Or set up the med tent out here?"

"Both?" asked MedTech Chambers. "Several people, especially the Major, need immediate attention as quickly as we can manage."

"Right, so set up the equipment as we look for a better bivouac." He turned and looked before waving several people over. "Cpl Robertson. Cpl Knight. I need you and the rest of the ship crew to assist the medtechs with getting the med tent up and secured. After that, Pfc Fox and Anderson will perform as orderlies until they're relieved."

The two corporals saluted and said, "Yes, Lieutenant."

"Let's start moving the container here," MedTech Chambers said as she walked over to the large plastic box that held the med tent.

Dewey left them to it and stepped past the airlock threshold.

"Anyone who's not already been given a job," said Dewey through the comm, "fall in."

By the time Dewey had given the open space a general pass with his eyes, the rest of the Hospitallers were in formation.

Both squad sergeants were present, as were the other fifteen who had not yet been given a current assignment. This did not include the wounded. Well, it wasn't supposed to.

"Cpl Alexander," Dewey said. "I thought you had a concussion and were supposed to rest."

"I'm fine, Lieutenant."

"Really?" Dewey reached for his comm. "I'll just verify that with MedTech Chambers?"

"No, Lieutenant." Cpl Alexander smiled. She'd been caught. "I'll go and do some more strenuous resting."

"Don't worry, Alexander, we'll need you soon enough."

"Thank you, Lt Tyler."

Dewey scanned the rest of the Hospitallers present. Was anyone else trying to sneak in from the wounded side of the roster? There was one person not visible, but he knew where she was.

"SSgt Castro."

"Lieutenant," said Castro from just behind Dewey's right shoulder.

"Three teams, Castro." Dewey pointed to the doors on the two side walls and the one at the far end of the building. "One hour. Clear as much as you can. Lockdown what you can't get to. We'll come back to it later. And if you can find me a map, that'd be great."

"One hour, Lieutenant. You got it." SSgt Castro saluted and turned to the rest of the Hospitallers. "Sgt Perry. Sgt Parks. Grab a fireteam and assemble. If you're short a person, grab from Garner's fireteam. Everyone else, assemble on me. We got some rooms that need clearing."

Dewey left Castro to her task. He knew that she would do exactly what he expected of her, a great job. He'd been surprised when she'd turned down officer training, but was secretly glad so that he still had her as his right hand.

While SSgt Castro got the Hospitallers working on the building, Dewey returned to where the med tent was now up. Cpl Knight was outside the tent, unlocking a crate.

"Cpl Knight," Dewey said as Knight popped to attention. "How's the med tent shaping up?"

"Good, as far as I can tell, Lieutenant." She returned to her task as Dewey waved for her to continue. "Dividers are up, and Chambers has everyone out of their suits."

"And how do they look?"

Knight Grimaced. "I've seen acid burns that looked nicer."

"I see. Thank you, Cpl Knight." Dewey opened the door to the med tent and entered.

For a tent, it was enormous. It was fortunate the interior of the building was large enough, or the med tent might have filled all available space. Once it was inflated, the tent had plenty of rooms for surgeries, outpatient procedures, and overnight guests.

"Chambers?" Dewey asked loud enough to be heard through the entire tent.

"Down here, Lieutenant."

Dewey went down the hallway to find MedTech Chambers in the second room on the right. She was sitting on a stool, inspecting Maj Simmons's wound.

"You'd better not laugh, Lieutenant," Maj Simmons said. Her voice sounded tired, almost drunk.

"Wouldn't think of it, Major," Dewey said. Even if he'd been inclined to do so, the look on Chambers's face killed the thought. "How're you doing?"

"Oh, just great," said the major. "I've got a seeping wound in my butt and a spreading rash that itches so bad I'm about to request MedTech chambers secure my hands to the bunk, so I don't scratch off all my skin."

"Sounds serious."

MedTech chambers stood, flipping a sheet up to cover the major's backside. "It is serious."

"I told her not to play doctor with her comments," Maj Simmons said. "We don't have time for obfuscation."

"Says the major who didn't report the nature of her injury right away."

"Point taken, Chambers. Now, am I dying?"

Chambers shook her head and heaved a sigh. "I don't know. Something is spreading through your skin. The civilian, Zeledon? He's in the same boat. It's slower on him because he wasn't hurt as badly as the major. Anyone who was just exposed to the air, they have a rash, but it's not the same kind."

"Can we stop it?" Dewey asked.

"I'm not sure yet, Lieutenant. I was hoping that their bodies would correct the problem on their own. So now I'm trying an antibiotic spectrum to see if anything responds. Soon as my machines are set up, I'll do an analysis. Till then, pain-killers."

"I think she drugged me so I'd stop giving orders," Maj Simmons said. Her smile was sloppy, her eyes half-lidded.

"Maybe, Major," Chambers said. She motioned toward the door with her body blocking her hand movements. "I'll be back, Maj Simmons. I need to check on my blood testing equipment."

Maj Simmons's eyes were closed. She didn't respond to Chambers's comment.

Dewey followed the medtech into the hallway.

"These walls are paper thin." Chambers whispered her information.

In the same volume, Dewey said, "You told the major the truth but not all of it."

"No, Lieutenant." Chambers took a deep breath. It was the type people took before delivering bad news. "It's definitely a poison. It's spreading through her systems. Zeledon, too, but like I said, just slower. I'm hoping that the blood chemistry analysis will help. Maybe we can counteract it with something as simple as aspirin or increased oxygen. Even a total transfusion would be nice, Lt Tyler."

"And if those don't solve the problem?"

"Then, things are going to get very complicated."

"All right. And what about those with the rash?"

Chambers flashed a brief smile. "At least there's some good news. We've several creams for burns and rashes that are having a positive effect. I'd like to get Cpl Garner in here, but he says he has orders to stay put."

"Well, that's mostly true," Dewey said. "I'll get him in here."

Dewey's comm buzzed. It was Cpl Garner.

"As if he was listening in," said Dewey. He tapped his comm to speak. "Garner, MedTech Chambers says you refuse to come to medical."

"Yes, sir." The humor Dewey expected was absent. "I'd like to. Hate this itch. But the civilians are getting restless. And now they're also getting angry. I could use a little authority out here."

18

Dewey had almost forgotten about the civilians. As much as he liked most civilians, especially the children, he wasn't feeling very fond of Capt Aunztequi. If it weren't for his mess, Dewey would still be on an intact ship, potentially even reading a book.

Here they were, though, on an alien world with an unbreathable atmosphere, no ship, and surviving the A.P. gunning for them every step of the way. And despite his feelings for the civilian captain, they had taken all of the civilians under their wing. They would protect them to the very last Hospitaller. All because of their oath to provide aid and comfort, and occasionally defend.

"When are we going to be allowed to move about?" The demand came at volume from an irritated looking Capt Aunztequi.

All of the civilians were together. Their evac suit helmets were on the ground, not even within arms reach. It contrasted poorly with Cpl Garner, who had his hanging from a lanyard at his waist. It might be awkward to walk around with the helmet banging against your leg, as Dewey's currently was, but it was more awkward to be gasping for air and unable to remember where you put it.

"Move about?" Dewey feigned surprise while enjoying Garner's look of annoyance.

"Yes, 'about.' You've got Hospitallers wandering off any old where and we're made to stand here."

"In my defense, Lt Tyler," Cpl Garner said. "I did inform the captain that his people were welcome to stand over there."

Garner had pointed down the line of the seal in the floor. They would still be inside the airlock space, just ten meters to the side. Dewey could well imagine the look of indignation on the captain's face.

"Cpl Garner, MedTech Chambers insists you report to her immediately. I will talk to the civilians until you return."

The only person who looked relieved at the change of guard was Cpl Garner.

"Right away, Lt Tyler." Garner saluted and quick-walked away.

"Now, Capt Aunztequi, about your question."

"Yes."

"You will not be allowed to move about."

More than the captain erupted in displeasure. Dewey held up his hands and waited until they got the hint and silence took over.

"That is absolutely not fair," one of the other civilians muttered into the silence.

"You're the XO of the smuggler ship, Juvenal Mecolaeta. That right?" Dewey knew he was right, he'd read each of their names and seen their faces as he did. It was a permanent part of his memory.

"XO?" Juvenal Mecolaeta seemed momentarily confused, which Dewey found interesting.

"Yes, he is," Capt Aunztequi said. He looked at Mecolaeta as he spoke.

"I am," said Mecolaeta, but without the confidence of someone sure of his answer.

"Well, XO Mecolaeta," Dewey said. "To rebut your comment, it's not about being fair. It's about being safe. We know nothing about the station. That is why my teams aren't wandering about, but are actually clearing rooms to make sure that the A.P. haven't also found a way into the building."

"There's more than one building," said another civilian that Dewey had previously spoken to. The engineer, Temistokles Aurrano. "They probably connect."

"Agreed," said Dewey. "And so we'll want to know where they connect and then how can we secure those passages. What we don't need is someone without training wandering off and getting hurt. Or, killed. Or captured by the A.P."

"But we can't just stand here," said Capt Aunztequi.

"No one is making you stand here." There was a long-drawn-out silence while Dewey let that piece of information sink in. "There's plenty of places to sit, even to lie down."

"Just so long as we stay on this side."

"It shouldn't be more than a few hours," Dewey said. "You can rest. You can eat. I can have my people set up a couple of portas if anyone needs to use them."

"Food?" someone else asked.

"If you'd like. It's all rations, but I can have someone else set up a reheater so they're at least warm. Probably be able to heat a pot of Insta, too."

The civilians seemed less impressed by the offer of Insta than the other suggestions.

"But, we will get to move around more after things have been cleared?"

"Perhaps," Dewey said. "Is there someplace in particular that you'd like to go?"

The question seemed to startle the captain. "What? No. I'm merely asking for information."

"We'll discuss that after my teams have reported back to me. In the meantime, stand by here or over where Cpl Garner suggested, and I'll get food and portas taken care of. Oh, and you might want to keep your helmets close by. Just in case."

The last comment seemed to raise a worry in a few of the civilians. They quickly reclaimed their helmets and held them in their hands as if decompression was imminent. Engineer Aurrano seemed to be one of the few who knew what to do with her helmet, and she quickly turned to the others, demonstrating how to secure their helmet.

Dewey made his way back toward the med tent.

"Pfc Fox," Dewey said. He caught Fox unaware. She hastily jumped to attention. "Stand easy, Fox. Where's Anderson?"

"Inside," Fox said.

"Great. If he's not busy, I'd like the two of you to find a couple portas and set them up with ballistic shields as privacy screens."

"Yes, Lieutenant."

"After that, break out rations and a reheater, so the civilians have some way to keep themselves busy."

"Will do, Lieutenant." She paused. "Now?"

"Now would be good."

Fox disappeared inside the med tent, passing Cpl Garner, who was on his way out.

"Did I stall long enough, Lt Tyler?" Garner asked with a followup grin.

"Long enough, Garner. But I still want you to keep an eye on Capt Aunztequi."

Garner nodded. Dewey knew he was feigning a somber attitude. "But from a distance, of course."

"Cpl Garner," Dewey said, trying not to smile, "Just so long as you don't lose sight of him. You can oversee Fox and Anderson. Maybe go ahead and start an urn of Insta. Civilians might not want it, but I think we could all use a little punch of energy."

"I'll get right on it," said Garner. He saluted and started back towards the airlock.

"Hold up, Garner." He stopped and turned back toward Dewey. "How's the arm?"

"Arm, Lieutenant?" Garner did a slow windmill with it. "Little sore, but the itch has gone away."

"Good. Back to work, then."

Garner nodded and left.

Dewey now stood alone outside the med tent. He could hear the buzz of quiet conversation from inside. In the distance, by the crawlers, the garbled sounds of conversations and the clink and thunk of equipment being moved and unloaded were multiplied off the walls around him.

Staying alive and getting here were the goals. They'd had their heads down, pushing forward, not thinking about what happened next. Now they were here. And now they had to think about what was supposed to happen next. Or, more optimistically, what they wanted to happen next.

Was the beacon still out there in space? Had it managed to send a message? Or were they just twiddling their thumbs, waiting to die?

With a shudder, Dewey threw off the growing shadow of negative thoughts. He was a Hospitaller and an officer. He would continue forward until there wasn't any more forward in which to continue. He tapped his comm.

"SSgt Castro? How are we doing out there?"

Static greeted his questions, and then, SSgt Castro was talking.

"Hey, Lt Tyler. This place is huge. There aren't just stairs to lower levels, there are ramps almost big enough for a crawler. Certainly an A.P.C, for sure."

They didn't have any armored personnel carriers. If they'd had them, there'd be a few less dead.

"Did you find connections to the other buildings?" Dewey began walking toward the open space beyond the med tent and in the direction that the three teams had gone before separating.

"I haven't," Castro said. "But Sgt Parks did. I told her to check the length and then see if there's a way to secure it or at least put a hand out as sentinel."

Hands, named because of their uncanny similarity to an actual severed hand, were a discreet way to monitor for movement.

"Good thinking. What about Sgt Perry?"

"She seemed impressed or excited about what she'd found. Said it looked like barracks, medical, labs. The business wing, I would hazard."

"What about a map?"

"Oh! Yeah, thanks for reminding me, Lieutenant." There was a pause, and then Dewey heard a muffled ding coming from inside his EVA suit. "Just sent it to you."

"Thank you, Castro. Thirty minutes and get everyone back here. We've got Insta going and a reheater for the rations."

"Sounds like a party," Castro said. "Be back in thirty."

The comm line went quiet. Dewey started opening the EVA suit, digging for the tablet that would be in the side pocket of his pants.

When he found it, he pulled it out and opened the file SSgt Castro had sent him. He scanned the floor plans. They were a captured image from an emergency evacuation plaque. There were two full floors and then four stairwells and ramps that went down five levels. Each of the levels below the top two floors were smaller, having fewer rooms.

The very bottom level, however, was almost as big as the top two, and it didn't have the little gray lines that were used to mark off enclosed spaces like storage rooms or offices. It looked like one big open space, much like where he was standing now. Why would they need that kind of space that far down?

He'd like to explore more, but first, he had to secure one area and be able to control and defend it. Then they could get creative.

"Sgt Perry," Dewey said after activating the comm again.

Static again and then, "Sgt Perry, Lieutenant."

"What's the state of the dorms?"

"Crazy, Lt Tyler." Perry chuckled. Someone near her had said something. "The plumbing works, the lights work. There are supplies like mattresses, toiletries. All of it sealed and ready for use. It's the dates on them that's the real crazy."

"Dates?"

"Yep. This stuff's been here for less than seventy years. I've had rations older than that."

Seventy years? That was the date the supplies were sealed and likely shipped. That meant that someone had been here less than seventy years ago. Who had been here less than seventy years ago?

Clearly, it had something to do with the A.P. If it had been them, it might explain why they seemed determined to keep it a secret? But even the Hospitallers had small bases on unclaimed moons and a few ice planets. If someone discovered the out-stations, they certainly wouldn't be killed for it.

No, it wasn't the fact they'd been here. It had to be the reason why the A.P. had been here. They'd been up to something and didn't want anyone to know about it, even after they'd clearly abandoned the place.

"Perry, can we used the barracks?"

"Sure can, Lieutenant. Medical looks in good condition as well."

Chambers might appreciate that. "What about a command station?"

"Nothing yet. Maybe the next level down?"

"Maybe, we'll look later. I'd like you to secure that section of the building, with the barracks and medical. We'll start moving supplies and personal in there for at least a couple shifts so everyone can get out of their evac suits and gets some real sleep."

"We'll get to it now."

"Let me know when you're ready, Sgt Perry." Dewey tapped the comm to close it. The civilians wanted to move about. Dewey touched the part of the map where the barracks were located. The civilians could move right about there.

"So now we're under guard?" asked Capt Aunztequi. He sounded even more annoyed than when he'd been confined to the airlock area.

"You're not under guard, Captain," Dewey said. They'd had this conversation not twenty minutes ago when they'd been guided down the side corridor and into the barracks.

The barracks were extensive, almost as big as the loading bay on the Shnel Shnek. There was also a mess wall with working heaters and built-in urns for hot water and coffee. Then, there were two shower rooms with ten showerheads in each. The bunks were doubles and weren't crammed together. There was plenty of room for everyone.

"There's a guard at the door," Capt Aunztequi said. He walked to the door and then into the corridor, pointing meaningfully in both directions. "And guards at both ends of the hall. It seems obvious to me that we are under guard."

Dewey sighed. Capt Aunztequi and the other civilians were a little too eager to get loose in the buildings. And as he had no idea as to why he wasn't about to let them off the leash. He'd learned that turn of phrase from a Wutenigel trainer. The creatures were curious enough to the point of self-harm when off their own planet.

"If you're under guard, then we're all under guard," Dewey finally said. "We have to be alert for any attempt at attack by the A.P. So, please, just relax. Once we are sure of how much space we can or do control, we can let you stretch your legs. Now, excuse me."

MedTech Chambers had stepped out of the medical offices. She'd probably heard Capt Aunztequi's overly loud voice. She appeared to take advantage of the opportunity to wave Dewey in her direction.

"Thank you," Dewey said after joining Chambers.

"Thank you? Oh, for Capt Aunz-something?" She waved off the captain's name. "You're welcome, Lieutenant, but that wasn't why I waved for you."

She re-entered the medical offices, and Dewey followed.

"Then why did you wave for me?"

"Because I didn't want anyone else to hear." She stopped at a table that was now the station for the Hospitaller medical equipment. A large box-shaped machine with a glass door at the bottom right and a screen at the top center was now Chambers's focus. "I've got bad news. Really bad."

19

Dewey looked at the screen on the chemical analysis machine. It was a reflexive reaction as he didn't have the training or experience to interpret what he was seeing.

"Care to explain?"

"It's a poison," MedTech Chambers said. She tapped the screen, enlarging some data that Dewey still wasn't comprehending.

"Poison, okay, got it," Dewey said. "Don't we carry meds for most types of poisons? Antidotes?"

"Yes and no, Lieutenant. The really common ones, sure. I have enough to treat everyone on the ship if needed. But rare poisons, no. The shelf life of most of the antidotes for rare poisons is short. So we just print them as we need them."

Dewey scratched the back of his head. He could use a shower. But that looked like it was going to have to wait. The chem printer on the ship was bolted into place. A lot of the surgical and scanning equipment was, too. Why not? It wasn't like they were ever going to need it anywhere else.

"Do you have the formula for the antidote you need printed?"

Chambers nodded before taking out her tablet and tapping on the screen. She flipped through several screens and then flicked sideways across it. Dewey's tablet vibrated. Now he had the formula.

"Do we have a deadline?"

"I can't say," Chambers said. She tapped the screen on the analyzer, putting it to sleep. "Slower heart rate has a delaying effect. So, I put both of them to sleep. But Maj Simmons is worse off than Zeledon.

Sooner than later?"

"I was hoping to at least give everyone a chance to rest," Dewey said. "So, if a couple of hours won't hurt?"

"Should be fine, Lt Tyler, just as long as whoever you send doesn't dawdle."

"Thank you, Chambers. Keep me updated on their condition."

"Will do."

Dewey had almost laughed when Chambers had suggested that he would be sending someone. Out into that world? No, he was going to go. Not only because he wasn't going to subject his people to a world he wasn't willing to face, but because he had to.

However, a few hours rest and a shower, first. Then, he'd find a fireteam of volunteers. He was certain that finding them would be less difficult than finding people who didn't want to volunteer.

He opened the door from medical into the corridor only to realize there was chaos. At the far end of the corridor, several of the civilians were being pushed back by Pfc Horton and Pvt Hart. Behind them, Cpl Chavez and Pfc Schultz stood with their backs to the doors. Down the corridor in the other direction, Sgt Parks and Cpl Mitchell's fireteam were standing at the open doors looking into the open bay they'd migrated into after the airlock opened.

Dewey started in the direction of the civilians. "What's going on here?"

"You can't stop us from looking around," one of the civilians said.

"Ms. Barindano," Dewey said. "Yes, we can. And it's about safety."

"You're people went," she said. "We should be able to as well."

Sometimes civilians were frustrating. "They went out there to make sure the place wasn't a danger to any of us. But they haven't cleared all of it. So no one should be out there without supervision."

"Okay." Ms. Barindano turned. "Come on, let's go."

The other civilians followed her without a single backward glance. Dewey eyed them suspiciously. They'd given up too quickly, too easily.

"Tell me what happened," Dewey said. He was still watching the civilians as they turned into the barracks.

"They rushed us," Cpl Chavez said. "They'd managed to push past

Horton and Hart before getting the doors open. Me and Schultz were on the other side. They tried to slip past, but we managed to grab them and get them all back on this side."

Dewey nodded and then tapped his comm. "Sgt Perry? Report, please."

"Hey, Lieutenant. Some of the civilians wanted to go stretch their legs. Gonzalez and Foster were at the doors and said they had to stay here. They rushed them, and several got through. But we got them all rounded up and back to the barracks. That was about the time they did the same thing at the other end."

"Are all the civilians accounted for?"

There was a long pause which gave Dewey all the answer he needed.

"I can't say for sure, Lt Tyler."

"Thank you, Perry." Dewey tapped the comm again, raising Cpl Garner. "Garner, do you have eyes on Capt Aunztequi?"

Garner answered in a whisper. "Pretty much, Lieutenant."

"Where are you, Corporal?" Dewey said. He looked around as he spoke, as if he had the ability to see through walls.

"Next level down," Garner whispered. "I've got my tablet on, you can ping it."

Dewey pulled out his tablet and used it to locate Cpl Garner. One level down, as Garner said and back several corridors. What was Capt Aunztequi doing there?

"Cpl Mitchell," Dewey said into the comm. "You and your fireteam on deck, A.S.A.P."

Mitchell's response did not come through the comm. Instead, Dewey heard his voice echo through doorways and the corridor. "Fireteam! Gear up. Move it now!"

Again on the comm, Dewey requested SSgt Castro to report.

In less than a minute, Cpl Mitchell appeared at the doorway to the barracks. He nodded at Dewey and then waved his arm like he was going to scoop each member of his fireteam from the room and deposit them in the corridor.

"Form up!"

Movement beyond Mitchell's fireteam drew some of Dewey's

attention. SSgt Castro had appeared, stepping through the doorway that separated the corridor from the central chamber where they'd put up the med tent. She said something to the Hospitallers guarding the doors and then trotted toward Dewey. At the same time, Cpl Mitchell moved to report in with Dewey, turning their easy gaits into a friendly competition. They arrived in tandem, grinning and saluting.

"SSgt Castro reporting."

"Cpl Mitchell reporting."

Dewey returned their salutes. "Mitchell, you and your fireteam are going with me to round up some missing civilians."

"Capt Aunztequi?" Castro asked.

"Surprised?" asked Dewey. "He and two others are missing. They created several diversions and then made a break for it. Cpl Garner seems to have anticipated their moves. He's got a bead on them now."

"You want me to make sure the rest stay put?"

"I want a better way to keep them secured, Staff Sergeant. They're here on purpose. And I think we're about to learn why. After that, I would like them locked down so they can't get in the way or get themselves hurt."

"I'll get right on it." SSgt Castro saluted and dismissed herself.

"Bring your team, Cpl Mitchell. And let's go gather civilians."

Dewey heard the civilians before he saw Cpl Garner. Cpl Mitchell's fireteam was split, two along each wall of the corridor that Garner's mark on Dewey's tablet map had led them. There were lots of wide windows between doorways, which slowed the fireteam's progress. Several of the doors were open, and that was the only reason they had Capt Aunztequi and the other civilians' positions marked.

"Lieutenant," whispered Cpl Mitchell. When Dewey looked his way, he motioned that Dewey should look further up the corridor.

Past the third open door, at what looked like a narrower side corridor, Cpl Garner was waving for attention. Dewey returned the wave.

"Keep a lookout, Mitchell," Dewey whispered. "I'm going forward."

Mitchell nodded, and Dewey gave him a quiet clap on the shoulder before crouching and duck-walking under a window. He quickly stepped across an open doorway before duck walking again.

Within the next doorway was the source of voices. Dewey could tell they were upset about something not being where they expected it to be, and that they were also considering where else to look. Oh, and one of them needed to find a working toilet.

Dewey took a deep breath and leaped across the space with the speed and skill of a ballet dancer. From there, it was a short walk without windows to where Cpl Garner waited.

"Nice leap there, Lieutenant."

"Dorm mother was big on dance and gymnastics. I guess some of it must have stuck. Now, any idea why they're here?"

"Not really. I'd heard them talking about creating a diversion and slipping out of the barracks area. I could have put a boot on their plans, but I figured it might be nice to know what they were looking for."

"So, you were sure they weren't doing this just to stretch their legs?"

"Even a Marine isn't that thick, Lt Tyler."

"Good point. Did they come right here?"

"No." Garner pointed to the opposite wall. "They started with the corridor that way. Almost accidentally caught me following them. I had to be a little more cautious and almost lost them. Fortunately, they talk a lot."

"And loud." Dewey stepped into the corridor. "All right. Let's go see what's got them all excited. Other than a potty break, that is."

He walked back toward the doorway the voices still drifted from. He motioned for Mitchell's fireteam to close in and then signaled for Mitchell to take the room.

Under Cpl Mitchell's guidance, they came in high and low. Dewey was sure that Mitchell knew the civilians weren't going to resist. He was also sure that Mitchell was making a point with his entrance. It was a point Dewey approved of.

"Down! Down! Everybody Down!" Mitchell roared as his team breached the doorway.

Inside the room, someone screamed while Capt Aunztequi cursed his surprise.

"I said down!"

Dewey hurried to enter the room to ensure that Mitchell didn't take the situation to another level. As he crossed the threshold, he slowed down. The three civilians were down, arms out, palms on the floor. Mitchell's fireteam had them boxed in. Only Capt Aunztequi was looking up and around.

"I don't know what you're thinking," he said, "acting like this."

"I think he's following orders," said Dewey. His voice seemed to surprise the captain, who had to turn his neck at an awkward angle to see Dewey. "Something that you might attempt when they are given to you."

Capt Aunztequi started to rise from the ground. Mitchell growled something that changed the captain's mind. He'd been cowed into staying down, but his attitude was still in play. "We are not part of your military, Lieutenant. We do not have to follow your orders."

"You were willing to do so when the A.P. were trying to kill you and you needed saving." Dewey motioned for Cpl Mitchell to pull his fireteam back. When they'd moved to give the civilians more space, Dewey continued. "And I'm still trying to keep you safe, you're just making my job more complicated. You can get up now."

Capt Aunztequi and the other two civilians hurried to their feet. Dewey wasn't surprised to see that the XO, Juvenal Mecolaeta, was present. But the other person was a surprise.

"Medic Izu," Dewey said. "I hope your patient is in good hands while you run around and play explorer."

"He's in an induced coma, Lt Tyler. MedTech Chambers is watching over him." She appeared a little ruffled by the situation.

"Why are you here?"

Izu looked at Capt Aunztequi. "I was asked to come along."

"Right. But why are you here? For real. Why are you all in this system? Why were you attempting to reach this planet? Why are you searching the rooms down here?"

"I told you," Capt Aunztequi said, "we were chased here by the A.P."

"No, Captain, you weren't. I'm pretty sure they were already here. I'm also sure their job was to ensure that anyone who came here never left here. So, again, why are you here?"

"We're with Knowledge Freedom Foundation," XO Mecolaeta said. "Well, I am. Anua Izu is, too. Capt Aunztequi is who he says he is."

Knowledge Freedom Foundation. Dewey knew some things about them. They were an independent organization that sought to unveil government and corporate secrets. Secrets that they deemed important enough to know that all people should be granted access to the information. They'd made several unsuccessful attempts to infiltrate Hospitaller-owned companies.

Mostly, though, Dewey understood their actions to be made with good intentions.

"KFF," Dewey said. "What's here that is worth risking your lives over?"

"Genetic manipulation," Medic Izu said.

Dewey studied her for a moment before asking, "GMO? That kind of manipulation?"

He had a feeling he was wrong. As long as humans had been expanding through the second radial arm of the galaxy, they'd been manipulating the genes of plants. That was how they were able to get so many of them to thrive in non-native soil. Then there was the manipulation of native plants, too, so that they could be beneficial to humans as a food crop. Dewey didn't think that was a big enough of a secret to die for.

When she shook her head, Dewey didn't even blink.

"No, Lt Tyler." She took a breath and then said, "Human genetic manipulation."

20

For a moment, it seemed to Dewey as if all the air had been sucked out of the room. It was quickly returned with a snort of disbelief by Pfc Beth Gonzalez.

"Human genetic manipulation," she said. Her smirk revealed her opinion on the matter. But if the wasn't clear enough, she also said, "That's just fodder for Friday night vids."

"Actually," said Dewey, and he couldn't help himself. He'd read about the history of genetic modifications. It had included several chapters involving human gen-mod. "There are records of attempts to modify human genetics as far back as pre-First Expansion."

"No one's been successful," said XO Mecolaeta.

"That we know of," added Pvt Foster.

Gonzalez laughed, earning a glare from Foster. "What kind of tab-vids have you been watching?"

"None. But you can be sure that if someone was successful, they'd keep it a secret. Use it for nefarious reasons."

"'Nefarious reasons.' That's rich."

"Stand down," Dewey said, killing the budding argument. "Besides, Foster has a good point. A point that brings you all here." He turned his attention back onto the three civilians. "Did you find evidence?"

Medic Izu chewed on her lip before saying, "No."

"Not yet," said Mecolaeta.

"The information we were given," Izu said, "indicated that we'd find the data down here."

"But you didn't," Cpl Garner said.

Mecolaeta shook his head, looking somewhat defeated. "No, the data banks were removed."

"But there's more rooms, more levels," said Izu. "We just have to keep looking."

Dewey recalled the large, lower level without its interior walls. What was that space for?

"Well, we don't have time for exploration," he said out loud. "MedTech Chambers thinks she has a solution to the poison in Zeledon and Maj Simmons."

"Well, that's good." Mecolaeta seemed relieved. "But how does that keep us from looking for our evidence?"

"It keeps you from running around here unsupervised because I can't spare the resources while I'm gone. And there is no way I'm allowing you free roam until I know that every space is clear, and we can keep the A.P. out."

"Wait," Capt Aunztequi said. He stepped forward, moving Izu aside with an elbow. "You're going somewhere?"

Dewey temporarily ignored the captain. "Cpl Mitchell, let's escort the civilians back up to the top level and deposit them back in the barracks where they will remain."

"Yes, Lieutenant." Mitchell signaled to the rest of his fireteam. Gonzalez took point while Pfc Doug Wong and Pvt Foster bracketed Capt Aunztequi and the other civilians. He pointed with the barrel of his weapon in the direction of the door. "This way, please."

Mecolaeta moved first, his head hanging like he'd been defeated. Izu followed, a little less dejectedly. Capt Aunztequi didn't budge.

"You said you were going somewhere," he said to Dewey. "Where are you going?"

Dewey waved the captain into motion. "Back to the ship. We need to print the meds for the poison antidote."

"Who's going with you?" Capt Aunztequi asked.

This time it was Dewey who snorted. "Not you."

Dewey wasn't going to get the shower he wanted. He might as well of wished to read a book for all the good it was going to do. By the time they got Capt Aunztequi and the other civilians back to the barracks, SSgt Castro had set up a watch system that would keep the civilians under observation around the clock.

"There's less room here than in that airlock," Capt Aunztequi said in disgust.

"Then maybe you shouldn't have broken our trust," said SSgt Castro.

Dewey took a long look at the doorway that led to the showers before waving for SSgt Castro to follow him into the corridor. He commed MSgt Roberson and had him join them.

"How's the major looking?" Dewey asked Roberson when he entered the corridor.

"Asleep. Pale. You sure this is going to work?"

"The antidote?" Dewey asked. "Chambers says it will. That's what we have to work with. And I trust Chambers at her job."

"I do, too," Roberson said. "But this is an alien world and an alien poison."

"Still all chemistry," said SSgt Castro.

"Good point. Still worried." MSgt Roberson paused and looked down the corridor where fireteams guarded both doorways. "Who's going?"

"I'm going. Mitchell's fireteam already had some fun. So I'm thinking Sgt Perry and Cpl Chavez with what's left of her fireteam."

"You're the only officer," MSgt Roberson said. "Castro or I should go."

"Biometric locks," said Castro. "The only way to override the security on the ship without engaging a self-destruct is with the major's or Lt Tyler's biometrics."

"So you'll be in charge, MSgt Roberson," Dewey said. He was glad to see that Roberson wasn't going to push the issue. "SSgt Castro will be your XO. Keep everyone in this area. You can send a fireteam out to the crawlers if you need any of the supplies."

"Yes, Lieutenant," Roberson said. "Don't be too long."

Dewey laughed. "I can't run there, but I'll move as fast as I can."

"I'll round up Perry and the others?"

"Yes, Castro, that'd be appreciated. I'm going to look in on the major and MedTech Chambers. We'll use the airlock closest here."

The two staff NCOs saluted and left. Dewey stood in place for a few seconds, visualizing a hot shower before making his way to medical. Past the door, Chambers and MedTech Moreno were studying the display on the chem analyzer.

"Numbers are about the same," Moreno said. She was leaning closest to the display. Chambers was just behind her shoulder, both of her arms crossed.

"Higher than before is not the same," said Chambers.

"But, the delta is smaller this time."

"Delta?" Both medtechs turned, snapping to attention. "At ease. What delta? You mean difference?"

"Yes." Chambers turned and looked at the machine as if to verify her answer. "The molecules that are attacking Maj Simmons's body have slowed reproduction. So it must have something to do with activity, heart rate, body temperature, or something."

"Since it's slowed," Moreno added, "it means we have a larger window of time."

"Speaking of, Lt Tyler, I thought you'd already left."

"That was sort of my intent. That and a shower. Civilians purposefully wandered off, and we had to round them up. We're going now. Is there anything else you need from the ship while we're there?"

"The burn cream?" asked Moreno as she eyed Chambers.

"That's not a bad idea," said Chambers as she nodded agreement. "It's in a bottom cabinet in the first exam room."

"Burn cream, okay. Take care of the injured, I'll be back post-haste."

Back in the corridor, SSgt Castro, Sgt Perry, and Cpl Chavez with her truncated fireteam stood in a ragged line that instantly sharpened as they realized Dewey was there.

"Ready to go," SSgt Castro said.

"Let's do it, then."

"Sgt Perry?" Castro asked the sergeant.

Perry turned to face the other Hospitallers. "Fireteam. Move out."

The turned and followed SSgt Castro and Dewey as they passed through the doors held open by Pfc Schultz and Pvt Becker. Dewey returned their salutes and then continued down the hallway.

"Perry? Your team searched along here?"

"Yes, Lieutenant."

"You find anything interesting? Anything that stood out as unusual?"

"Not that I recall," said Sgt Perry. "The rooms were stripped of any identifiable materials. Nothing that would identify who'd been here or why they'd been here if that's what you were hoping for."

"Kind of, yes. Thank you."

Assuming it was the A.P. who'd built the bigger buildings over the old buildings, they'd removed proof that they'd been here. But they'd also left enough equipment behind that they could also re-occupy with little effort. There'd even been the essential medical supplies as Chambers and Moreno had discovered.

Unfortunately for the civilians, there hadn't been any proof of the genetic testing they'd hope to expose. Dewey didn't doubt the A.P., or whoever had been occupying the buildings, had been doing something they didn't want anyone else to know about. Setting up on a hostile planet with a hostile environment was as good a secure location as any.

The A.P. had taken an aggressive posture toward the entrance of the smuggler ship, the Tunkum Panri, almost obliterating it before the Shnel Shnek had arrived. And they'd continued to hammer at the survivors even as they struggled on the surface of Wenshen. That was a lot of work, but maybe not if they were desperate to keep a secret secret. Human genetic manipulation would be precisely the kind of secret they wouldn't want the galaxy to know about.

"Here, Lieutenant."

Dewey did an about-face-march and returned to where SSgt Castro and Sgt Perry waited. They were both smiling.

"Lot's to think about. Everyone ready?"

"Yes, Lt Tyler."

"Let's get this started so we can get it over with."

Dewey entered the airlock, followed by Sgt Perry and the fireteam.

The airlock was big enough that they could have gotten an entire platoon inside, but not so big that it would take hours to cycle.

Rechargers hung on hooks along the walls. Dewey took one down and snapped it to his EVA suit as he put on his helmet to call up the HUD. The recharger worked and would replenish his system to full capacity if he'd be willing to sit still for an hour. An hour was something he didn't have. He pointed at the other rechargers and then remembered to tap the comm on his suit, activating the external speaker.

"Top off while we wait for the airlock to complete its cycle."

The other Hospitallers moved to comply, donning helmets as they went. Dewey turned to find SSgt Perry, standing at the hatch to the airlock. She gave him a thumbs up. When he returned the gesture, she stepped back, out of visual. The door to the airlock swung on its oversized hinges, sealing the entrance.

Before pressing the button to start the cycling process, Dewey checked everyone's suit for proper seals. Cpl Chavez returned the favor. Once Dewey was certain they were all properly secure inside their suits, he gave the button a gentle punch with one fist.

The cycle took thirty minutes, which was longer than Dewey liked. However, it wasn't just evacuating an environment. It was replacing it with another. The protocols were different than a standard evacuation to zero atmo.

When the light turned green, Dewey signaled Sgt Perry, who gave the order to disengage the rechargers. When everyone was standing, Perry finger-punched the button that released the outside hatch lock. The door popped open about a half-meter and then stopped.

Over the general comm, Perry said, "Bit rusty. Horton, give it a push. Hart, watch his back."

Pfc Horton stepped forward and leaned against the door with both hands and slowly pushed it open. Next to him, Hart scanned the outside with the barrel of her weapon leading. Horton pushed until the hatch was open enough that everyone could exit without rubbing against the edges.

Hart went first, her weapon barrel leading the way. Cpl Chavez followed, moving to the right, allowing for Pfc Horton to come through the middle. They scanned the area for several minutes before signally the area was clear.

Perry led Dewey out of the airlock and then tapped the controls that closed the hatch.

Dewey had decided that since the original owners of the buildings left the inside hatches open as a great way to keep people out, it might be an excellent tactic to replicate. The only serious problem with the idea, though, was that they'd have to wait outside while the airlocked cycled again to put the planet's atmosphere into the airlock once more.

The comm in Dewey's helmet buzzed.

"Lt Tyler," he said after tapping the comm.

"SSgt Castro, Lieutenant. How's it looking?"

"Same as before," Dewey said. "But without the incoming shoulder rockets."

"Ouch, Lieutenant. I get to live that one down, right?"

"As I'm still alive, I'll say that it's possible. We're moving. I'll try checking in after an hour's march."

"I'll hang out in the big airlock and see if that improves the signal."

Dewey acknowledged the idea and then switched his comm to speak to the fireteam. "Sgt Perry, as quick as we can."

As quick as they could was not a run or a trot. It was barely at force march speed. The EVA and evac suits slowed them, but not as slow as the crawlers. Still, they had to wind their way around the different plants that could slice or stab. And rather than the shallow pass, they went over the hill to reach the wide flat plain on which they'd crashed the Shnel Shnek.

An hour out, and they still had some communication with SSgt Castro. In the second hour, all Dewey could hear was static. The tether had been cut, and they were on their own. As long as they kept moving in the right direction, they would be okay. If nothing hindered their progress, they'd reach each goal on time.

Their first goal was to reach the abandoned crawler and supplies. Dewey wanted to make sure that any other munitions left behind couldn't also be used by the A.P. That was assuming that they hadn't already taken it.

Despite the restraints of space suits, gear, and deadly plants, they were making better time than they had on the way in. It was three hours by the time they reached the crawler. It was apparent, based on the disorderly distribution of the abandoned supplies, that the A.P. had picked through everything.

"SSgt Castro said there were munitions, too," Sgt Perry said. "But the rockets they fired at us constituted all that we'd left behind."

"Are ammo won't work in their weapons anyway," said Dewey as he nudged a crate of emergency rations. Whoever had opened the box hadn't bothered to shut it. Something else had disturbed the contents and scuffed the boot marks on the ground in the process. They'd only met one other creature on this planet besides the A.P., and they'd been even more deadly.

The thought of the giant monster ants made Dewey uncomfortable enough that he shuddered. He didn't want to be out here in the dark if they came once more.

"Okay, let's move out," Dewey said. He was confident that they could reach the ship and be inside before it was too dark to maneuver without task lights. Task lights would be like bullseyes painted on their foreheads for the A.P. and who knew if it was an attraction for the ants.

Pfc Horton took point as they began the next leg of the forced march that would bring them to the ship. Horton had gone less than thirty meters when he stopped and held up his hand. Everyone paused and took up defensive positions.

Dewey could see that Horton was talking to Sgt Perry. After several seconds of waiting, Dewey's comm buzzed.

"Sgt Perry? What's the holdup?"

"Something's moving out there, Lieutenant. And it's coming this way."

21

Dewey didn't have to guess what was coming. If it had been the A.P., they would have led with gunfire. This had to be something more dangerous.

He tapped his comm for general communication. "Everyone, left flank, march. Keep in line. Horton, let us know if anything changes."

"Yes, Lt Tyler," Horton said. Dewey picked up a sense of anxiety from Horton's voice as everyone turned left at the same time. Knowing what the giant ant monsters were capable of, Dewey was feeling a little anxious, too.

They continued moving left, keeping each other in sight as they wove through the equally deadly brush. Twice, Horton reported that the movement was still there, but was also falling behind.

"Lt Tyler," Horton said after an hour had passed.

"Team halt," Dewey said. He watched as they turned to guard every direction. "Go ahead, Horton."

"We're not being followed, Lieutenant. I think whoever it was, or whatever it was, has gone elsewhere."

"Did they turn around?" Dewey wanted to avoid another encounter if he could.

"I don't think so, Lieutenant, no. The movement just sort of faded."

What to make of that? Dewey wasn't sure. What he was sure of was that they were running out of daylight.

"Okay, thank you, Horton." Dewey changed the conversation. "Sgt Perry, let's put someone fresh on point and head forward once more.

One hour and then we'll start angling back toward the ship."

"You got it, Lt Tyler. Cpl Chavez? You mind taking point?"

"I'm on it." A pause and then, "Excuse me, Lieutenant."

Dewey turned as Cpl Chavez came by. She saluted as she passed, and Dewey reciprocated. She'd been on the back end of the line. Now he was. He watched as Chavez wove her way up to the front. It was a few more minutes before the fireteam started moving.

"Lt Tyler," Sgt Perry asked as they moved, "you want me or someone else to take up the rear?"

"No need, Perry, I'll handle it for now."

The next hour went without incident. While paused to change point, Sgt Perry taking his turn, Dewey attempted to make a comm connection with SSgt Castro once more. As expected, he got nothing.

The ship was now visible as a straight-lined hump on the near horizon. It was in shadow. The sun had moved well past its zenith. Two more hours of fast moving would see them at the ship. Getting in was going to be a different matter.

"Coming, Lieutenant?"

Dewey snapped out of his revere and moved, closing the too-wide gap between him and Pvt Hart.

They continued to walk, weaving through the foliage, always mindful of what it could do to a suit or a person. The ship grew steadily larger with their approach, and just as the sun tapped the horizon, they stood next to the Shnel Shnek.

"How do we get in?" ask Pvt Hart.

"This way," Dewey said. He led the way around the ship to the aft loading bay. They'd done an emergency drop of the front bay's door, which rendered it unable to close. That was why they'd destroyed the airlock. But the aft bay had been cooperative, and the loading hatch was firmly in place.

In a less secretive way than the panel at the buildings, there was a small panel next to the loading bay entrance. Behind it, there was a one-hand keyboard and a biometric reader. When the panel was removed, the system came online. Dewey quickly pulled the outer layer of his EVA glove off and pressed his hand to the reader.

His hand was now partially exposed to the atmosphere via the thin metal skin of the inner layer of Dewey's glove. It would corrode quickly, but hopefully, it would last long enough for Dewey to receive the go-ahead. Then he only needed to get the outer layer of his glove on before the burning sensation became too much to bear.

The delay in time from when Dewey pressed his hand to the reader to the time the light winked green made Dewey more nervous than the itch beginning to build in his hand. But the light did turn green. As Dewey slipped the outer layer of glove back on, he could see that the edges of the metal skin had begun to rust. If he had the chance, he was going to need a new glove.

Now that he had access to the ship systems, Dewey entered the lengthy control code that he'd never forgotten after the one time he'd seen it. That gave him the ability to direct ship systems to lower the hatch to the bay.

Dewey pressed enter, setting the command in motion. The door began it's slow grinding of gears as it moved downward. Then it dropped as if cut loose from the gears that controlled it. The hatch slammed into the ground, throwing up a cloud of dust. Dewey staggered backward in surprise.

"Good thing we weren't standing any closer," said Cpl Chavez as she caught Dewey and kept him from tripping over his feet.

"You enter the wrong command, Lieutenant?" asked Sgt Perry. Her question was punctuated with a grin.

"Has the lieutenant ever forgotten anything?" asked Pfc Horton.

"Good point," Perry said. A round of laughter filled the comm. Dewey joined in once he was sure he still had his toes.

"The corrosion must have gotten to the gears," he said. "Or the damage from the landing may have been enough that we got one good operation out it before things broke. Either way, we're in. Let's go."

Pvt Hart stepped onto the hatch that now served as a ramp when Pfc Horton called through the comm. "I found something weird," he said. "It looks like a footprint."

"A footprint?" Sgt Perry joined Horton. "Probably one of ours. Or an A.P. boot."

"Yeah, it's not a boot print, Sergeant. It's a footprint."

This wasn't the first time that Dewey had heard the comment made. Still, he was curious and joined Horton and Perry. It certainly looked like a footprint, very much like the one he'd seen outside the research buildings.

"Well, I feel sorry for anyone who lost a boot on this planet," Sgt Perry said. "That's got to burn bad."

"Could be another creature we haven't met yet," said Dewey.

"Like the ancient Yeti?" asked Hart from where she stood on the ramp.

"That would have been hard to miss," Horton answered.

"Like giant monster ants, Horton?" Cpl Chavez asked. "We missed those."

Dewey studied the ground. He saw several other prints that could easily be mistaken for a human footprint, too. "It could be a lot of things. Overlapping prints might give the impression of a human footprint. The way the dirt settled. Whatever it is, it can't be human."

"Looks human," Horton said as he stepped around the print and continued to the ramp.

Dewey agreed, but he wasn't about to say it out loud. Sometimes things really were just coincidences.

The loading bay was in the same state as when they'd left it. They went around the crawler lying on its side and reached the airlock that would let them into the center of the ship. They passed through in two groups. While Dewey waited for the second group, he ran a diagnostic on the air quality. MSgt Roberson had mentioned a small leak that was affecting the ship's atmo.

"Okay, we got air," Dewey said as the second group exited the airlock. "Oxygen is still at normal numbers. If you get a funny taste in your mouth, it's the air from the planet. It's about one part per billion, so nothing on you should melt."

Dewey unlocked and removed his helmet and then his gloves. The others followed suit. Pvt Hart's reluctant first breath raised a smile on Dewey's face.

"Sgt Perry, set a guard here. I'm going to get a glove. Then I'll meet you up in medical. Start checking the first exam room for burn cream." Dewey looked at his hand, the palm was redder than usual. "Definitely the burn cream."

"Hart, you're on guard duty," Sgt Perry said. "Everyone else, follow me."

While the others went up the spiral staircase, Dewey went to the EVA lockers and rooted out a replacement glove. He hung it on the same lanyard as his helmet and then gave Hart a nod before taking the stairs up.

By the time Dewey reached medical, Sgt Perry had a stack of burn cream canisters on the table in the center of the room.

"You want me to look for anything else?" Perry asked.

"I don't think so," answered Dewey. Then, "Maybe put together some food? We're going to be here awhile. Might as well get something in our bellies."

MedTech Chambers had been exact on the time it would take to print the antidote to the poison. She also hoped that Dewey would have enough time to print extras, just in case.

"Cpl Chavez? You and Horton want to take care of that?"

"Will do, Sergeant." Chavez waved for Horton to follow, and they left in the direction of the dining hall.

Dewey had crossed to the bank of machines on the far wall of the room. One looked similar to the machine Chambers had used to analyze the major's blood. He recognized one of the others as a centrifuge. It was the machine on the far right that he needed.

A tap with a finger on a small panel woke the printer. Dewey dug his tablet out from inside his EVA suit and pulled up the message from Chambers with the code he needed to enter. It was a long string of random digits and letters. He read it twice and put the tablet away.

It took a minute to enter the string and push enter. Dewey waited as the machine seemed to mull over the data. He wasn't a hundred percent perfect in his ability to recall. Despite the joking outside, he did get things wrong. Though it was a rare event. Had he done it now? Was the machine going to kick back a failed entry? Or worse, would it print the wrong medicine? Would it print something useless that wouldn't help the major or the civilian?

Dewey read through the string as he waited for a red light to tell him he'd done it wrong. However, he was positive that he'd done it right. The chime and green light reconfirmed his belief. Lines of information scrolled up, pushing the string of numbers out of sight. The data was an initiation of the printing process and the request for quantity. It was one pill per person, so Dewey tapped in a request for ten pills. The data scrolled more and then indicated it would take two hours for the process to complete.

"Two hours?"

"The compounds are complicated," Dewey said in answer to Sgt Perry's question. "And we can't leave until daylight. Shall we see about getting some Insta?"

As Dewey had the time, he took a shower. It was longer than a standard shower, so he had a few moments of guilt while the hot water poured down over him. He justified his time under the water by reminding himself the ship was going to be written off anyway. No one would be using this ship after they were rescued.

Still, he had a decade of training that said to not waste resources. So after two extra minutes, Dewey was out and dry. He did put on fresh everything as he dressed and before climbing back into his EVA suit. He wanted everyone to be in their evac suits or as close to them as possible in case something happened.

Once he had his suit on, Dewey took a half-hour to read a book. It was a history of the A.P. government. It was written by someone who did not look favorably on the Allied Planets. Fortunately, he'd read several other books on the history of the A.P. government and was able to identify the inconsistencies between the authors. This was the worst of the bunch in Dewey's opinion.

However, there were plenty of conspiracies in the book, which was the reason for reading it. Unfortunately, there wasn't anything mentioning Wenshen or human genetic manipulation. If the A.P. had been experimenting, they'd done an excellent job of keeping it secret enough that even those predisposed to seeing conspiracies hadn't ever gotten a whiff.

After finishing the book, Dewey went to the dining hall and had a cup of Insta after putting a breakfast tray in the warmer. Based on the time and the guard schedule, Cpl Chavez was at the airlock while the other three were either asleep or resting. Sunrise was a couple of hours away.

Dewey sat and ate in the silence of the abandoned ship. He knew he should get some sleep, too, but he was worried about the major, the rest of the Hospitallers, and the civilians. His cup came down hard enough to slosh Insta over the rim and onto his hand.

Why hadn't he thought of it before? The ship's comms.

After disposing of the tray and refilling his cup, Dewey made his way to the bridge and stopped. The emergency airlock. He'd forgotten about it. Was the bridge at full atmo, or was it poisoned by the planet's atmosphere? He could put on his helmet and gloves before going in, but he couldn't take his Insta. Reluctantly, and after two long swigs, he put the cup on the deck and donned the rest of his EVA gear.

Once through the emergency airlock, Dewey tested the air. It was five parts per billion here, so it might scratch his throat as he breathed. Better to stay in a full suit.

At the comm station, Dewey had to wake it up and enter passwords and command controls before he could reach out to SSgt Castro. She answered almost immediately.

"Are you back already?" Her voice was a little weak with distance and interference.

"Still on the ship. Using its comm. Should have thought of it sooner."

Castro laughed. "One of us should have. Did the printer work?"

Dewey tapped his chest. The plastic box with the ten large pills was safe inside his suit. "They're all done. Just waiting for daylight. How are things on your end?"

"The civilians are irritable but cooperating," SSgt Castro said. "Maj Simmons and Mr. Zeledon are still under. They're a little worse than before but holding. Chambers tried to clean their blood but it didn't make much of a difference."

Dewey was about to respond to Castro's comment when the connection was suddenly filled with static. The comm was being blocked. By who? He moved over to the nav station and woke it. He tried the exterior cameras, but the only ones that were working saw only dirt. The other scans showed something different. Once he identified the source of the interference, Dewey tapped the comm for everyone on the fireteam.

"Suit up, we need to go now."

"Lieutenant? What's going on?"

"Dropships. And they're not ours."

22

Twice Dewey's heel slipped on a stair and almost dropped him on his butt. He knew hurrying wasn't going to make any difference in the time they had. But sometimes the body took on an urgency of its own.

At the bottom, he jumped down over the last two steps, sliding to a stop. Sgt Perry and the rest of the fireteam were already suiting up. Cpl Chavez was checking Horton and Hart's suits as they sealed their helmets in place.

"A.P. dropships?" asked Sgt Perry.

"Four of them." Dewey went to the airlock and tapped the controls to open the door. "Everyone in, we're doing this in one go."

Dewey did a double check on each of them as they passed into the airlock. He backed in after Sgt Perry so she could verify his suit was good to go, too. After getting a thumbs up from Perry, Dewey punched the buttons to start the airlock on its cycle.

And this was why trying to kill himself coming down the stairs didn't make sense. For all that hurrying, the airlock was the bottleneck. There was an override that would have opened the second door immediately. In a vacuum, it would have been problematic but sometimes necessary. However, it would have taken almost as long to initiate the override as it would be to wait for the cycle to complete. It was the famous hurry-up-and-wait scenario.

"I think I left the Insta urn on," Cpl Chavez said. She earned a chuckle from some of the others.

Pvt Hart asked, "Don't they have an automatic shut-off?" To which he received several groans.

Fortunately, the cycle finished, and the green light came on.

"Everyone, night vision," Dewey said. "Horton, the hatch, please."

"On it." Horton pushed the button, the hatch clicked, then swung open.

Horton, Hart, and Chavez came out of the airlock at the ready. They had the butts of their weapons pressed into the space between shoulder and arm, the barrels up, prepared to fire. They moved outward, creating a half-circle of clear space. Sgt Perry and Dewey followed, also ready for action if needed.

The night vision made the work of moving through a dark space at night easier, but it didn't make them invisible. There was always the telltale light that bled off the face shield and onto the wearer's face. It wasn't a lot of light, but if someone knew what they were looking for, it was like a beacon.

"Let's stay back," Dewey said. Even though his voice was only heard inside everyone's helmet, he still whispered. It was a natural reaction to the moment's concern. "We want to get a view outside without giving ourselves away."

"Without out getting shot," Pvt Hart said. This time he did earn a chuckle.

"That's right, Hart, let's not get shot."

Back on the bridge, Dewey had learned what kinds of ships were coming into atmo. The ship systems had also plotted a likely trajectory and landing. Dewey really wanted the computer to be wrong. But like him, the ship was rarely wrong.

The Hospitallers moved in a long, drawn-out line along the back wall of the loading bay. The open hatch provided a limited view that they panned by continuously moving to the aft end of the bay. Halfway across and Dewey knew the ship's calculations for the dropships' landing locations had been nearly perfect.

As they landed, the four dropships' engines lit up the night, filling the Shnel Shnek's rear bay with harsh orange light. Dewey stooped behind several pieces of equipment they'd left behind on their exodus. Down the line, the other members of the team did the same thing.

"Hey, Lieutenant?"

"Yes, Perry?"

"Do they know they're in our way?"

This was why he'd hoped the computer had miscalculated. The four dropships had come down about where the giant ant monsters had attacked the convoy. They might have even crushed the crawler that had been left behind. The worst of it, in Dewey's opinion, was that the dropships now stood between the Shnel Shnek and the research buildings.

To get back to the buildings and join the rest of their team, they would need to walk a wide perimeter. That was going to take more time.

"They might know," Dewey said. "If they had any communication with the other A.P. on the ground."

"We're going to have to go around?"

"Yeah, Sgt Perry, we're going to have to go around. Soon as their engines are off and the darkness returns, let's move around to the back of the ship. Might block any scans they point in this direction."

"Got it," Sgt Perry said. "I'll take point."

They all remained where they'd taken shelter from the artificial light until the dropships touched down, and the glow of the engine exhausts began to fade. With his night vision back on, Dewey could see Sgt Perry as she walked in a crouch toward the open hatchway. Hart followed and was followed by Pfc Horton in turn. Chavez went, and Dewey followed her.

One by one, they slipped out of the bay and hustled along the exterior of the engineering section, past the fins, and then turned at the exhaust cones. Before Dewey turned, he stopped for a look at the dropships. The sun was beginning to rise, highlighting some of the edges of the ships. Small pinpoints of light marked the open hatches where the A.P. soldiers were likely to already disembarking.

Dewey didn't like to admit it, but he was feeling like they were going to arrive back at the buildings too late. The A.P. might still be unable to get inside, but it also meant that Dewey and his team wouldn't be able to get in. Maybe they wouldn't, but maybe they would. Dewey was going to hold on to that thin ray of hope.

Before turning away, he pulled out one of the Hospitaller eyes. He engaged the magnetic lock on it and tossed it up and at the exhaust cone. There was a deep click that he more felt than heard as the eye stuck to the metal side of the cone. There wasn't any reason for them to be blind.

As he joined the rest of the team near the engineering airlock, Dewey could see Sgt Perry looking into the distance. Her hands were manipulating VR controls only she could see. He tapped the comm so she would know he was about to talk and not surprise her.

"What's going on?" He asked.

"Maps," Perry said. Her voice was distracted. "I've overlaid the topography data we collected coming in for our landing with the old data we'd pulled up from the archives. I'm looking for a way around that will minimize the chances of discovery."

"Hopefully, without having to go too far out of our way." Dewey switched the comm. "Cpl Chavez, I put an eye on the side of the ship. Can you keep watch on the A.P.?"

"Will do."

"Horton, Hart, keep watch fore and aft, please."

"Yes, Lieutenant."

"You got it."

Horton moved forward a couple of meters while Hart moved past Dewey to watch aft. Waiting until they had light was going to take time. However, it might also allow them to move faster. Again, Dewey didn't believe they'd make it back before the A.P. arrived at the buildings, but he wasn't going to let that belief stop him from trying.

For the next few minutes, Dewey stared into the distance. Ideas rolled up onto the visual in his mind, showing him a variety of scenarios in which he would be successful. After a half dozen of them, he huffed in annoyance. He could formulate all the plans he wanted, but it wasn't going to matter until they were near the buildings.

"Got it." Sgt Perry said across the comm. "Good path. A couple of low hills for cover. Should be able to make good time."

"A.P. are formed up, but they haven't moved away from the dropships," Cpl Chavez said. Her stare was still distant as she continued to monitor through the eye."

"Everyone recharged, yes?" Dewey asked. If they hadn't, they could likely use the recharge in the engineering lock. Hopefully, they had. Dewey didn't want to wait anymore.

"We're all good, Lieutenant," Sgt Perry said. "I made sure of it."

"Good work, Perry. Good work, team. Okay, Chavez, drop out, let's get moving."

"Doing it now."

"Horton," Sgt Perry said. "You got point."

For an hour, Dewey's team moved away from the Shnel Shnek, keeping the ship between them and the A.P. dropships. At fifteen minute intervals, Dewey or one of the NCOs would access the eye and check on the A.P. forces. Perry, checking at the forty-five-minute mark, brought the bad news.

"They're moving."

"Can we start turning?" Dewey asked. He motioned toward the hills as he spoke.

Perry's eyes took on the stare of someone pulling up and monitoring their HUD. She was gone for less than a minute.

"Five minutes," she said. "Then we can angle left. There's a dip in the land that runs the direction we want to go."

"I'll take point," Dewey said. He moved past the others.

"Lieutenant," Cpl Chavez said. "Are you sure?"

Dewey paused and grinned at Chavez. "You think I've gotten rusty?"

"No, Lieutenant."

What Chavez had alluded to was the same thing he'd often felt as an NCO. Officers were somehow more important than the NCOs and general enlisted. After several years as a lieutenant, Dewey wasn't so sure anymore.

Yes, he had a lot of specialized training and a brain full of information that the enlisted weren't always privy to. But he also knew anyone in the team could assume leadership if called upon to do so.

"Thank you, Chavez." Dewey turned and kept moving forward. "I'll take that as a compliment."

Dewey led, winding between the plants known to be dangerous and those not yet known to be dangerous. His weapon was across his chest, his hand resting on the pistol grip, ready to be called into action if need be.

If something did happen, Dewey expected it to be the ant monsters or some unknown local threat. He doubted the A.P. unit that had initially been harassing them would have come this far back. And there hadn't been any signatures of other dropships entering atmo before he'd bolted from the bridge. There were many unknowns that had to be taken into account. Unfortunately, unknowns were also difficult to account for.

"Lieutenant, the left turn."

Dewey slowed. Several meters more and the land dipped a meter. He stepped down into a wide furrow. It ran to his left and his right. He moved left five meters and stopped, turning to watch as Horton stepped down the short but steep slope. Dewey moved forward, turning every few steps to make sure that the others were still following.

Once everyone was on the new path, Dewey picked up the pace.

Life was full of regrets. Though, Dewey honestly felt that he had few. The last few days had been the exception and seemed to be nearly bursting with them. The most recent was the idea to keep the EVA suit rather than a combat evac suit, which was lighter and only a little less sturdy.

A unit was only as fast as its slowest member. Dewey, despite being on point, was feeling like the slowest member. That was one of several reasons he'd taken point. This way, no one would feel as if they had to wait for him.

They traveled for several more hours. They'd been pausing to check the eye, but there didn't seem to be any more movement at the dropships. They had no idea where the A.P. forces had marched off. They had a good guess, though.

The path they were on had taken them behind low slung hills. They could no longer see the open plain where the dropships had landed.

They were also unable to see the buildings as they approached.

Another hour and Dewey noticed the shallow ditch they'd been forced marching through was beginning to arc in the direction of the buildings.

He paused and commed Sgt Perry. "How're we looking?"

"Two more hours at this pace, Lieutenant. You want someone else to take point?"

"Naw, I'm feeling selfish." Dewey switched to general comm. "Everyone holding up?"

There was a general assent, so Dewey closed the comm and started moving forward once more. He was tired, there was no denying that. If it weren't for the EVA suit's systems, Dewey would also be uncomfortable. But, if he could get the team back into the buildings, get the medicine to MedTech Chambers, and then find a way to hold back the A.P. forces, he'd reward himself with another shower.

He just had to get there first.

One hour and a half later and Dewey realized getting to the buildings had just gotten more complicated.

"Hold up, everyone," Dewey said into the comm as he took a knee. He could see the buildings just a few kilometers away. Adjusting the data on his helmet's HUD, he could also see the forms of several hundred A.P. soldiers spread out around the main building.

"Lieutenant? Everything okay?"

"I'm okay if that's what you were wondering, Sergeant. But beyond that, no, things aren't okay. I expected we might have to deal with the A.P. forces that landed, but they're already posted around the main building. Not sure they'll let us waltz by."

"What do you want to do?"

Take a shower. Read a book. A beer, that'd be okay, too. Those were the thoughts that bubbled into Dewey's brain. They weren't the ones he shared. "Sit tight for the moment. Let me see if I can raise SSgt Castro on the comm."

"You heard the lieutenant," Perry said. "Sit tight, but keep watch."

Dewey adjusted his comm and tapped it. He mentally willed it to reach SSgt Castro. The comm hissed and crackled quietly for several seconds. Then, like someone whispering across an empty room, SSgt Castro was on the comm."

"Lt Tyler? How's everyone holding up out there?"

"Okay," Dewey said. "How's everyone holding up in there?"

Castro laughed. "Well, we've got company. They've knocked a few times. Hard. But the engineers who put this place together were serious about it lasting."

"We have eyes on them. They have the main building surrounded."

"They told us that," Perry said. "I didn't believe them at first."

"Right, we probably should have set up some eyes on the outside."

"Too late now." Castro paused and then said, "Oh, we found the station's control room. There are monitors that connect to cameras, but the cameras are either missing or defunct."

"Understood. What we need most of all, SSgt Castro, is a way back into the building."

"I was hoping you were going to come up with a brilliant plan, Lieutenant."

"So was I," Dewey said just as his comm beeped. "Stand by Castro."

Dewey switched the comm over as he turned back to the rest of the team. They were all facing outward. Cpl Chavez, who'd commed Dewey, was facing the way they came.

"Chavez? You got something?"

"Yes, Lieutenant." There was a pause, and even though they were all suited, Dewey saw the faint move of a quizzical tilt to Cpl Chavez's head. "Someone's coming."

"Someone? More A.P.?"

"That I could explain away," said Cpl Chavez. "But not this. Maybe I'm hallucinating."

Dewey moved past the rest of the team as he approached Chavez. "Did you check your oxygen levels?"

"Twice." Chavez giggled. "This is crazy."

"What's crazy?" Dewey stepped up next to Chavez and used his HUD to verify that her oxygen levels were in the green. They were, and there was no sign of other contaminants in her air supply.

"That," Chavez said. She pointed toward the bushes and trees that hugged the sides of the shallow ditch they'd been using for passage.

Dewey followed Chavez's finger and used it as a guide to direct him to a section of trees that were quivering. Something had pushed past them. Dewey blinked several times. It wasn't something, it was as Chavez had said. It was someone.

It was someone without an evac suit or EVA suit. They had no suit at all.

And they had company. Behind them, several more people sans suits were making their way down into the ditch. Four people. Their skin was reddish, where it was visible. The rest was covered by rough-looking cloth and gray plating. Two of them carried spears. The other two carried what looked like ancient crossbows.

"Lieutenant?" It was Sgt Perry. "Maybe we're all hallucinating?"

"Perhaps," said Dewey. "But only if we'd been hypnotized and given the same suggested imagery. And as I don't believe in hypnotism, I think we have to accept this as real."

"Are they with the A.P. forces?" asked Pvt Hart.

Dewey realized that they were all focused on the approaching group of suitless people.

"Guard the perimeter," he said. "Let's make sure this isn't a trap. Chavez, watch my back."

The others shifted to guard the other sides of the team as Dewey stood. He patted Chavez on the shoulder and started walking toward the new visitors.

"Lieutenant? Are you sure about this?"

"No. And, yes, Chavez. Just keep at the ready."

Dewey continued forward. If the people approaching were human, they were young, in their late teens or early twenties. Except for the one in front. He had a short beard with gray streaks in it. He looked to be in his forties or fifties. That was assuming they were human. Dewey was sure they were mostly human.

The group stopped and seemed to wait for Dewey. They seemed aware of the tension of the situation. They kept their weapons visible and pointed off to the side at all times. The one in front turned his head and said something that caused the other three to step back several meters.

When Dewey reached the lone leader, he tapped the comm for the external speaker.

"Any chance you speak standard?" He asked.

The man facing him smiled and nodded his head before saying, "Yes, we do."

"You don't have a suit on. How is that possible?"

"Oh, that's easy," the man said. "We were born here."

23

Anyone else might have scoffed or been stunned to silence by the declaration of the red man claiming to be native to Wenshen. After all, the planet had an atmosphere dangerous to humans. Yet, here they stood, their skin looking like they'd spent too much time in the sun without UV blockers.

Dewey, however, nodded. He hadn't expected to see the Wenshens, but he wasn't surprised they existed. Not if Capt Aunztequi and the other civilians had been speaking truthfully. Admittedly, he was surprised about how human they still looked.

Besides the red skin, there wasn't much difference. They all had hair that was short and tight-curled. One of the three that had stepped back looked female, but maybe that wasn't true. He wasn't going to ask as that seemed presumptuous and perhaps a little rude.

A smile and tilt of the lead Wenshen's head alerted Dewey that he'd been staring and not talking. How long had he been staring? How long had he been thinking?

"I'm sorry," he said. "I'm just honestly surprised to meet you."

The man nodded. "Normally, you wouldn't have. But Panorea said you weren't apes. So we came to look."

"'Apes'?"

"Those people." The man indicated the direction of the A.P. forces and the buildings.

"Allied Planet forces," Dewey said. "But aren't they the reason you exist?"

Dewey had made the quick assumption that the A.P. researchers were responsible for the genetic manipulation that made it possible for humans to exist on the planet unencumbered by suits. In which case, they should be allied.

"Yes, they are the reason." The man's face tensed, looking like stone for just a moment. Dewey couldn't miss the emotion. "And that is why they are the enemy."

"And we're not?" Dewey didn't bother hiding the concern in his voice.

"Not yet," said the man. He smiled away the statement and held out his hand. "I'm Neoklis."

Dewey took the other man's hand in his. "Lt Dewey Tyler, Hospitallers."

The man laughed. He looked over his shoulder as he released Dewey's hand. "Good call, Panorea."

One of the three, who must have been Panorea, punched one of the others in the arm. "Told you."

"Lucky guess," the other said, rubbing his shoulder as he spoke. He chuckled after that, joined by Panorea and the other man with them.

Neoklis turned back to Dewey. "Panorea reads. A lot. She's the one who said you weren't apes but might be someone that could be allies."

"I think that's entirely possible," said Dewey. He paused and looked at his team, who seemed to suddenly remember there was a perimeter to watch. He then looked a little higher, where the buildings and the A.P. forces were gathered. "We could use an ally."

"From what we saw come down from the sky, yes, you could." Neoklis paused, his gaze grew temporarily distant. Then he blinked and said, "You should come with us."

He turned before Dewey could speak. "Wait. The rest of our people. We can't leave them." Dewey's hand moved, covering the hidden packet of antidote pills.

"And we won't," said Neoklis. He didn't turn back to face Dewey. Instead, he continued walking. "But, you can't go through the front."

Dewey tapped the comm. "Sgt Perry. Get everyone moving. We're following the locals."

"They're legit?" asked Sgt Perry.

"So far." Dewey moved slowly, checking over his shoulder for the rest of the team. The Wenshens were already stepping up the side of the ditch. One of them had used their spear to move aside the fronds of one of the razor plants.

When it was Dewey's turn up the shallow side, one of the Wenshen remained in place, their spear continuing to hold back the plant's dangerous edges. Past the plant, the space opened up, allowing for freer movement. Dewey moved far enough out of the way so that the rest of the Hospitallers could come up. When Sgt Perry passed the waiting Wenshen, the spear was moved, and the foliage allowed to cover the gap they'd all just passed through.

"I'm sorry, excuse me," Dewey said through the speaker on his EVA suit. He'd pushed the volume, confident that the sound wouldn't carry to the A.P. "Where are we going?"

The Wenshen who'd been holding back the plant with his spear was moving quickly by Dewey. "We got us an outpost not far from here. We're going there."

"An outpost?"

The young man paused and looked at Dewey. "We certainly wouldn't want to live this close to the enemy," he said and then continued walking.

Neoklis had also paused. He stayed until Dewey had caught up with him. "What Stathis means is that they've come back at other times, too. Usually, it's just a small ship that will fit inside the big building. They stay for a day or two, and then they leave. Sometimes they come looking for us."

"What happens then?"

"Then, someone has to come looking for them." Neoklis shrugged and started to walk again. Dewey kept with him.

"So, why are we going to your outpost? Shouldn't we – shouldn't my team – be looking for a way into the buildings? I can't just leave them like this. And some of them are sick."

"Sick?"

"From the plants. I have antidotes for them. But if I don't get in there, it'll be too late."

"I see," said Neoklis. "One of the changes to our genetics makes us immune to the plants. And many of the smaller animals."

"Well, we don't have that sort of immunity," Dewey said. "And if I don't get the antidote into the buildings, we're going to lose some people."

"People die."

Neoklis's comment felt harsh to Dewey even though he knew it was a fact. But the energy in the words was cold in a fatalistic sort of way. That caused Dewey to wonder how many people Neoklis had lost.

"Agreed," he said rather than pursue more answers to more questions. "But if there is a way to save them, then that's something we should also do. If you can't help us, then maybe we should part ways."

Neoklis stopped once more. Ahead of him, the other Wenshens stopped, too.

"We didn't say we weren't going to help, Lt Tyler." He pointed his spear and arm back toward the buildings. "But you can't go that way. Unless it's you who wants to die."

"How are you going to help?"

"In our way. Come, please. And maybe be a little patient."

Dewey nodded, and Neoklis started walking again. The other Wenshens turned and started walking, too. The last thing Dewey wanted was to be patient. But at this moment, what choice did he have?

Every kilometer they moved away from the buildings weighed heavily on Dewey. Distance equaled time. Time wasn't something that Maj Simmons had. In an almost obsessive way, Dewey repeatedly tapped the hidden packet of pills each time he thought of the major's condition, the distance from her and they other Hospitallers they were traveling away from, and the time he felt they were wasting.

Fortunately, the distance came to an end after three and one-quarter kilometers.

Dewey had initially thought they were going to wind their way up a hill. But the path they walked split just behind a clump of trees that looked like anorexic conifers with extra long needles. As they moved past them, Dewey wondered if these plants were as dangerous as the ones they'd already encountered.

More trees blocked the entrance to a narrow canyon. A small brook trickled past where they walked. Several times there was a break between the trees where Dewey could see the buildings in the distance. Then, they were at another building.

It could have been a house or a warehouse. Dewey wasn't sure what the intention of the building was; It was a mashup of stone and logs and rusted corrugated metal sheets. The windows, assuming they were windows, were narrow slits. The door looked like something Dewey would have expected to see in the buildings back where the rest of the Hospitallers and civilians waited for their return. They were bulky looking. The difficult-to-penetrate kind of bulky looking.

Inside was much the same as the outside. There was a lot of natural materials that made up the floor and rafters that supported the rusted steel roof. But there were also tables, chairs, and bunk beds there were clearly not manufactured on Wenshen.

"Some of this was scavenged from the research buildings," said Neoklis. "Some of it from the trash heap. You may not have seen that."

"No, we didn't," said Dewey.

"It's pretty much been covered by dirt and bushes over the years."

"How did you get inside the buildings?" as Sgt Perry. Dewey had put them all on the comm so they could start to understand more of what was happening. "Can you operate in both atmospheres?"

"Definitely cannot," Neoklis said. "It's not deadly. Not like if you tried to breathe our atmosphere. It's more like a slow suffocation. No, an area was set apart for us as we were born and grew up. We took some of this when we left."

"Wait," said Pvt Hart. "You grew up in the buildings? The research place?"

Neoklis nodded. His face did not beam with the pride many people displayed when declaring their place of birth. His look was much grimmer. "Yes, I grew up there. I'm part of the first viable generation."

"'Viable'? Do I even want to know?" asked Cpl Chavez.

"Probably not," Dewey said. "But there's a bunch of civilians with us that would like to know and then make sure the rest of the radial arm is made aware."

"Someone in the universe cares? That's interesting." One of the young men had wandered over and was standing just behind Neoklis.

"This is Demetre," Neoklis said. "My nephew."

"Which raises another question," said Sgt Perry. "How many of you are there?"

"Fifty from the first viable generation. Hundred and forty of the second generation." Neoklis paused and looked at Demetre. "Forty-five third generation?"

"Forty-seven."

Neoklis nodded and said, "That's right. Forty-seven. Eliana had twins. Now I remember."

"How many were born outside of the research facilities?" Dewey asked.

"Hundred forty-seven," Demetre said. He looked away and then put a hand on Neoklis's shoulder. "The others are returning."

Dewey turned and looked. He saw no one.

"Are you psychic as well?" asked Pvt Hart.

The Wenshens laughed. All of them.

"Not psychic," answered Panorea. "But it's said we have exceptional hearing and vision."

"By-product of the genetic manipulation," Neoklis said. "They weren't trying to do anything else but create people who could breathe this atmosphere."

"For colonization," said Pfc Horton. She'd been quietly watching the Wenshens.

Dewey noticed that Neoklis's look grew even darker. "No. Purely for scientific purposes. That's what caused the revolt. Once we figured out what they were doing, what they had done to us, and what they were planning to do to us once they'd proven they could do it, we resisted. And when they tried to kill us, we killed them and then escaped."

"I'm sorry to hear that," Dewey said.

"Not the part where you killed them," Sgt Perry added. "But that they were going to kill you."

"Yes, that," said Dewey.

"We tried to negotiate with them at first," Neoklis said. He was watching the door as he spoke, drawing Dewey's attention along. Someone was coming up the trail. They weren't in EVA or evac suits. "There wasn't any reason why they could just let us live. We were stuck on this planet as it's the only atmosphere we can breathe."

"But they couldn't risk anyone ever finding out what they did," said Dewey. Demetre and one of the other young men had left the building to greet the others now less than ten meters from the doorway.

"That's what one of them said. He felt guilty. He was the one who showed us how to escape. They killed him and then came after us. We lost tens of people before we managed to stop them. They had the weapons, but we had the atmosphere. I'm assuming that you know what happens when you are exposed to our air?"

Dewey nodded. He knew.

"Excuse me," Pvt Hart said. "If you can't breathe our air, how did you escape?"

"There's a tunnel," said Neoklis. "A construction ramp. At the bottom of the facility, there is a large space, a man-made cavern that we lived in. It was designed to replicate the surface. But the ramp had been sealed off. None of us knew it was there until Dr. Jackson showed us."

Now Dewey understood how the Wenshens could help. "Where is the ramp?"

"Around the other side of the building site. The entrance is another kilometer along."

"Excuse me, Lieutenant," said Pfc Horton. "But if the A.P. built it, wouldn't they already be using it to get in the back door, so to speak?"

"Agreed," Dewey said. But he also didn't think the Wenshens would suggest it if they didn't know some other important piece of information. He looked to Neoklis and waited for an explanation.

"They blew up the entrance after we escaped."

There it was, the information that mattered. The A.P. wouldn't bother checking on it since they destroyed it. But it would also mean they couldn't get in. Unless the Wenshens had thought of that, too.

Sgt Perry gave a voice to Dewey's concerns. "We have to dig it out?"

Dewey kept his eyes on Neoklis even as more of the Wenshen entered the building.

"No." Neoklis grinned at Dewey as he answered.

Dewey was certain Neoklis was aware of his thought process. "We got through a few years ago. But we've covered the entrance, so it still looks impassable."

And yet Dewey noticed they hadn't been inside. "What's the catch?"

"The airlocks. To open the next interior door, the air automatically cycles to the other type. If there's a way to override it, we don't know what it is."

"But you got out," said Sgt Perry.

"We did, yes," said Neoklis. "Dr. Jackson did something to the system so that it was all opened to us. We didn't have to open and shut the airlocks. We only recently discovered the new situation. It came at a high cost."

People had died. Dewey knew what the phrase, 'It came at a high cost," meant. He'd seen the cost paid out a few times as a Hospitaller.

"Is there something in there that you want?" Dewey asked. "That would be the primary reason for you helping us?"

24

The other Wenshens, who'd been moving about and talking to the newly arrived members of their party, paused, turning to watch the conversation and its sudden change. Neoklis was looking at Dewey as he, in turn, watched the Wenshen leader.

"We've no interest in your people or the apes. You are right. If it weren't for some things in our prison-home that we've been after for decades, we would have sat back and let you all have at each other."

"At least they're honest," Pvt Hart said. Dewey recognized that Hart had only spoken through the comm system, which meant only the rest of the Hospitaller team had heard him.

Through the speaker and across the comm, Dewey said, "As long as we know where we stand. But I'd also like you to know that we would have been glad to help you anyway. That's why we're here in the first place."

"You came here to help us?" asked one of the other Wenshens. They'd come in with one of the other groups and looked around the same age Neoklis.

"Not exactly," Dewey said, turning to the other man.

"This is Theophilus," Neoklis said. "He grew up in the facility, too."

Dewey nodded and said, "We came into the system to help someone else. That's how we ended up on your planet. But as we are here, there's no reason not to help you, too. If Panorea read enough about us, you would know that it's what we as Hospitallers do."

"Hopefully, you can understand that we have never trusted anyone that wasn't one of us," Theophilus said.

"We're used to trusting our own, too," Cpl Chavez said through her speaker. "We've also learned that by earning others' trust, we can get a lot more accomplished."

"We have to earn your trust?" asked Neoklis.

"I mean that we have to earn each others' trust," said Chavez. Her response earned a nodding approval from the Wenshen and Dewey.

"When can we get moving?" Sgt Perry asked.

"We need to get our people out before the A.P. gets in."

"We have time," said Neoklis. "They'll have to get into their computers and make some changes to make the doors obey."

"Not this time," said Theophilus. "It looks like they're cutting through the doors. They might be doing what they should have done a long time ago."

"Destroy all the evidence," said Dewey. "Which means we need to hurry."

"I'll get everyone ready," Theophilus said. He clapped Neoklis on the shoulder and then turned away, calling several of the young people by name as he moved.

"Sgt Perry," Dewey said over the comm, "give everyone a gear check. Make sure we're ready, too."

"On it."

Fifteen minutes passed, and the Wenshens were ready to go. The Hospitallers had been prepared for ten of those minutes. But they'd also had a lot more experience and carried everything they needed with them.

During Sgt Perry's quick check on the team, they found that Pvt Hart's filter system had one damaged filter. That left just one to filter his air and supply his oxygen. That did more than just halve the ability of his suit to feed him oxygen. The extra strain on the remaining filter meant it was going to fail faster than normal.

"He'll make it fine the rest of the way," Sgt Perry said when Neoklis voiced his concern for Hart's situation. "But if the second filter gets damaged, then we'll have a problem."

"One of you could share a filter if that happened," said Neoklis.

"In vacuum, it might not be a big deal," Dewey said. "But here?

Both people would get an ugly dose of acidic atmosphere."

"And they'd have to breathe it until the filters cleaned it out," said Cpl Chavez.

"Not to mention the damage it would do to the filters," said Pvt Hart. "They'd start failing almost immediately."

"You have some of these filters in the facility?" asked Neoklis.

"We do," said Dewey.

"Then we really do need to get going."

The trip out of the hills brought them past the thin pine trees, and through a forest of trees that looked like stick versions of broccoli stalks, took another hour. Several times, Dewey attempted to make contact with SSgt Castro or anyone inside the facility building. Once, he'd heard Castro respond, but the connection was lost as quickly as it was made.

"You're lucky to have any contact with the inside of the building," said Theophilus. "We were told the buildings were designed to mask the presence of people inside."

"It may be decades old tech," Cpl Chavez offered. "We're running with systems only a few years old."

"And the local environment could be deteriorating whatever systems they were using back then to mask human presence," added Sgt Perry. "We should have better communication as we get closer."

For the next hour, they didn't get any closer to the buildings and the A.P. that surrounded them. Even on magnification, Dewey's face shield couldn't see as well as the Wenshen could with their natural vision. They had to inform Dewey that the A.P. were still working on cutting through the large airlock hatch and that they had made little progress so far.

After another hour, the Wenshens on point began to veer left, slowly bringing them closer to the buildings and the location of the unblocked entrance to the lowest level of the facility. Dewey attempted comm contact on a more frequent basis, waiting for the moment of sustained communication.

They had just forded a small creek when MSgt Roberson's voice came through the comm. It was carried along with a crackling and popping noise, but his voice was clear enough to understand every word.

"Lt Tyler. We were beginning to worry about you."

"Thank you for the concern, Master Sergeant. We're all still standing. And we've added to our numbers."

"You mean," said Roberson, "besides the people knocking at the front door?"

Dewey laughed. "That would be the A.P. They want to get inside and say hello."

"I don't think they want to say hello. Did our reinforcements also arrive?"

Dewey stopped walking, stepping aside to let several more of the Wenshens pass by. "More Hospitallers? No. But we have someone else that will surprise you and please the civilians."

"And what would that be?" Roberson sounded genuinely curious.

"We found the locals," said Dewey. He paused, partially because he was smiling and partly to let it sink in. "The experiments the A.P. were doing? They're alive and well and helping us."

"Why would they help us?"

"Because they hate the A.P.," said Dewey. He briefly explained the situation and the genesis of the Wenshens.

MSgt Roberson's response was natural. "I'd hate them, too. Heck, I'm not fond of them anyway."

"Neither are we," Dewey said. "Now, what's the situation inside the building?"

Roberson explained that Maj Simmons was stable. The civilians had been behaving themselves though they'd become agitated by the presence of the A.P. forces outside the building. SSgt Castro and half the remaining Hospitallers were pulling the other crawlers into the open space beyond the airlock. Then they could seal those doors and add one more layer for the A.P. to force themselves through.

"That's a good idea," Dewey said in response to the last information. "After that, I need you and Castro to get everyone, and as much of the supplies as you can, down to the bottom level. You'll need to suit up when you get down there. It's the same atmosphere as out here."

"How are you going to get there if you don't mind, Lieutenant?"

"The locals know a way." Dewey knew it sounded cryptic, but it also had a bit of humor to it.

MSgt Robeson understood. "Always trust the locals for the best routes and the best food, Lt Tyler."

"Always," said Dewey, though he had his concerns for the moment. Hopefully, they would be alleviated soon enough. Then, getting back to business, "I'm not sure where the exit out is once you're down there, so just be ready when we arrive."

"When will that be?"

Dewey turned and looked at Neoklis. "How long until we're in?"

"Hour and a half, more or less."

Over the comm, Dewey said, "seventy-five minutes, maybe more. We've several airlocks to get through. Oh, and Master Sergeant, tell MedTech Chambers we'll need that emergency med tent."

In less than thirty minutes, Dewey, the rest of his team, and twenty Wenshen arrived at a stand of trees. There were other clumps of trees nearby, but not as many as were gathered here. And some of these were different. They were stubby, their branches close to the ground.

The stand of trees hid a pile of rock and manmade debris. Rough-shaped concrete blocks bristling with rusted rebar were jumbled together with boulders and tree stumps. It was, in Dewey's opinion, a daunting mess, if this was the way into the research facility.

"I thought you said you'd cleared the way," Sgt Perry said as she joined Dewey and the two older Wenshens, Neoklis and Theophilus.

"We did," Neoklis said. "But we didn't want the apes to know we had."

"So, you filled it back up?"

"Would you have?" asked Theophilus.

"No," said Sgt Perry. "We'd have made... Oh, right."

The two Wenshens laughed. Dewey joined them. Like the Wenshen's had done, the Hospitallers would have created some sort of camouflage to hide what their work. But the Hospitallers also had access to a host of equipment that would have made the job easier. The Wenshens had only the natural elements around them.

"We should get to work?" Dewey asked.

"We'll get to work," Neoklis said. "We don't want your people risking a tear in your suits or damage to more of those filters. Don't worry, it won't take us long."

"All right," said Dewey. He didn't like the idea of not being able to help. Though he only had four people, they would be bouncing on the balls of their feet, agitated at the sight of others working while they stood idle. Perhaps he could fix that. He tapped his comm. "Sgt Perry, Cpl Chavez, put everyone on perimeter guard. That includes both of you. Use the trees for cover. The A.P. starts moving this way or even shows mild curiosity, I want to know."

Sgt Perry grinned as she saluted, revealing the fact she understood what Dewey was up to. "Will do, Lt Tyler."

Several more commands by Sgt Perry and the four Hospitallers were moving around the debris and into the trees. Now it was only Dewey left to bounce on the balls of his feet, wishing he could help.

Fortunately, it took as long as Neoklis had stated. Which meant that it didn't take long before the debris had been cleared to reveal a layer of dried branches that were then removed to reveal thirty logs. Only the center logs were removed, providing a narrow doorway into the darkness and a ramp that was not constructed by nature, though it was cracked and no longer smooth.

One of the younger Wenshens paused next to Dewey and pointed. "One kilometer. That way." He walked away, laughing.

The humor alluded Dewey, so he chalked it up to a local thing. There had been many times he'd been unable to follow what passed for local humor on many worlds. He did here what he did there, which was to smile and nod even if the young man couldn't see Dewey's face inside the EVA helmet.

Contemplation of the local humor was interrupted by Theophilus, who was waving his spear. Dewey looked his way and realized he'd been trying to gain Dewey's attention.

"We're ready to go if you are."

"Roger that. Let me call my team back in." Dewey turned off the external speaker switched to the team's comm. "Sgt Perry, pull everyone back."

The comm made several sharp popping noises before Perry responded. "On our way, Lieutenant."

While he waited for the rest of his team, Dewey joined the Wenshens near the opening.

"We'll be ready when you're people get back here," Neoklis said.

Dewey started to respond before he realized he'd turned off the external speaker. He tapped the comm button before asking, "Will you be leaving a guard here to watch the entrance?"

Neoklis seemed momentarily surprised by the question. "Normally, no. But considering the eagerness of the apes to get inside, it might not be a bad idea."

"I'd like to leave Sgt Perry here, too. She can use her comm to contact us if anything changes up here."

"That should be fine." Neoklis pointed with his chin. "Here they come."

Sgt Perry was coming around the rubble that had been shifted into two piles parenthesizing the entrance to the tunnel.

"Hart, you doing okay?" Dewey asked. Hart seemed to be sweating more than would be reasonable for a combat evac suit. The temperatures were usually within a specific range unless the external temperatures were at some extreme. They were not in extreme temperatures right now.

"Doing okay, Lieutenant. System's running a little warm."

"Pvt Hart's suit is at fifty percent, Lt Tyler," said Cpl Chavez.

Dewey nodded. "Then let's get him down the tunnel and get it fixed, A.S.A.P. Sgt Perry, I'd like you to stay here with the Wenshens who'll be guarding the entrance."

"Do I get a spear, too?" Perry's question was punctuated with a grin. The grin broadened when one of the young Wenshen men handed her his spear. She took it and jabbed the empty space in front of her. "I almost wish I could find a reason to use it."

"Let's hope it doesn't come to that," Dewey said. He turned to Neoklis. "Shall we go?"

Neoklis responded by waving several of the younger people forward. Once they started down the ramp, he motioned for Dewey to proceed.

In turn, Dewey nodded to Pfc Horton. "You have point. Let's go get our people."

25

Dewey followed the rest of his team through the opening and across the broken surface of the tunnel. In the initial gloom, he could see that several more timbers had been used to support the ceiling; the beginning edge was in worse shape than the floor. Ahead, where Dewey had expected to see Hospitaller task lights, he saw a bright glow with a slight yellow tinge to it.

"You don't have some sort of flashlight here, do you?" Dewey asked Neoklis as the Wenshen native came alongside him.

"In a way, yes," said Neoklis. They continued, following the other Hospitallers and Wenshens in the lead. "It's a recent discovery."

Neoklis produces several sticks that he then bent in half. The sticks were green and didn't break into separate pieces. Instead, the outer surface split along the length of each stick, excreting thick sap. Around the bent sections of the sticks, Neoklis wrapped several dry leaves. The leaves crackled while being wrapped around the sticks. Dewey noticed small sparks running along the lengths of the cracks of the leaves.

"Takes a few seconds," Neoklis said.

They continued to walk as Dewey eyed the leaf-wrapped sticks. They reminded him of the torches that intrepid explorers always seemed to have at the ready on the Saturday morning vids. He didn't think that was going to happen here. Even if they did suddenly generate enough heat to burn, there wasn't enough oxygen in the atmosphere for more than a weak flame.

There was no flame, as it turned out. Dewey didn't know when it started, but the leaves were now glowing a bright yellow. He had to turn away. Neoklis lifted the torch over their heads, removing it from their field of view.

"Everyone is encouraged to explore and test ideas," Neoklis said. "We still know very little about our world. The apes never showed an interest in what lay beyond the confines of their buildings. For our part, we'd assumed the outside was the same as where we lived down here, except without the walls and a ceiling.

"We didn't understand where we were going when we escaped. The caretakers never showed us pictures of skies, mountains, other creatures. Several people panicked and wanted to return to our' home.' They reasoned it would be safe there now that we'd kill all of the apes. But I knew that more apes would come, and we wouldn't be safe down here or on the surface nearby.

"Everyone carried what they could, and we began walking. That first night, the flat-tails attacked. We had the ape guns. We used them as best we could, but we still lost ten people. We moved for another day. That night more flat-tails came. No one died that night, but we were also short of the ammo the weapons used.

"We'd already made the painful discoveries of the plants, but we did manage to make weapons with those and the other plant life we encountered. There were less of the flat-tails the third night. It turns out we were on the edge of their territory by this time. Three people died that night, but we were able to put our new weapons to use.

"So, from that time, we always explored and tested. These light-sticks, one of the third generation, Stefania, had been testing leaves for different uses. Some had dried out after being collected. She is not a tidy person. The mess she'd made one night began to glow. Thus, we have light for the dark."

"I know this wasn't the point," Dewey said, "but you mentioned the flat-tails having territory?"

Neoklis laughed. It sounded on the bitter side to Dewey.

"This valley is filled with warrens of flat-tail colonies. That's why we watch from the hills and only come down here if necessary."

"Something I wish we'd known," Dewey said. His mind went once more to MedTech Phillips's mutilated body.

"If it makes you feel any better," said Neoklis, "we're still trying to understand our world."

"I can assure you that you have at least one ally. We'll give you as much help as you want."

They came to a stop. The Wenshens and Hospitallers in the lead had spread out. Before them was an airlock almost large enough for a crawler to fit through.

"And what if what we want is to be left alone?" Neoklis's head tilted slightly to one side as he seemed to wait for an answer.

"If that's what you want, the Hospitallers will help you with that, too."

"That remains to be seen." Neoklis pointed at the airlock with his light-stick. "The airlock."

"Cpl Chavez?" When Chavez turned Dewey's way, he said, "Open it up, please."

Chavez and Horton advanced toward the hatch. Hart had moved to help, too, but Chavez made it clear he needed to stand by and conserve energy.

Dewey understood Neoklis's concern. The only experience they'd had was with the A.P. The Allied Planets government was only a few degrees worse than the other multi-planet governments. But even the Dark Worlds seemed less notorious than the A.P. had evolved into. But what Neoklis might not know was that the Hospitallers were not a government and only existed to help others. The help might be providing temporary shelters and food. It might be helping with natural disasters. Unfortunately, it was often fighting back oppressive forces, liberating those being forcibly oppressed and then helping them take care of themselves.

"It's cycling," Cpl Chavez said over the comm. "Ten minutes. More than someone could hold their breath."

"Good work, Chavez. Let me know when it's open." Dewey turned back to Neoklis. The area around them had gotten brighter with more of the light-sticks being gathered in one place by the other Wenshen joining them. He asked Neoklis, "What supplies are you hoping to retrieve down here?"

"Whatever we can find that's still useful. Clothes, household items, maybe the digital learning devices they let us use."

Dewey had his doubts about the last one. "Might depend on the battery life in them. They might be useless without a way to charge them."

"Maybe that's one of those things we can use help with in the future."

"Sounds like a good place to start," said Dewey. He'd noticed the airlock hatch starting to move at the same time that Cpl Chavez was turning and lifting her arm. He waved an acknowledgment. To Neoklis, he said, "We'll move as much as we can into the airlock."

"It will be appreciated."

Dewey walked to the airlock, indicating with a wave of his hand that the rest of the team should proceed him. Cpl Chavez stepped through and to the side just ahead of Dewey.

"Now, Lieutenant?"

"Now, Cpl Chavez." Dewey turned and gave a nod and a wave to Neoklis and the other Wenshens as the airlock began to shut.

As the hatch crept closed, Dewey turned and looked down the length of the airlock. Horton and Hart had turned on their task lights, filling the lock with a dim light. Dewey felt that the light-sticks the Wenshens used were better for illuminating the space. He should have asked for a couple of them.

"Cycling now, Lt Tyler," Cpl Chavez said through the comm. She was standing next to him as she spoke.

"Ten minutes?"

"Maybe eleven. The system is old."

Dewey started walking the fifty meters of the airlock. He could feel the buffeting as air currents kicked up to storm level as the air cycled. Sodium Borate snow began to fall. It was picked up by the whirling air, creating miniature snowstorms.

They all gathered at the opposite airlock. Dewey remained silent as Horton and Chavez mused over the Wenshens, comparing and contrasting them to themselves and the A.P. forces. The A.P., based on what parts of the conversation Dewey focused on, were getting the worst of the comparison. Hart was silent, his helmeted head drooping.

"Hanging in there okay, Pvt Hart?"

"Doing okay, Lieutenant. Be glad to get on the other side."

"Glad?" asked Cpl Chavez. "Did you miss the memo, Hart? There's one more airlock just like this to get through."

"There is?" Dewey didn't think Hart could sag any lower without collapsing to the ground. Yet, he somehow managed.

"It's why the Wenshens needed our help," Horton said. "The next airlock is all our kind of atmo. They'd suffocate trying to hold their breath or breathe the atmo until it switched over. Not to mention the air changing here. One of the Wenshen told me they lost four people in this airlock."

"Oh," was all Hart could manage.

"You'll make it, Hart," Dewey said. "Soon as we get through, we'll pull your filters, and you can use one of mine."

"Thank you, Lt Tyler."

Then, as if benevolence was the signal, the airlock winked a green light. The hatch began to open. No one hurried through as it would have to open all the way before they could signal it to shut. While they waited, Dewey opened the filter system on his suit and removed one filter. Pfc Horton had done the same thing for Hart. They quickly removed the broken filter and replaced the overworked one with Dewey's.

"That should hold you until we can both get a new set," said Dewey.

"Closing the hatch," Cpl Chavez said.

As the hatch swung shut, they began to walk the next fifty meters. A thought occurred to Dewey as they walked. "Chavez, any chance we could override the airlock systems?"

"Probably. Depends on what you want to do with it."

They stopped as they reached the next airlock. "I'm thinking we should force both airlock hatches to open at the same time and stay open."

"I don't know if I could do that," Chavez said. She'd stepped over to the control panel and tapped it awake.

"Cpl Robertson might," said Pfc Horton. "Or Cpl Knight."

"Thank you, Horton." Dewey tapped the comm for SSgt Castro and MSgt Roberson. The walls of the airlock tunnel were thick. He only heard the ghost of someone attempting to respond.

"Five minutes," Chavez said.

The longest minutes were always the last minutes. It seemed true here just as it was before the back hatch of a dropship or RapRes slammed down to the ground, and the Hospitallers inside rushed out to face the newest danger. But the longest minutes he remembered had to be sitting outside the interview room after the final exams for officer candidate training were completed. That and the last panel of senior officers he'd faced. It had only taken them two minutes to confirm Dewey had passed all the tests with the highest marks and had earned the privileges and responsibilities that came with being an officer. Dewey had been certain he'd aged several years in that one hundred twenty seconds.

"Time, Lieutenant."

Dewey focused on the present, nodding to Cpl Chavez. She punched a button. The airlock hatch clacked and whirred before it swung open to reveal a second airlock that was also a hundred meters in length

It began to open, flooding the airlock with light. The airlock had opened less than a meter before someone poked their head through the expanding gap.

"Lt Tyler, good to see you." Even the EVA suit's comm couldn't hide the humor in SSgt Castro's voice.

"Everyone through, Castro?" Dewey asked.

"Not yet," said the staff sergeant. "Medical and the injured are still on the other side. Everyone else is staged on the lawn."

"The lawn?"

Castro grinned and stepped back as the hatch revealed more and more of the space beyond it. She gave a theatrical wave and bow as she added, "Welcome to wonderland."

Wonderland was one word for it. Dewey stepped over the threshold of the airlock. If he hadn't looked up, he would have thought he'd magically appeared on the surface of the planet once more. The ground looked the same here as on the surface. The big difference being the absence of plants that could kill an unwary person. But there was a path, what passed for grass on Wenshen, and a village of prefab houses. Most of the civilians and Hospitallers were present.

The ceiling was more than fifty meters overhead. A series of large circles were backlight by the light reflecting off the ceiling to illuminate the ground as brightly as being on the surface.

SSgt Castro seemed to follow Dewey's thoughts. She said, "It was pitch black before. Took us a while to find the power and switch it all on. It was almost like watching a sun come up over the horizon."

"Some of the Wenshen grew up here," Dewey told Castro. "This was all they knew until they rebelled and found the surface."

"Not much different than living your life on a station," Castro said.

Dewey agreed to a point. At least on a space station you could look out a port and see stars, maybe planets.

"We need to get moving, Staff Sergeant." Dewey pointed at the waiting civilians and Hospitallers. "Move all our stuff into the airlock and stage it on the starboard side. Then, start stripping the buildings of anything that isn't bolted to the ground. Stage that to port."

"Yes, Lieutenant."

"I'm going to go and see to Maj Simmons." Dewey tapped the spot on his suit where the antidote pills still waited. He turned and then called through the comm, "Pvt Hart, with me."

"Yes, Lieutenant." Hart approached and saluted.

"Come with me," Dewey said. Then, back to SSgt Castro, "You have it under control?"

"Sure do, Lieutenant."

Dewey returned Castro's salute and started walking. The change of filters had been beneficial to Pvt Hart. He had no problem keeping up with Dewey, who was taking long strides to cross the only world Neoklis had known as a young man. He was glad to see that Hart was feeling better. Still, they both needed two filters if they wanted to make it out. A new question queued in Dewey's mind: Out to where?

26

Dewey steered Pvt Hart towards the pitifully small piles of supplies salvaged from the crawlers. Sgt Parks called the Hospitallers near her to attention as Dewey approached.

"Good to see you back, Lt Tyler," she said as she saluted.

"Good to be back, even if only just for suit filters."

"Suit filters?" Parks turned and still on the general comm asked, "Wong, where'd we put the suit supplies? We need filters."

Several of the other Hospitallers turned and did a quick rummage through one pile. They pulled out a plastic tote about the size of two EVA helmets.

"Here we go," Sergeant," said Pfc Wong. He opened the tote and then looked toward where Dewey was standing with Sgt Parks. "How many?"

"Two sets," Dewey said. Once Wong had passed along the filters, still sealed in their packs, Dewey said to Sgt Parks, "See SSgt Castro about moving the supplies."

After an exchange of salutes, Dewey walked away with Pvt Hart close behind. He tapped on his comm and did a general call for Cpl Knight and Cpl Robertson. When they both responded, he switched to a closed comm. "Do you think that either or both of you could override the controls on the airlocks?"

"Maybe," said Cpl Robertson.

"What did you have in mind, Lieutenant?" asked Cpl Knight.

"The Wenshens can't get in here because the airlocks cycle through oxygen-rich air that they can't breathe."

"You want us to make it so it doesn't?"

"Yes, Knight, unless you can't. Then maybe try something else?"

"We'll see what we can do," said Robertson.

"Thank you. Check back in as soon as you have something."

"Will do," they said simultaneously.

Dewey waved Hart into motion, and they continued walking. They'd just reached what Dewey assumed to be Neoklis's village when he saw several civilian suits jogging in his direction. Capt Aunztequi he recognized right away. With him was his XO Mecolaeta, who really wasn't an actual XO, and one other civilian, Iturraeta. They were waving their arms as they hurried in Dewey's direction. He could see their mouths working. Soft plumes of steam spotted their helmet shields, indicative of people yelling fruitlessly inside their helmets.

It took Dewey a moment to remember that the civilians were on a different comm. He adjusted his so that he could hear them and instantly regretted the action. "No need to yell, Captain." He adjusted the comm to dampen their voices.

"We didn't think you could hear us," Aunztequi said.

"I can hear you now."

"Is it true, then?" asked Iturraeta. "They exist?"

"If 'they' are the Wenshens, then yes," said Dewey. "They do exist. If you'll excuse me."

Dewey started to turn away but was stalled by Mecolaeta's hand on his arm. "What are they like, Lieutenant?"

"Friendly enough, for the moment. You'll meet the Wenshen once we can get through the airlocks. For now, SSgt Castro will need your help with moving supplies."

He stared them down until all three seemed to grow uncomfortable.

"Right, well," Aunztequi said. "We'll go see what help the staff sergeant needs."

"Thank you." Dewey nodded deep enough to make his helmet bob and then returned to his mission.

The buildings of the town were simple prefabs made of thick plastic walls and thin plastic roofs. Dewey doubted that the A.P. scientists had ever made it rain or caused a wind storm to happen. In some ways, Dewey was surprised that the A.P. had done as much as they had. He could easily have imagined the scientists keeping the Wenshens in cages or cells.

Neoklis had said one doctor had felt bad about what was going to happen. Perhaps others had felt something, too, and pushed for this artificial landscape to give the Wenshens some bit of scenery and freedom of movement.

None of it made sense to Dewey. The very idea of messing with human genetics was scary enough. But to create an adapted version of people for experimental purposes and knowing at the end of the experiment, they would be terminated, Dewey wasn't sure he could do it. One of the A.P. scientists couldn't, and that was all it took to change everyone's future. Some, like the Wenshens, were lengthened. Others had been drastically shortened.

Dewey and Pvt Hart crossed a bridge that arched over a dry creek bed. The houses here showed signs of damage. Combat damage, evidenced by lines of bullet holes. Fire damage, evidenced by melted and blackened plastic that turned at least two homes into tortured blobs.

There was a larger building here, too. The doors were missing, and Dewey noticed tables and chairs, some overturned, some damaged. He guessed either a classroom or dining hall. A classroom seemed less likely. Why would the scientists bother educating the Wenshen when they had no intention of allowing them to live past the experiment. If he had the chance, he'd have to ask Neoklis.

All the speculation would have to wait until later. He and Hart had arrived at the airlock that allowed passage into the rest of the facility. Dewey wanted them on this side of the airlock. Even now, at the surface, the A.P. were still trying to break in.

Dewey tapped his comm, signally for MSgt Roberson. "Airlock clear, Master Sergeant?"

"It is, Lieutenant." A pause, and then, "Oh, looks like it isn't shut. I'll start the cycle from this side for you."

The airlock, while still more extensive than the ones on the Shnel Shnek, was quick to cycle the air. A minute and the light winked green, and the hatch began to swing open.

"In you go, Hart."

Hart entered the airlock ahead of Dewey, who tapped the button that started the cycle once more. Sodium borate fell like dust and was quickly whisked away as the air went from acidic and deadly to benign and breathable. When the light turned green, Dewey started replacing Hart's filters. He took his turn standing still while Hart reciprocated. Past the now opening hatchway, Dewey could see the two cots, their occupants, the medtechs, Medic Izu, and MSgt Roberson, his helmet hanging by its lanyard.

"There you go, Lieutenant," Hart said. Dewey felt the gentle push as Hart shut the flexible hatch, pushing it into its seal.

"Thank you, Hart. Stand by for now." Dewey stepped out of the airlock. "Roberson, how's everyone holding up?"

"Well enough, thank you. You brought the antidote?"

"I did." Dewey looked at MedTech Chambers as he added, "It's pill form."

"You wanted it to print a liquid, Lt Tyler?"

Dewey smiled. Though the voice was weak, Maj Simmons's voice was still unmistakable.

"Good point, Major." Dewey unsealed his EVA suit and extracted the packet from where he'd been keeping it safe. He passed it to MedTech Moreno, who'd moved to accept it.

"So, the A.P. were messing with nature?" Maj Simmons asked.

"Even our scientists mess with nature," said Dewey. He walked over to look down at the major. Chambers was pulling a pill out of the packet and passing it to Maj Simmons. "I just don't think ours would mess with human DNA."

Maj Simmons allowed the medtech to press the pill to her lips. She used her lips to pull the pill into her mouth and then used the drinking nozzle in her suit to wash the pill down. After she swallowed, she said, "If they did, Tyler, we'd be some of the last to ever know."

Dewey couldn't deny that possibility. He just hoped that they hadn't become like the A.P. or the other multi-planet governments.

Chambers, in the meantime, had passed a second pill to Medic Izu who was now giving it to Zeledano.

"How long until we know it's working?" Dewey asked.

MedTech Chambers was standing, stretching out her back. "I don't know, Lieutenant. All we can do is watch vitals and hope we see improvement."

"I've no idea what you're talking about," said Maj Simmons. "I feel a hundred percent better. Help me up."

While Dewey chuckled, Chambers said, "If you're feeling that good, Major, stand up on your own."

"Clever move, Chambers," Maj Simmons said, but she also stayed on the cot, on her back.

"If we're all done playing around," said MSgt Roberson, "Maybe we can seal up and get going?"

The master sergeant's request got everyone moving. Between Dewey, Hart, and the medics, they carried the stretchers and remaining supplies into the airlock. Dewey noticed that Pvt Hart moved with more energy now that he had two working filters.

Inside the airlock, all the open space that had been there when Dewey and Hart came through was now filled with boxes, crates, and the slowly recovering injured. Dewey and the others sat or stood on the supplies while they waited for the airlock to cycle through, filling the chamber with Wenshen air.

On the other side of the airlock, as the hatch swung open, people were waiting. They were all civilians. Dewey was confident he knew why they were hanging around.

"We moved all of the supplies," Iturraeta said before any of the other civilians could explain.

"The Wenshen items, too," said Capt Aunztequil. He put a restraining hand on Iturraeta's shoulder. She shrugged him off.

"Well, good," said Dewey as he hopped off a case of medkits. "Because we have a bunch more that needs to be moved."

"We wanted to ask about the Wenshens," said Mecolaeta.

"Now that we're done doing your chores."

"Thank you for the help, Iturreata. Stand by, everyone." Dewey adjusted his comm and called for Cpl Garner. "Ganer? I thought you had eyes on Capt Aunztequi."

Dewey noticed someone moving near the schoolhouse building. They waved just as Dewey heard Cpl Garner's voice. "I do have eyes on them."

Of course, Dewey hadn't directed Garner to control where the civilians went, only to watch where they went and what they did.

"Good job," he said. "Now, come take control of them. We need all these supplies moved to the other airlock.

"You got it, Lieutenant."

Dewey switched the comm once more. "Cpl Garner will show you where to stack the supplies waiting in the airlock."

"But what about the Wenshens?"

"In time, Ms. Iturraeta, you will get to ask them yourself. We have to get out of here first."

Dewey left them to cart supplies. Pvt Hart, with his newfound energy, remained behind to help the medtechs move Maj Simmons and the civilian. He sought out and quickly found SSgt Castro.

"Were pretty much done here, Lieutenant," Castro said as she saluted Dewey.

He returned the salute. "Good work, Staff Sergeant. The civilians are bringing the last of the supplies, and the medtechs have the major."

"How's the major doing?"

"I can't say for sure," said Dewey. "It's only been a few minutes. I would imagine it'll take a while for her body to recover. I'd almost be willing to remain in the outer airlock until she recovered, but we don't know what the A.P. are up to. We don't want to get caught unaware. I'm pretty sure they won't be taking prisoners."

SSgt Castro grinned.

"What is it, Castro? Spill."

"It may be a waste, Lt Tyler," Castro said, "but we placed the remainder of our eyes in strategic locations throughout the building and stairwells. I then assigned one person to an eye. They'll get a motion alert if anything moves. Then they can do a double-check with visual."

Dewey grinned, too. "Excellent thinking. As was putting the crawlers up against the airlock doors."

"All the more reason not to be around here when they finally get through," Castro said. "They're going to be in a pretty foul mood by then."

"Good point. All right, then, let's get the last of the supplies in the airlock."

Again, Dewey had people waiting for him. Fortunately, it was not more civilians.

"It's a yes and no situation," said Cpl Robertson. "I don't know enough about their coding or airlock systems to throw the doors open, so to speak."

"So that would be the no of the answer," Dewey said. "What's the yes."

"We can control what cycles," Cpl Knight said. "What I mean is we can tell it what kind of atmo to cycle to."

"I know that it sounds like that's what it already does," said Robertson, "But this is a bit different."

Knight smiled and then, with a nod to Robertson, said, "She came up with the idea. We set the system so that once it cycles to Wenshen type of atmo, it always cycles to Wenshen atmo."

"So even though the hatches are shut," said Roberston, "The Wenshens can use the locks because it'll always give them breathable air."

"And the sodium bicarbonate?" Dewey wasn't sure if it would affect the Wenshens' skin, but he also didn't see a need to take chances.

"Oh, I didn't think of that," said Knight.

"Me neither, Lieutenant. We'll go back. I'm sure we can turn that off."

They both saluted and headed back to the hatch and wall between the two airlocks. Dewey watched them leave, confident that they would soon have the problem solved. They would have to do it quickly, the last of the Hospitallers, carrying Maj Simmons and Zeledon, were now entering the airlock. The rest of the Hospitallers had already filed in.

The civilians had clumped together near the opposite side of the airlock, near Knight and Robertson. Maybe they'd forgotten that there was one more airlock to go.

SSgt Castro was standing near the controls for the open airlock. She had one hand on the wall near the panel, ready to tap the controls that would take the airlock cycle to a breathable atmosphere one last time.

Dewey switched his observation of the staff sergeant back to the medtechs and Maj Simmons when his comm beeped. It was Castro.

"Staff Sergeant?"

"Fox just reported in, Lieutenant. The A.P. have breached the inner doors of the airlock up top."

That was that. Unless the A.P. found a way to control the loss of atmo quickly, the entire facility would fill with Wenshen air. It would take a long time to cycle the whole space back to breathable air, assuming they wanted to reclaim the space.

"Thank you, Castro," Dewey said. "Let's have whoever is monitoring the next few eyes keep tabs on them for now. Once we're in the next airlock, we're likely to lose signal."

"Will do."

Dewey tapped the comm to close the line. His comm buzzed a request a second later. This time it wasn't Castro. It wasn't anyone in the airlock.

"Sgt Perry? What's going on?"

"We've been attacked, Lieutenant. I'm sorry."

27

Time was now elastic, seeming to stretch out further than trying to get through the airlocks the last time. Seeming to stretch further than at any other time in Dewey's life. Sgt Perry's call had come through just as the cycle had begun for the first airlock. Ten minutes seemed to forget how to tell time and ran on longer than Dewey thought possible. He left one fireteam with the civilians, the injured, and MSgt Roberson. They would have to wait a cycle and then bring all of the supplies through.

Dewey had been on more than one rescue mission in his career in the Orphan Corps. There was always that anticipation as they dropped in from above or hurtled down broken roads in a RapRes. Someone needed their help. The time it took to get there might be too long, and there could be no one to rescue. It had happened. He wanted very much for this time to not be one of those.

When the airlock flashed green and began its slow swing open, Dewey pushed through. MedTech Moreno was right behind him. The other Hospitallers followed, grim-faced, with SSgt Castro bringing up the rear. She came last to dissuade any civilians from trying to join. She also had to stand by the hatch. Once it was fully open, she would push the button that would direct it to close and the next cycle to start.

Everyone else followed Dewey to the other end of the airlock. They checked their weapons and each others' gear. Part of that came from habit, the other part out of nervous energy that preceded any military action.

Sgt Perry's comm had cut out before she could offer any further information. They'd been attacked, and Perry was apologizing. Had she been captured? Were they now walking into a trap? Both ideas stirred an anger in Dewey. He didn't mind a fight. He'd grown up training for them. But even a boxer could get tired of taking punches and decide to do something to stop it. If the A.P. had Perry and wanted a fight, Dewey was primed to give it to them.

He was tired of taking punches. Punches that seemed to keep coming from the moment they'd entered the solar system.

"Five minutes," SSgt Castro said. She'd joined them at the hatch that would lead them to the tunnel that would take them to the surface. "Anything else from Perry?"

"Nothing." Dewey had attempted contact twice since they'd entered the second airlock. Bringing everyone onto the comm, Dewey said, "Four minutes, people. Let's do this like we know what we're doing it."

They did know what they were doing. Sgt Parks stepped in and began positioning everyone. The hatch swung inward, which put them in an awkward, defensive position. Cpl Mitchell's fireteam was on point. They had little to hide behind other than the few ballistic shields they'd brought forward from the first airlock.

The next fireteam, Cpl Fleming's, would be exposed as the hatch opened further. Dewey waited with Cpl Chavez's team despite the look that SSgt Castro gave him. But Hospitaller officers didn't hide no matter how important their staff NCOs thought they were.

"Here we go," said SSgt Castro. She still looked displeased with Dewey's placement just behind Cpl Chavez.

Then it didn't matter. The light near the airlock hatch turned green. There was a clicking noise just before it began to swing open. Everyone was prepared, weapons to shoulders, barrels pointing at the widening gap being left behind by the opening hatch.

Dewey watched Cpl Mitchell. Normally he could see his people's eyes. From that, he could guess at what was happening. Lacking eyes to watch, Dewey studied Mitchell's posture. When the corporal relaxed, Dewey was ready for the comm call.

"Lieutenant, I think it's one of the Wenshen? He isn't wearing a suit. Correction, she isn't wearing a suit. And she's waving."

Dewey stood and approached the still moving hatch. He leaned for a look around and then stepped into the widening space. The Wenshen that Mitchell identified stood just on the other side of the opening. She was highlighted by the glow from the light-sticks that seemed to have been left behind. He tapped his comm, activating the external speaker and mic.

"My sergeant said you'd been attacked."

The Wenshen nodded solemnly. "Flat-tails. We hurried to the surface as soon as we learned what was happening. Your soldier helped. She used one of our spears. Neoklis said to tell you she was very brave."

That explained why he hadn't been able to get Sgt Perry on the comm.

"Thank you for letting us know." Dewey pointed into the airlock. "We have to get everyone out of the other space, and then we will come up to the surface."

"I'll tell Neoklis. Do you want us to leave the soldier where she is?"

"For now, thank you."

The Wenshen nodded and then turned. She started to jog up the tunnel, quickly disappearing into the gloom. Dewey took a moment to breathe and collect his thoughts. He'd been hoping that he was done with losing people on this mission. Did he dare hope that Sgt Perry was the last? He banished the thought, knowing it would only make him feel worse.

Dewey turned to face the rest of the Hospitallers. "Everyone hear?"

"Yes, Lieutenant," SSgt Castro said. "Never forgotten."

"Always remembered," said Dewey and the rest of the Hospitallers present.

After a silent count to ten, Dewey started giving orders. "Cpl Chavez, your fireteam and MedTech Moreno will come to the surface with me. Everyone else remains here with SSgt Castro to help move supplies."

"Will do," said SSgt Castro.

"Let's go, Chavez." Dewey turned and started up the tunnel. His external mic was still on. He could hear the feet of Cpl Chavez's fireteam following him.

He would have liked for time to drag now. He was in no hurry to see what had happened to Sgt Perry. Unfortunately, too fast or too slow, time didn't care about his feelings. The trip to the tunnel entrance felt as if it had only taken seconds.

The Wenshens were there at the opening. They stood in what seemed to Dewey to be a poor example of a squad formation. Only when one of them looked over their shoulder and back to Dewey did he realize they were attempting to create a shield to protect him from what lay on the other side.

"I know it may have seemed that we don't value life as much as you do," said Neoklis as he stepped over to Dewey. "But I assure you we do. It is just that we know that it can be taken from us even when we're not ready."

"Then we're on the same screen," Dewey said. He noticed only enough behind the shield of Wenshens to determine the presence of just one body.

"Your soldier –."

"Perry," Dewey said. His voice surprised him with its sharpness. "Sgt Shelley Perry."

"Of course." Neoklis paused for a moment and then continued. "Your Sgt Shelley Perry was more vigilant than Acamas who was keeping watch with her. She saw the flat-tails before he did. By doing so, she saved his life. I'm sorry that we could not save hers."

"Our job, or purpose, is to aid, comfort, and defend. Sometimes our lives are given in that purpose. We know this and do our best to make sure that a high price is paid for it."

"I'm not sure what you mean about price," said Neoklis. "But if it has to do with taking as many of the flat-tails with her as she could, then she has certainly made them regret attacking while she was guarding here."

Dewey'd had enough. He nodded and then moved forward. None of the Wenshens attempted to stop him. It could have been the way he moved, but it also could have been the three Hospitallers close behind him. Either way, they cleared a path.

The Wenshen had moved the parts of Sgt Perry so that they were close to each other. It said something that they only found large pieces. Sgt Allen and MedTech Phillips had been so severely cut up that Dewey hadn't been sure they'd gotten all of each of them into the body bags.

"She stepped right in the way," Neoklis said. "She used the spear like she was born to it. She made them pay a heavy price."

Neoklis pointed. Dewey followed the direction with his gaze, seeing five flat-tails splayed on the ground. When they'd been attacked the first night, they'd used their rifles. The bullets tore through the flat-tails with much less grace than what the flat-tails used when eviscerating the Hospitallers. These creatures, though clearly lifeless, did not appear to be damaged.

"They're dead?" Dewey asked. "How?"

"Between the head and the body. There is a narrow gap between the protective plates. It takes some strength, but if you push hard enough, it reaches a vital point, and they die instantly."

"There were too many."

"Yes, Lt Tyler. Neither Sgt Shelley Perry nor Acamas saw the one come from behind. It attacked your sergeant. Acamas heard the scream and killed the attacking flat-tail. But there were others." Neoklis paused and breathed a deep breath. "We arrived, then, but it was too late. Several other flat-tails had gotten to Sgt Shelley Perry. We could not stop them."

"If you're worried that we blame you," Dewey said, turning from the remains of Sgt Perry, "we don't. You did your best. That's all we can ask of anyone."

"Pardon me, Lieutenant." It was Cpl Chavez. "May we take care of Sgt Perry's body?"

"Yes, please, Chavez. And thank you."

The fireteam would put Perry's body into the bag that they would find in one of the outer pockets of her evac suit. If it was damaged, someone else would surrender theirs. Everyone carried their own body bag. Dewey's was in the pouch at the small of his back. He always put it there with the belief that it was the least likely place to get damaged.

Some people the Orphan Corps encountered across the Second Radial Arm thought it was a morbid idea, carrying your own body bag. Dewey knew it served as a reminder of what they were doing and what the outcome could be. Sgt Perry knew. Every Hospitaller knew.

Dewey stepped aside and let the three Hospitallers look after the remains of their friend. Some of the Wenshens observed from a few meters distance. One of them moved to help. He had a short conversation with Chavez that Dewey didn't hear. Rather than reject the help, Chavez appeared to agree to allowing the Wenshen to help.

"That's Acamas," Neoklis said.

The information explained why Chavez had allowed him to help.

It took more time to move pieces of Perry into the body bag than it took to put Pfc Cruz into one when she'd been killed by an A.P. bullet. By the time they were finally sealing the bag and cracking the small chemical vial inside it to preserve the remains, more Hospitallers were coming up the tunnel. They weren't alone, and they weren't in the lead.

Dewey met the civilians as they emerged into the light. Several of them stumbled over their feet. Already off balance with the loads they were carrying, Dewey had to step forward to stop one from falling. He missed the next one.

"Up you go," he said as he helped the second civilian off the ground. They'd been carrying a tote of emergency rations that had managed to remain shut after being dropped and landed on. Then he got a look past the helmet shield. "Engineer Aurrano, I'd have thought you'd be more careful."

"Normally, I would," she said as she brushed off her evac suit's knees. "Someone said there'd been an attack by the giant monster ants."

"The flat-tails, yes," said Dewey. He picked up the tote and passed it back to Aurrano. "They've been convinced to go away. Or killed. Please take this over to the side, with the ones my people are stacking."

"Yes, of course." Aurrano looked around and then slowly made her way over to where Cpl Mitchell and his fireteam were stacking the supplies brought up from the tunnel.

"I thought they'd look stranger."

Dewey turned to face Capt Aunztequi, who'd emerged from the tunnel and approached after a pause. He was still carrying two small cases of ammunition.

"What?" asked Dewey? "Like extra arms? Or gills?"

"Maybe gills," said the captain. "Or larger eyes or scaly skin. Honestly, I never really considered it until now."

"You didn't believe they existed?"

Capt Aunztequi shrugged. "I didn't know what to think. I'd thought it was the monster ants they'd created. I might have thought they'd done a gen-mod on human DNA, but I'm also sure I quickly dismissed it, too. Who would be that crazy?"

"You have your answer to that last part. The A.P. are that crazy. At the least."

"Well, I'd like to talk to them," Capt Aunztequi said. "But I think we should probably bring up the rest of the supplies. And their belongings, too."

"Maybe they'll talk to you while everyone works." Dewey pointed a thumb in the direction of the tunnel entrance. The Wenshens, mixed in with the Hospitallers and the civilians, were entering the tunnel.

"Maybe." The captain grinned through his face shield and then hurried over to join the thin procession into the tunnel.

28

With the Wenshens helping, the Hospitaller supplies and the items from the Wenshen subterranean homes were in two stacks before another hour had passed. Dewey explained to Neokis and Theophilus what they had done to the airlocks.

"Hopefully, we'll never have to go back in there," Theophilus said. "But if we do, your efforts will make it easier. Thank you."

Maj Simmons and Zeledon came up around the same time as the last of the supplies. Dewey gave the major a succinct report of what had happened to Sgt Perry. At the same time, he realized that not everyone was present, and he hadn't seen them appear on the surface.

"MedTech Chambers? Where are MSgt Roberson and Pfc Anderson?"

"Anderson had reported movement at the eye she was monitoring. The master sergeant went into VR to look, too. He wanted to scan all the other eyes as well and said he'd be along shortly."

"Thank you," Dewey said. He adjusted his comm and tapped it. "MSgt Roberson?"

"Lt Tyler." the master sergeant sounded distracted.

"Everything okay?"

"For the most part," Roberson said. "The A.P. are in the facility, and they've cleared the first level."

"So they know we aren't there."

"Clearly," said Roberson. "But that's not the thing that has my curiosity tingling."

"What does?"

"The number of people the A.P. have in the buildings. I've been trying to keep track, but I don't think that all of them are inside."

"They're keeping a rearguard," suggested Dewey. It was a half-hearted suggestion, given while his mind whirred through scenarios. "But they wouldn't need that many."

"No, Lieutenant, they wouldn't."

"Okay, if you're still in VR, drop out and hustle to the surface, Master Sergeant. I think we may need to get moving as soon as possible."

"Will do."

Dewey adjusted his comm for externals and sought out Neoklis. "I have a feeling the A.P. are going to search the other buildings and the area around them. We might want to get moving as quickly as we can."

"I'll send a couple of people to the edges of the tree line to check," Neoklis said. "But we also want to cover the opening here. They might know it's here, but we don't want to make it easy on them."

"Right," said Dewey. "We might also want to determine what supplies to leave just inside? We won't be able to carry everything, not even with your help."

"I see your point. Do you have suggestions on what we should leave?"

Dewey wondered if this was a test. Did Neoklis expect him to suggest leaving all the Wenshen property behind? If he did make that suggestion, how would that affect their relationship? It hadn't occurred to him to ask the Wenshen to sacrifice everything. Not after they'd just retrieved it.

"We'll need our medical, food supplies, suit parts, and ammunition. My people can carry most of that. I'll need a few of the civilians to help us."

"They're chatty, the civilians," said Neoklis said.

Dewey laughed. It was long and refreshing and unconcerned about the quizzical look on Neoklis's face. Dewey's eyes had tears that he couldn't wipe away with the back of his hand. They'd have to stay until they dried.

"You're right, Neoklis, they are exceptionally chatty. But they'll work. We'll send half of them to help carry your property. Anything that's left from either stack, we'll put back in the tunnel."

"That will take a little more time."

"It will," said Dewey. "But, you'll have help."

Dewey commed SSgt Castro and explained what was going to happen and then tasked her with setting out the supplies to go with them and splitting the civilians between Wenshen and Hospitaller supplies. Dewey then indicated they were to help haul logs and rocks. While the Wenshens and Hospitallers worked on closing the tunnel.

While the different teams got to work dividing supplies and hauling the extras back into the tunnel, Dewey went and checked on Maj Simmons. He found her sitting on the stretcher. MedTech Moreno was kneeling in front of the major. She was fixing a ration to the inlet that would allow her to draw on the nutrients as she needed.

Maj Simmons looked up as Dewey approached. She reached between Moreno's hands and tapped her comm. "Lt Tyler. How are things looking?"

"About the same, Major."

Simmons chuckled. "So, not good?"

"They've been worse," Dewey said. He'd been caught inside a building with his fireteam, back when he was a corporal. The Druiins, a fanatical separatist group, had them pinned down and were chewing the building to pieces with mortar fire. Most of the building had been brought down around the fireteam's ears before help had arrived. That had been a worse day. But then, he'd never had to look on a friend's body after some creature and sliced them to pieces.

"Well, I'd love to take on some of the burden," Maj Simmons said.

"You can't, Major," said MedTech Moreno. "You still need time to recover."

"I know, Moreno, I know." Maj Simmons looked up at Dewey, rolling her eyes. "I didn't say I was going to. I said I would like to."

"Sorry, Major." Moreno pressed the seal on the compartment that now held the suit ration. She tapped several other buttons that cleared the line and the chamber of external atmosphere.

"I appreciate the care, Moreno."

"Then lie down, Major, so the care works."

Dewey heard the lightness in Moreno's voice. So, it seemed, did the major. She laughed as she spun on her uninjured buttock and lay back on the stretcher with the medtech's help.

"When are we moving out?" Maj Simmons asked.

"Soon as we have the entrance to the tunnel hidden," Dewey said. "Hopefully, we'll be able to put distance between us and the A.P."

"Good, good. And where are we going?"

"Good question, Major."

With the extra help, the Wenshens had the entrance covered in a little more than half the time it took to uncover it. The supplies had been stacked inside to port and starboard. Dewey wasn't sure if they would ever need or have a chance to come back for the Hospitaller supplies. If they didn't, he hoped the Wenshens would take advantage of them.

But for now, they were done, and everyone was ready to move. Each civilian, Hospitaller, and Wenshen carried one or two containers, depending on size and weight. What Dewey still didn't know where they were going. But he was sure of one thing.

"You're camp," he said to Neoklis and Theophilus, "isn't big enough for everyone here."

It was also a lousy place to try and defend, but he kept that to himself.

Neoklis's face grew a confused expression that he turned from Dewey to Theophilus. Theophilus had a similar expression. Dewey wasn't sure why they were confused. Unless they either hadn't come to the same realization or they knew something about the site that he didn't know. The last one was likely as he'd only been there a few hours.

"I just had it in my head that you would tell him," Theophilus said.

Neoklis laughed, the confusion now washed from his face. "And I thought it was obvious and didn't need an explanation."

"Clearly, it does," Dewey said.

"I apologize for not making it clear before. There is only one place that we know of that is safe, and that is our home."

"We live in a cut in the hills less than a day from here," said Theophilus. "The apes have never found it. We believe it is the safest place around here. It has been for us."

"We can't stay in our suits forever," said Dewey. "The power won't keep that long."

"The civilian, Augias Aunztequi, said that your people were coming here to rescue you."

"We hope, Neoklis, we hope. We have no confirmation that the beacon survived and transmitted our distress signal."

"More apes came," said Theophilus. "Surely, your people will as well."

"That's our hope."

"Can you call them from anywhere on the planet?" asked Neoklis. "If they come here?"

"If they're in orbit above us and are listening, yes. If they come into the atmosphere, we'll have to be able to see them."

"Until then," Neoklis said. "Do you want to wait here and fight the flat-tails and the apes? Or do you want to go someplace safer?"

Dewey laughed this time. "Oh, I didn't say we didn't want to go. And I think the civilians are even more eager to go."

"They said the galaxy would soon learn about our existence," said Theophilus. "That will be a good thing?"

"It should," said Dewey. "The A.P. can't exterminate you if the radial arm knows you exist. Others, though, might come with the hopes of exploiting you."

"But not your people? The Hospitallers?"

Dewey recalled Maj Simmons's comment about her and him being some of the last to know if HQ was messing with human genetics. As loyal as he was, he hoped they weren't. But he also believed in the tenants of the Hospitallers to aid, comfort, and defend. He was going to hold firm to the belief that this would hold sway over any other desires or intentions.

"My people," he said after a long pause, "will work with you to provide the aid you want."

"We shall see," Neoklis said. "Until then, let us go home."

Dewey nodded agreement. The Wenshen home had to be better than here. He tapped his comm. "SSgt Castro? The Wenshens have point. Let's move out."

"You got it, L.T."

Dewey muted his comm while SSgt Castro gave the orders. While he couldn't hear for the moment, he could see the Hospitallers forming up, each with their load to bear. Ahead of them, the civilians were formed up exactly as Dewey would expect them to form, which meant more of a gaggle than precise lines. At the front, the Wenshens were already moving. Four of the younger Wenshens led the way. With them, Cpl Lindsey Alexander from engineering walked with them as Hospitaller liaison. Every Wenshen carried a bundle from homes most had never seen. Ones Neoklis and Theophilus probably would never forget.

In the middle of the Hospitallers were the medtechs, MSgt Roberson, and ships crew. They carried the two stretchers and what was left of the medical supplies. They would all take turns at carrying Maj Simmons and Zeledon.

Dewey looked back, as most of the Hospitallers filed by. Again, they'd been forced to leave one of theirs behind. Sgt Perry's body was just inside the tree line. They'd dug a shallow grave and then piled rocks to protect what remained. The cairn was low so as not to draw attention. Even Dewey had to scan, squinting his eyes, to pick out the location.

One more name to be etched onto the wall in the commanding officer's office. One more name to be chiseled into this year's obelisk flanking the entrance to headquarters.

If he could get through this action without adding another name, Dewey would count himself lucky. The only problem with that idea was that Dewey wasn't feeling lucky.

The march was slow. Everyone was carrying extra weight. The Hospitallers were doing okay, but even they were flagging, having done so much with so little rest. The Wenshens were wearing a little bit more than even the Hospitallers. Dewey found a little pride in that, outperforming the native population on their own planet.

It was the civilians that were the real drag parachute on the march. It was clear to Dewey that none of them had ever had to walk long distances while carrying an extra load. They'd forced the Wenshens to slow the pace or risk losing them and the Hospitallers who were behind them. SSgt Castro was frequently reminding the others to not bunch up. Sgt Parks, at the rear of the column, was stopping and starting frequently as the line of people stretched and bunched like a worn-out spring.

Dewey tapped his comm. "Cpl Alexander? Check with Neoklis. We need to break and rest for a while."

"Will do, Lieutenant."

The line continued to move. Dewey had to sprinkle some encouragement for the civilians. He hadn't received confirmation from Cpl Alexander, but he told them anyway. They would be breaking soon. Hang on a little longer.

Just about the time that Dewey was wondering if he should comm Alexander again, he noticed the Wenshens were slowing spreading out. As the civilians reached the Wenshens and the rest stop, Dewey understood why Neoklis may have chosen to wait until they reached this point.

They'd been walking a winding trail with trees and killer bushes on either side. Most of the time, there'd been room to walk side by side, but occasionally they were forced into a single file. Where the Wenshen were coming to a stop, there was more space. There was a lot more space as it turned out.

Neoklis had brought them to a halt in a clearing. Based on the stumps, Dewey had a feeling that the clearing existed for a purpose. Perhaps this was one of the places the Wenshens had stopped during their original exodus? Dewey would have liked to ask Neoklis. His curiosity would have to wait because they were suddenly being attacked.

29

"Flat-tails!" one of the Wenshens shouted.

While the civilians milled about in fear, the Wenshens and Hospitallers took action. The Wenshens pushed ahead of the Hospitallers. Dewey caught a few glimpses of the confusion on some of the faces through their shields. They weren't used to being behind someone else when danger raised its ugly head. Their natural response was to jump forward to protect, not stand and be protected.

"Stand easy, Hospitallers," Dewey said. He set the comm to include the civilians. "Ship's team, control the civilians, keep them out of the way."

"Yes, Lieutenant." MSgt Roberson and Cpl Knight had spoken at the same time. Their voices disappeared off the comm as they switched their comms to deal with the civilians.

In the trees and scrub back in the direction they'd recently passed, the ground seemed to move. Dewey realized he was looking across the backs of several dozen flat-tails. They were approaching in a broad line, weaving past the trees and ground plants. The first of the flat-tails coming in a rush towards the Wenshens.

With a skill that could only come from obsessive practice, the Wenshens jabbed forward with their spears. Some of them worked in pairs as there was currently less flat-tails than Wenshens on the line of defense. The spears found the weak spots in the flat-tail exoskeletons and were then shoved home by the Wenshens, leaning hard on the spear shafts. Some of the flat-tails thrashed for several heartbeats and then collapsed. Other flat-tails had dropped as quickly as if someone had flicked a switch.

Behind the first rush of flat-tails, the other flat-tails slowed and then stopped. Some of them moved backward. Others could not move because of the press of more flat-tails behind them. They began to spread out, creating a near unbroken line of giant ant bodies with razor-sharp tails.

With his external mic on in case the Wenshens needed to communicate with him, Dewey heard for the first time the sounds of the flat-tails. There was the rustle and clatter as they moved past plants and scuttled across dirt and rock. That was just the sounds of their motion. The other sound was a mix of clicks, pops, and hisses. Dewey's mic wasn't designed to deliver stereographic projection. So, he could only determine that the sound came from different places by watching the actions of the Wenshens.

The Wenshens, having extracted their spears from the dead, appeared to change the direction they faced when the hisses of the flat-tails changed in volume. Dewey could only surmise, but the hissing seemed to indicate the direction of the most significant threat. Either the flat-tails knew what the Wenshens were doing, or they were completely random in their action. Either way, the danger seemed to switch places as the flat-tails continued to advance on the waiting Hospitallers and Wenshens.

"Hey, Lt Tyler," SSgt Castro said over the comm.

A light on the inside of Dewey's helmet screen informed him that Castro was speaking on a closed line. "What do you got, Castro?"

"Couple things. There's eighteen Wenshens with their spears. Might be a few more flat-tails than that."

"Seems that way." Dewey had tried counting them, but their movement and the foliage that provided some cover made an exact number difficult to determine. "What else?"

"We took out more than this our first night on the planet. Bullets make short work of these creatures, and no one has to get close to them."

"Agreed," said Dewey. Then, he added, "But we didn't have an option at that moment. We gave away our position when we did."

"Oh, right, I see," Castro said. "Definitely don't want an entire company of A.P. to get a lock on us."

"Definitely do not." Dewey paused and then said, "But be ready, just in case. I don't want anyone dying just to keep our location a secret."

Castro laughed. "Neither do I, Lieutenant. Neither do I."

"Lt Tyler."

Dewey turned, scanning for Neoklis. He found the elder Wenshen waving for attention. He and one other Wenshen had unearthed a long trench. Dewey trotted over to their position.

"What do you have here?" he asked Neoklis. The question answered itself when Dewey looked into the long trench in the ground.

In much the same way that they'd hidden the entrance to the facility tunnel, the Wenshen had covered the five-meter-long trench with sticks, leaves from the razor-sharp bushes, and dirt. Now uncovered, it revealed a stash of spears.

"Spares," Dewey said. A young Wenshen had stepped down into the hole and passed a spear up to Dewey.

"There are many where the hills touch the plain," Neoklis said. He accepted several more spears from the young Wenshen as he spoke. "The spears are not unbreakable. Their length makes carrying extras complicated."

"And you only really need them when dealing with the flat-tails."

"Not exactly," Neoklis said. "But with the flat-tails, we lose more spears than at other times. Pass these to your people."

Dewey accepted a bundle of spears. He turned intending to carry them to SSgt Castro, but she was already behind him.

"Excellent," Castro said. "At least we won't be bored."

Castro turned and left with ten spears, moving to the right of the line of Hospitallers. Dewey accepted more of the spears and carried them to the left. The Hospitallers, in their turn, received the spears. Some with uncertainty as spear training hadn't been part of their curriculum. Others seemed to be eager to embrace the new challenge. There was no time for wondering. The flat-tails had once more surged forward.

The only flaw that Dewey saw in the flat-tails' assault was the space they had to allow between each other. While they did have pincers that would likely do serious damage to anyone or anything they grabbed on to, it was the tail that was the real danger. But to use their tail, they had to bend their bodies into a U. That brought the tail into play, and it was nothing but lethal.

That was the catch. Their tails shredded anything they contacted with, including each other. Already, one of the flat-tails was down, several meters back, its face slashed out of recognition after stumbling and then moving into the path of another flat-tail moving past.

The foliage had also suffered under the attack of the flat-tails. The dangerous bushes had been turned into confetti by the flat-tails. A few of the skinny trees were down, and others showed a profusion of scars from the passing razor-sharp tails.

The bushes and trees could not defend themselves. The Wenshens and Hospitallers could.

Dewey stepped forward as one of the Wenshen youth was struggling to remove her spear from the body of the flat-tail she'd taken down. Another of the monster ants had started forward, its body beginning to bend, bringing its tail toward the young Wenshen. Dewey shoved forward, spearing the flat-tail.

He felt the pressure as the tip contacted the skin below the exo-skeleton. As he continued to push, the resistance collapsed. The spear slid another half-meter into the flat-tail. The creature spasmed once before collapsing. It landed on top of the one from which the Wenshen had finally pulled her spear.

The Wenshen gave Dewey a nod before she turned away and speared another flat-tail.

Here and there along the front, Hospitallers and Wenshens fought side-by-side. There'd been only one pause in the attack. It came when a flat-tail killed one of the Wenshen. Their scream pierced Dewey's ears through the mic and speakers before the system could adjust for volume and pitch. Collectively, everyone took a step back. That caused the flat-tails to pause for a moment, too.

Just as it happened, it ended. The Wenshens stepped back into the fray. This time they did so with more force, more passion. Even before the Hospitallers could step back in, several dozen more flat-tail were down. Behind their dead, the rest of the flat-tails had paused.

"Who did we lose?" Dewey asked.

"We're all okay," SSgt Castro said over the comm. "The Wenshens lost one."

"I heard."

Dewey looked around and located Neoklis. Keeping his head turned so that the flat-tails were still in his vision, Dewey stepped over to where Neoklis was in conversation with Theophilus and several of the young Wenshens. They, too, were keeping a watch on the flat-tails.

"Lt Tyler." Neoklis acknowledged Dewey's presence with a nod of his head. "Your people fight well."

"They'll be pleased to know they've earned your respect." Dewey paused as he glanced at the remains of the one Wenshen casualty. "Who did you lose?"

"Dimoniki," said Theophilus. "She was my family."

"I'm sorry," Dewey said.

"Anyone of us could have died in the fight," said Neoklis. "Could have been one of yours. Could have been you or me. That is life here."

"Sometimes, the best idea is to not be in a fight," Dewey said. "I'm also not sure how long we can hold this position. I don't know how smart these creatures are, but they may soon figure out they can go around and box us in."

The younger Wenshens agreed. One of them said, "Another kilometer, and we'll have the canyon walls to help us."

"So, a rearguard action?"

"If you mean that we fight from the rear, then yes, Lt Tyler, that is what we'll do," said Neoklis.

"Can we put one of my people on point again? With yours?"

"Phaedon," Neoklis said. He looked at one of the two young Wenshens standing with him and Theophilus. "You and Antonis go with the Hospitaller, lead the way up to the pass."

Phaedon didn't look happy with the idea. Dewey could well imagine that the young man wanted to be at the rear, fighting the flat-tails. He was sure that whoever he picked for point would feel the same way. However, also like a Hospitaller, Phaedon did not argue with orders given.

"Pfc Dunn, report to my position," Dewey said over the comm. In seconds, Pfc Dunn appeared next to Dewey.

She saluted. "Yes, Lieutenant?"

"We're pulling back to the hills where we can better resist the flat-tails' advances," said Dewey. "I need you up there with Phaedon and Antonis to keep us in contact."

"The front, Lieutenant?" Dewey could see her eyes through the shield as she took a quick look back where the flat-tails were still milling. Then, her eyes snapped back to Dewey, and she said, "I'm on it. But who are Phaedon and Antonis?"

"I'm Phaedon." The young Wenshen lifted his spear to draw attention. "Come with me, and we'll gather Antonis."

"Dunn, turn on your external mic."

Dunn laughed through the comm and then through the speaker. "I guess that would be useful. You're Phaedon?"

"I am." He smiled, seeming to be aware of the error on Dunn's part. "Come, let's find Antonis."

Once they left, Dewey turned to Neoklis and Theophilus. "We'll probably want to move soon? Before the flat-tails regain their courage?"

"I'll pass the word," Theophilus said. He nodded to Neoklis and then started toward the line of waiting Wenshen.

"I'll get the medtechs and wounded ready," Dewey said to Neoklis. Neoklis nodded, and Dewey left, walking another five meters to where the medtechs were standing. They weren't standing alone, Maj Simmons was also standing. He saluted as he approached. "Should you be on your feet, Major?"

"I think I should," she answered.

"I don't think you should," said MedTech Chambers.

Dewey remained silent, watching and listening to the exchange with some amusement.

"Is that an order, MedTech Chambers? Am I still too ill to move on my own?"

There was an audible sigh over the comm before Chambers said, "No, Major, you aren't too ill to stand, nor to walk. But rest would be better."

"I think it'd be better for a whole bunch of Hospitallers and Wenshens," Maj Simmons said. "But I don't think those overgrown bugs are going to let them have a rest. What's going on, Lt Tyler?"

Dewey pulled down with his mouth, erasing the small smile he'd been allowing to grow on his face. "We're getting ready to pull a rearguard action, Major. Another kilometer and there's a narrow pass that will be more defensible and allow us to spell some of the Wenshens and our people."

Maj Simmons clapped her hands together. "There you go, Chambers, we got to move. And I move faster on my feet than on my back."

"As you wish, Major," Chambers said. There was movement near Chambers. Zeledon was climbing to his feet. "You, too?"

"I don't want to be the only one taking it easy," said Zeledon.

"You sure you're not a Hospitaller?" asked Maj Simmons.

Zeledon groaned and said, "Oh, I hope not."

Those who'd heard the tone of his voice as he spoke enjoyed a brief laugh.

"Okay, Major. We need everyone here ready to march," Dewey said. He saluted and turned to brief the rest of the Hospitallers.

Even though he'd turned and he was walking away, Dewey was still close enough to hear the conversation behind him.

"You might be walking, Major," MedTech Chambers said, "but you are not allowed to carry anything."

"Just my wounded pride, Chambers."

Dewey chuckled as distance cut him out of the conversation. Humor always made the weight of a situation easier to bear. Major Simmons had never appeared to have a problem with laughing at herself. That attitude was picked up by Dewey and the staff and senior NCOs. But laughter wouldn't cure the wounded, especially the type of wounds the flat-tails could cause. They had to survive this situation so they could laugh about it later.

"Lieutenant." SSgt Castro and MSgt Roberson saluted as he approached.

Roberson asked, "What's the word, Lieutenant."

Before Dewey could respond, his speakers growled with the sound of gunfire.

30

Dewey spun around, looking for the cause of the sound. "Who fired?" he asked across the general comm and the speaker.

SSgt Castro started moving, pointing past Dewey toward the medtechs. "Back there, Lt Tyler."

Dewey followed. "Who's firing? And at what?"

"Sorry, Lieutenant," said Maj Simmons. "One of the civilians. Justified, though."

Dewey broke into his lumbering EVA-suit trot and returned to where the major was standing with one of the civilians. They were holding one of the MUWs passed along from one of the dead Hospitallers. Several meters away, partially hidden by a razor bush, a flat-tail lay on the ground, legs sprawled out to the sides. An automatic burst of bullets had shattered its head.

"I'm sorry," the civilian said. The voice clued Dewey that it was Urbano Marieta. "I turned and saw it was approaching, and I just fired. I didn't want it to attack."

Before Dewey could respond, there was another, shorter, burst of gunfire. Dewey wanted to shout at everyone to stop firing. They'd resorted to using just the spears for a reason.

"That's on me," said SSgt Castro.

Dewey located her on the other side of the medtechs and civilians. A few meters past her, another flat-tail lay prone with its legs splayed. This time, the head remained undamaged.

"I know we aren't supposed to," said Castro as Dewey approached. "But if the A.P. heard the previous burst of fire, one more hardly makes a difference."

"And if they didn't?" asked Dewey. He was eyeing the flat-tail. There were three holes in the carapace just behind where they would have driven a spear.

"Then, really my bad," said Castro. "But I learned something. We'd wasted a lot of ammo that first night. If it comes down to it, we can do three-round bursts in the same place. Which means we can do it from a distance."

"Yes, good information," Dewey said. He clapped SSgt Castro on the shoulder. "But let's not use it unless we absolutely have to. We may need those rounds for the A.P. I don't think they'll be so easy to spear."

"You got it, Lt Tyler."

Dewey moved back to where Neoklis and Theophilus had gathered once more. He noticed that the Wenshens and his Hospitallers were standing more relaxed now.

"I think your weapons have given the flat-tails pause," Theophilus said. "They've turned and scurried back into the brush, probably heading for their burrows."

"I'd cross my fingers," Dewey said and then held up a gloved hand, "but it's hard to do in this suit."

"I'll cross mine for you," said Neoklis. "Though I'm not sure how that helps."

Dewey laughed. "It doesn't. It's just something we say."

Beyond the dead forms of flat-tails, the ground that had been churned up by the living flat-tails was now barren. What had been alive with plants and moving giant ant bodies was now empty and dead. Several Wenshens were squatting near the remains of Dimoniki, gingerly pulling the dismembered pieces into a single pile. Her head, which had been sliced open by the flat-tail, was just visible in the slowly growing collection of flesh and was, Dewey was relieved to see, turned face down.

"How do you handle your dead?" he asked.

"We have a place in the cliffs, on the edge of our village," said Neoklis. "They rest there."

"Out here," Theophilus added, "in situations like this, we'll dig a hole and line it with rocks, then add more on top."

It was similar to the cairns the civilians and Hospitallers had built. Except, they remembered to layer the bottom.

"And the dead flat-tails?"

Neoklis shrugged. "They eat their own."

"Who else eats them?" When both elder Wenshen looked at him, confusion knitting their brows, he added, "Their natural self-defense. It existed long before you came to the surface. There's something as big or bigger than the flat-tails. Or there was."

"Four-points," said Neoklis. "But they are rare. Seen a few. That's where we got the idea to use the spears."

"They have spears for legs," added Theophilus. "They stay away from us. We stay away from them."

Dewey nodded. "Speaking of staying away, maybe we should do the same from this area."

"Before the apes come, true," said Neoklis. "We'll make faster time now."

"To your village?"

"Safest place we know of."

It had only taken an hour to dig the hole for Dimoniki's remains. After that, they started up the slope toward the Wenshen village. A kilometer along, they'd entered a slowly narrowing pass split down the middle by a fast-flowing stream. The pass turned into a narrow canyon after another kilometer and a half. In the middle, the stream took up most of the floor, and the walls were high, casting everything in shadow. The data on Dewey's HUD showed a ten-degree drop in temperature. The cool air would feel good against his skin if it weren't so acidic.

In a half kilometer, the canyon began to widen once more. Two hundred meters more, and it was like stepping into a different world.

"That's impressive," said Dewey.

"It's like an adventure vid come to life," Maj Simmons answered back over the comm.

Dewey had forgotten that the comm line was open and that he'd spoken out loud rather than keeping his thoughts to himself.

"Welcome," Neoklis said as he stepped past Dewey, who'd unknowingly come to a complete stop as he took in the view.

The walls here were higher than the narrow section of the canyon. They were also fifty to sixty meters apart, depending on where along the walls one might measure. Dewey noticed that they were closer at the top than at the bottom. This may have been a giant cave at one time. Either way, the curved walls provided a protective overhang for the homes carved into the walls beneath them.

"You can see why flyovers never revealed their location." MSgt Roberson was standing next to Dewey.

"I'm not sure that was their intent, but it's a good location anyway," said Dewey. He pointed as he talked. "There's a stream. I assume that means fresh water for them. And it's wider here, so a gentler flow, easier to cross, easier to use. Then, trees, there and there, that look like they have some type of fruit on them. Either native to the canyon or transplanted. And deeper in, it looks like they are growing something like crops."

"The homes look defensible, too," Roberson said.

Dewey agreed. The homes started a good ten meters above the ground. It looked like the Wenshen had adapted natural shelves and then dug rooms into them. Ladders permitted access to the upper levels. Unlike stairs, they were easy to remove if anyone, or anything, got into the canyon. The doors to each home were half-height, and the windows, though prolific, were all narrow. Lots of light could get in, as with air, yet still serving as defensive barriers.

"Hey," Dewey stopped one of the Wenshen carrying supplies into the canyon. He mimicked his question as he asked. "Do you also have bows and arrows?"

"Yes. But no good against the flat-tails."

"Good against apes?"

The young Wenshen laughed. "I'd like to find out."

There were shouts of excited voices that echoed off the walls of the canyon. Heads appeared at windows. People leaned out of doorways. Children appeared, moving too fast for Dewey to count accurately. They convened on Neoklis's position. Several adult Wenshens followed in their wake.

With a wreath of children around his legs, Neoklis turned to face Dewey, who'd been joined by the slower moving Maj Simmons and MSgt Roberson, who shadowed her.

"The children," said Neoklis. There was no mistaking the pride on the elder Wenshen's face.

For their part, the children seemed to suddenly realize that there were aliens amongst them. They went from surrounding Neoklis to using him as a shield.

"Hello," Maj Simmons said through the speaker that gave her voice a warble that seemed more alien than usual from Dewey's point of view.

True to the nature of children across the second radial arm of the galaxy, a few of them waved a tentative greeting.

Several other Hospitallers, Dewey included, spoke a greeting, too. With each added voice, more of the children waved a greeting. Some of them had come out from the safety of Neoklis's legs.

"Are they the apes?" Dewey heard one child ask as he tugged on Neoklis's hand.

"They'd be dead if they were apes," answered another child.

Neoklis chuckled, tousling the hair of the boy who'd had his hand. "They are not apes. They are friends who the apes are trying to hurt."

"But they're dressed like apes," said another boy. He was taller than the children near him and looked to be several years older. Dewey's judgment relied on his experience in the orphanage, which was more than a decade ago.

"We can't breathe your air," Maj Simmons said. "Like the apes."

"But you don't want to kill us?" This from the boy who'd been close to Neoklis.

"Absolutely not," said Maj Simmons. She knelt. Dewey noticed the slow speed that she performed the action. "I'm Helen. What's your name?"

"Orestes," the boy said after he first looked to Neoklis for approval.

"Nice to meet you, Orestes," Maj Simmons said.

"I'm Lidia," said a young girl who stepped forward, her hands wringing each other.

"I'm Pavlis."

"I'm Chloe."

The names came like a hard rain, so fast and quick that Dewey, despite his ability to remember, was sure he only grasped half the names and the connecting faces. Once that barrier had been broken, the children surged forward, milling amongst the Hospitallers and the civilians, touching the evac and EVA suits, asking questions, and answering questions.

Through the waist-high crowd, Neoklis waded with a woman accompanying him. They stopped in front of Maj Simmons. In her turn, Maj Simmons turned and waved for Dewey to join them.

"Maj Helen Simmons, Lt Dewey Tyler," Neoklis said before half-turning to include the woman who waited with a half-smile on her face. "This is my partner, Georgia."

"Greetings," Georgia said. Then, "So you cannot breathe the air?"

"No, ma'am, we cannot," said Maj Simmons.

Georgia turned to Neoklis. "Then we cannot invite them to join us for a meal?"

"I don't think they can eat the food either." Neoklis turned to the Hospitallers, the unasked question clear on his face.

"No, we cannot eat the food, either," said Maj Simmons. "But we can certainly sit with you if you will allow us."

"Seems wrong," said Georgia. "Sitting to eat with those who cannot eat."

"Excuse me, ma'am," Dewey said, drawing Georgia's attention. "We have food in our suits that we can eat."

"So you see," Neoklis said, "they can eat."

"Still doesn't seem right." Georgia's lips were pressed tight together when she finished speaking. She appeared to study the Hospitallers and civilians for eight or ten seconds. Then, she gave a curt nod and walked away.

"Georgia has less reason to like the apes than most of us," Neoklis said as he watched her leave. "She became pregnant while we were still in the facility. That was before we planned to revolt. They gave her a shot that caused the pregnancy to end. There was much blood, and they were going to leave her to die. Except for Dr. Jackson, who came that night and fixed the bleeding. It also meant that she could never have another child."

"That must have been hard," Maj Simmons said.

Many Hospitallers took a voluntary long-term birth control injection, male and female. After they turned forty-five, many Hospitallers chose never to have children, choosing instead to help raise the orphans by becoming a dorm mother or father. So, while most Hospitallers might not desire their children of their own, they were all very aware of what it was like to help raise them.

To have that choice taken away by some unfeeling person, might be beyond a Hospitaller's comprehension, it was still something they could connect to through empathy.

"Was," Neoklis said. "Still is. I imagine that seeing you all rubs that wound a little raw."

"Our apologies."

Neoklis turned back to the Hospitallers and shrugged. "Not that you knew. Not that it would make a difference. Now, come, join us for a gathering."

The gathering took place in what turned out to be a natural cave. It was reached through a hand-carved archway. Except for the hundred glow-sticks hanging from hooks in the walls, there was no other source of light. The room had a trench dug into its floor, forming a rectangle around a table of split tree trunks.

Across the tabletop were bowls of varying shapes and sizes. Dewey noticed that some of what he'd thought were fruit on the trees had been piled into several bowls spaced across the table. Other potential fruits and vegetables filled the remaining bowls. None of them looked like anything Dewey had ever dined on, and he wasn't even sure that calling them fruits and vegetables was appropriate.

Guided by several smiling Wenshens, Maj Simmons, Dewey, MSgt Roberson, and SSgt Castro were invited to sit. Each of them sat between Wenshens, who had followed them in and were now also taking seats. At one of the narrow ends of the table, Neoklis sat. Georgia sat beside him. Several younger Wenshens carried pitchers, filling cups with water.

Twice, Dewey had to explain to a Wenshen that he couldn't drink the water or eat their food. He'd been compelled to demonstrate how he ate and drank inside the EVA suit. Around the table, Dewey noticed that Maj Simmons and the staff NCOs were also doing the same thing.,

When it seemed that everyone was satisfied that the Hospitallers wouldn't starve, Neoklis raised his hand. The conversations evaporated as everyone turned toward him.

"As you have all heard by now," Neoklis said. "The apes have returned. They have returned in much larger numbers, putting their ships on the plain of the flat-tails."

There was some chuckling around the room.

"You've all met our new friends. While they may breathe the same air as the apes, it has been shown to us that not all who live in the suits are our enemy."

Dewey wished that he could point out that they didn't always wear the suits, but decided it probably wasn't worth the effort.

"For now," Neoklis added, "the apes remain on the flat-tail plain. The Hospitallers helped to retrieve many items from the facility village. We appreciate their help."

The Wenshens around the room applauded in a soft, polite manner.

Neoklis picked up one of the fruit and tore it in half. He held out half for Maj Simmons to take. "Let us eat in honor of our new friends and the memory of Donikis and the Hospitallers who have died this last day."

The other Wenshen picked up a single piece of food from the bowls and tore them in half as well. They then exchanged with the person next to them, which included the Hospitallers. Dewey politely accepted a piece of something dense and red. The juice from the torn fruit or vegetable in his hand trickled down the side of his glove. It flowed over a sealed rivet that began to bubble with corrosion. He set the food down on a wide, flat bowl that seemed to serve as a plate. Then, using the exterior water tube on his suit, Dewey discreetly rinsed away the juice.

"It is a shame you cannot taste our food," said the Wenshen to Dewey's left. "And thus, a shame that we cannot taste yours."

"Maybe one day we'll find a way to make it happen," said Dewey.

The Wenshen nodded before saying, "Until then, more for me, eh?"

They both laughed as the Wenshen scooped some small orange pea-shaped items onto his plate. He popped several into his mouth, munching on them and smiled contentedly in Dewey's direction.

The Wenshen not only proved to be kind hosts, despite the limitation of interaction, they were also good storytellers and conversationalists as well. Dewey was listening intently to one of the second generation Wenshens, describing seeing her first four-point, when he noticed a Wenshen youth rush into the room and kneel next to Neoklis to whisper in his ear.

After several back-and-forth whispers, Neoklis nodded. As the other Wenshine hurriedly exited the room, Neoklis stood.

"The apes have left the facility." He looked around the room, pausing each time his gaze passed a Hospitaller. "They appear to be coming this way."

31

Dewey stood on an outcrop high above the plain. A semi-hidden staircase in the Wenshen village had provided the access. It was a grand view with the distant horizon shrouded in haze. In the near distance, Dewey could almost make out the research facility. The A.P. dropships, which were much darker than the earth around them, were barely identifiable dots in the middle distance. Though only a smudge off to the right, Dewey was confident he'd identified the location of the Shnel Shnek.

What Dewey couldn't see were the A.P. forces.

"Three fingers below the facility," said one of the young Wenshen that had been keeping watch from the outcrop. "Then just to the left a finger."

"I hear you," Dewey said. He'd already held up two fingers, putting the research facility above them. He'd shifted his gaze to the left. Still, he couldn't see the A.P. "I just don't see what you see."

"Try magnification," SSgt Castro said. "It doesn't help much, but I see movement."

"Right." Dewey tapped controls and then used the V.R. controls to zoom his view of the plain below. He kept his focus on the spot the Wenshen guard directed him.

The magnified view was a little hazy and a little shaky. But it finally saw something. It wasn't distinct figures marching through the maze of trees and bushes. Rather, it reminded Dewey of the hazy, fuzzy vids he'd seen as a kid.

The vids purported to show real aliens lurking on the periphery of human civilization. Like many others, he'd wanted the vids to be real, but he'd known they weren't. There wasn't anything wrong with wishing unless the wishing was foolish, like the sudden appearance of a Hospitaller fleet above the planet.

"See them, Lieutenant?"

"I guess," said Dewey. "I see some grayish blobs moving in our general direction."

"That's them," said Castro before she laughed. "What do you see, Vasilios?"

Vasilios, the Wenshen who'd first spotted the A.P. on the move, laughed. "I see apes. I see them quite clearly. Is your eyesight truly that bad?"

It was Dewey's turn to laugh. "No, your eyesight is just that amazing."

"Did you get a count?" asked SSgt Castro.

"I did not," said Vasilios. "They're moving under some of the trees and taller bushes. But, I am certain it is close to a hundred."

"That's a lot," said Castro.

"We've faced worse," Dewey said. The Wenshens laughed, unaware that Dewey wasn't making light of the situation or throwing out false bravado. They had indeed faced worse, but only once had they taken the worst out of the conflict. The problem with some armies, especially those on planets, was that they mistook quantity for quality.

"Vasilios." Everyone turned as Neoklis spoke. He'd been the last person to step onto the outcrop. He pointed and said, "Can you look there? Behind the apes?"

Not just Vasilios turned to look across the plain just beyond the advancing A.P. forces. But unlike Vasilios, Neoklis, and the other Wenshens present, Dewey couldn't see anything but the vagueness that implied bushes and trees. Even on magnification, he saw nothing more.

"The apes are in trouble," Vasilios said.

"What is it?" SSgt Castro asked.

Dewey still couldn't see anything, but he had his suspicions. "Flat-tails?"

Vasilios nodded. "The most I've ever seen."

"Still," Castro said, "the A.P. can use their weapons. They aren't going to be too concerned if we know where they are."

"It's possible they could be overwhelmed." Dewey turned to Neoklis. "How much experience does the A.P. have with flat-tails?"

"Dr. Jackson never spoke of them," Neoklis said. "I would imagine that if he knew, he would have warned us."

"Any time the apes come to the station, they are only outside for a short time," added Vasilios. "If they had any experience, I would say it was long before we existed."

Dewey turned off his face shield magnification, remembering to close his eyes just before he turned the V.R. knob. He gave it a second and then opened his eyes, looking at the world with his normal vision. "And it's unlikely their experience was anything like what we have encountered."

"I've never seen this many flat-tails," said Neoklis. "I don't think the apes will survive."

"It's going to be ugly," SSgt Castro said.

Dewey agreed, which meant they couldn't sit by and watch. "Not if we help them," he said, surprising the Wenshens present.

"Help them?" said Neoklis. "They want to destroy us. Let them suffer the fate they would wish upon us."

"I want nothing to do with helping the apes," said Vasilios. "They are the enemy."

"You know how it is to see someone killed by a flat-tail," Dewey said. "Would you wish that upon anyone?"

"Yeah," Vasilios said. "On the apes."

It was clear to Dewey that making the Wenshens understand how helping the A.P. could benefit them was going to be difficult. However, he wasn't going to sit still and let others die as horribly as MedTech Phillips, and all the others had died even if it looked like he'd be doing it without the Wenshens' assistance.

"Neoklis," Dewey said. "Remember that we had to prove ourselves to you? We had to show that we were not like the A.P., not like the apes?"

"You have never tried to kill us."

"So far, neither have they." Dewey pointed toward the floor of the plain as he spoke. "Granted, that may be why they are here. But consider how the dynamic changes if you save them from a gruesome death."

"It would give you leverage," said SSgt Castro.

"And when the flat-tails are defeated?" asked Vasilios. "What then?"

"They'll honor a truce," Dewey said. "If not for you, then for us."

"And then you'll leave, back to your world."

"Yes," Dewey said, acknowledging the younger Wenshen's statement. "But not before we do our best to secure your safety."

"What if you can't?" Neoklis said. Dewey recognized in the elder Wenshen's voice the tone of someone who was reluctantly coming around to an idea.

"Then we'll stay and fight with you," said SSgt Castro.

Dewey nodded in agreement. After all, that was precisely what they'd been trained to do.

As it had seemed simple to convince Neoklis, Dewey had foolishly thought the rest of the Wenshens could so be convinced. That had not been the case. The detractors of the plan, lead by Neoklis's partner, Georgia, argued angrily against lending the apes any assistance.

It was only when Maj Simmons had stepped in and explained the benefits of helping a foe that the momentum swung in the other direction. When she managed to explain how it would look good to the other governments if the Wenshens had helped someone even as reprehensible as the A.P., even Georgia was forced to admit there was sense to the idea. Still, Georgia said she would not lift a hand herself.

"So that is what it comes down to," said Neoklis. "Only volunteers will come and assist you in helping the apes. Personally, I think many of them hope to see the apes destroyed. But that may be the fault of the first generation. We have allowed our hate to infect our later generations."

"But they will help, yes?" asked Maj Simmons. "Lt Dewey isn't going to have to worry about any last-minute betrayal?"

Neoklis laughed. It was one of those laughs that implies someone doesn't understand a subject as well as the amused person. "More than our hate of the apes - or maybe because of it - we've always held honor in the highest esteem. They will fight if needed. They will protect their families and you Hospitallers. And, yes, they will help save the apes even if they believe they aren't worth saving."

Maj Simmons turned to Dewey. "That's as good as a promise as you're going to get."

"I think it's enough," Dewey said.

The major, for her part, was not going to be coming back down to the plain. MedTech Chambers had been adamant. Even though Maj Simmons was making good recovery, she was still weak and would likely get herself in danger. Worse, she could endanger the lives of the Hospitallers near her, who might become distracted should she falter.

MSgt Roberson was coming, though his job was as liaison, reporting back to Maj Simmons. The medtechs would be coming along, but Dewey hoped their services would be little needed.

While the Wenshens gathered as many spears as each of them could carry, Dewey tapped his comm to check in with Cpl Garner, who had been sent back up to the outcrop.

"Well, I still can't see a thing, Lieutenant," said Cpl Garner. "But Fotini here, she's got amazing eyesight."

Fontini was a great-granddaughter of Theophilus. She would have volunteered for the battle if her great grandfather hadn't already volunteered her for the lookout.

"Well, then, Garner, what does Fontini see that you can't?"

"She thinks the A.P. have finally begun to realize that something is behind them. She says about ten of them are fanned out across the rear of their column. They're in pairs. Probably one watching the way they've come while the other watches their back."

The A.P. Didn't have the eye tech that the Hospitallers had. If they did, they could have dropped them along the way to serve as motion detectors.

"Thank you, Garner. We're about to depart. Keep us updated."

"Will do."

Dewey tapped the comm, closing the connection as Neoklis approached.

"Everyone is ready to march," said Neoklis. He looked around and then added, "I will not be attending. Georgia has made it very clear that she resents the idea of me risking my life for the apes."

"I understand," said Dewey. The lives of the Wenshens had so far been nothing but the struggle for survival. It was one thing to die protecting family and home. Risking one's life for the enemy, Dewey counted himself lucky that any of the Wenshen had agreed to come. "I'll try to bring everyone back."

"Watch the apes," said Neoklis. "You may be honorable people, but I do not believe they are."

"People can surprise you."

"Yes, they can." Neoklis laughed as he reached out and gave a fraternal arm-squeeze to Dewey's EVA suit. "You've shown us that already."

"Hopefully, we'll continue to earn your trust."

"Good luck, then," said Neoklis. He stepped back and gave a wave of acknowledgment to the spear laden Wenshens.

Across the floor of the canyon, shouts of good luck echoed. People crowded the grounds, gathering to wish the fighters well. In several cases, there were attempts to change someone's mind at the last minute. It worked once, but not in the intended direction. The expeditionary force was increased by one, much to several people's dismay.

"SSgt Castro, who's on point?"

"Two Wenshens and Cpl Chavez's squad," said Castro. "Bolstered by the addition of Pfc Fox."

"Let's move out, then."

"You got it, Lieutenant." There was a pause, and then over the general comm and external speaker, Castro said, "Chavez on point. Hospitallers. Wenshens. Move out!"

A ragged cheer rose up as the Hospitallers and Wenshens started moving. Several small children ran up to where Dewey was walking and waved vigorously. Dewey waved back, regretting that he hadn't yet found a toy from the T-n-T bag that he was confident could survive the acidic atmosphere. Maybe, when everything was over, and help had arrived, they could find something that the children could have that wouldn't corrode overnight.

The people behind Dewey surged forward. He had to take several quick steps to reclaim his space.

"This going to work?" asked Sgt Parks. She'd come up next to Dewey as she spoke. "Will the A.P. take the deal?"

"I can't see how they would have a choice," Dewey said. He took three balanced steps across a log that put him on the right side of the stream. "I know some of the government forces can be stubborn to the point of suicide. However, if any of them fall victim to a flat-tail, I think their commander will see the light."

"Time will tell," said Parks before she fell back to join her squad.

Dewey agreed. Time would tell. The real question was, did they have enough time? That and several other issues occupied Dewey's mind as they left the protected canyon and entered the narrow section that would bring them out somewhere above the A.P. forces, and the flat-tails.

The walk went quicker than it had on the way up. No one was slowed by the burden of carrying crates and totes. The wounded did not hold the abled-bodied back. And now gravity was on their side. So, in a third of the time it took to reach the village, they were coming out of the canyon and into the narrow pass. Here, the trees blocked any view of the plain, which was much closer now.

Over the comm, Dewey checked in with Cpl Garner.

"Well, I can't see a star blasted thing, Lieutenant." Garner followed up his comment with a short laugh. "But Ms. Fontini says you're about a kilometer away from the A.P.'s point. The flat-tails - which I couldn't see no matter how hard I try - are close behind. Ms. Fontini says the apes haven't made contact with the bugs, but that's only a matter of time. Oh, and there are a lot of the flat-tails."

"Thank you, Cpl Garner."

"No problem, Lt Tyler. Oh, Neoklis says hello, and good luck."

Dewey nodded to himself and said out loud, "Let's hope it doesn't come down to luck." He switched the comm to reach SSgt Castro.

"It's all quiet up here," Castro said.

"Good. I'm going to try and contact the A.P." Dewey changed the comm once more, setting to a general broadcast. He took a deep breath and said, "This is Lt Dewey Tyler, Hospitallers. Trying to reach the commanding officer of the Allied Planets forces on Wenshen, over?"

Someone started to respond, but Dewey was distracted by a distant sound of gunfire.

32

Within a single heartbeat, Dewey had several incoming requests for comms. At the same time, someone else was yelling at him over the general line he already had open.

"What have you set on us, Hospitaller?" The voice was loud and angry. The comm adjusted for volume, but there was no adjusting the anger.

"If you're speaking about the creatures attacking from your six," Dewey said, "that has nothing to do with us or the Wenshens. Those are native creatures. Tell your people to aim just past the head. And watch the tails."

"We know about the tails, no thanks to you."

The comm clicked, closing the communication with the angry A.P. Dewey started answering the other comms, beginning with Cpl Chavez.

"We heard the firing," Chavez said. "Do you want us to pick up the pace?"

"Not a good idea," said Dewey. "The A.P. are in a bad mood right now. Proceed with caution."

The second comm request came from Cpl Garner on lookout.

"What can you see?" Dewey said. Then, "Or to be more precise, what does Fontini see?"

"The A.P. rearguard is gone," Garner said. "I couldn't see it, but Ms. Fontini did. She's still crying. She said they were being slaughtered. If we're going to help the A.P., Lieutenant, we'll want to do it soon, while they're still some left to help."

"Got it, Garner. Keep watching." Dewey cut the comm, switching to reach SSgt Castro. "Change of plans. We need to double-time. The A.P. are getting chewed up in the back."

"Understood." The comm changed to local. Dewey heard Castro give the command for double-time.

Vasilio looked at Dewey. "The apes taking it hard?"

"Yes," said Dewey as he broke into a trot. "But let's not look pleased when we get there."

"We'll do our best," said Vasilios. He dashed away. Dewey hoped he was telling everyone to mind their Ps and Qs.

During the ten minutes of double-time, Dewey heard a nearly incessant growl of gunfire. Ahead of him, the line of Wenshens and Hospitallers became ragged with movement. Dewey didn't like how they were thinning out and separating from each other. The last thing he needed was for those on point to run into the A.P. and get mowed down by nervous soldiers. Worse, and it was the fear niggling at the edges of his conscience, was getting sideswiped by the flat-tails. They could inadvertently sever the line of Wenshens and Hospitallers, making it easier to take all of them out.

"SSgt Castro." Dewey decided that they should stop trusting to luck. "We need several lines along the front. Mix Wenshen and Hospitallers. Sharpest eyes to the outside."

"Getting right on that, Lt Tyler."

Dewey slowed to a quick march as he noticed the people ahead of him, spreading out to the sides. SSgt Castro was in the middle, using the speaker on her suit to direct people to either side, holding back half for a second line.

"How bad is it?" MSgt Roberson had appeared to Dewey's left.

"From what I got after talking to Cpl Garner on lookout? It's bad. I think they were caught off guard and underestimated the flat-tails."

"They seem to underestimate a lot of what lives on this planet," MSgt Roberson said. His barked laugh was harsh, clearly recalling how the Hospitallers had suffered after several attacks by the flat-tails.

"Hopefully, we can keep them from annihilating themselves." Dewey pointed at his comm. "Speaking of which, let me see if they're more approachable."

"I'll see if I can help SSgt Castro." Roberson threw up a salute and then trotted away.

Dewey switched to the general comm channel that had connected with the A.P. "Allied Planet commander, do you copy?"

The pause was shorter than last time, and nothing distracted either side.

"Seems you were right about the where to fire," said the voice on the other end. The A.P.'s voice still sounded angry to Dewey, but that could have just been the result of dealing with the flat-tails. Then, with some remorse, the voice said, "But I don't think we have enough ammo to deal with all of them."

"We're about a hundred meters away," said Dewey. "We're armed, and the Wenshens have come, too."

"Wenshens? You mean the experiments?"

Dewey took a moment to swallow back the harsh tone that wanted to coat his words. He kept his tone flat. "They may be what saves your life. Unless you want to die at the hands of the flat-tails."

"'Flat-tails'? That's what we're calling these creatures?"

"That's what the Wenshens call them." Dewey made sure to emphasize their name. "You want the help, or should we pull back?"

"It pains me to say it, but we can use the help. What's the deal?"

"No one fires on anyone from the other groups. And you surrender at the end."

"Surrender? You think too highly of yourself, Hospitaller."

"Do I? How's your body count?"

"Too high," said the other voice. "Unconditional surrender after it's all over. Assuming any of us are alive."

"We'll do our best to make sure we're all more alive than dead. We're coming in from the direction of the hills. If you can make three sides of a box?"

"Will do, Hospitaller. Just keep your word."

"Keep yours," Dewey said into a comm line after it disconnected. He switched to local comm. "MSgt Roberson. SSgt Castro. We have the green light from the A.P. They're making a box, we're the fourth side. Let's go."

Neither of the staff NCOs responded over the comm. Dewey heard their voices directing the two lines to hustle forward. He inserted himself in the second line, ready to join the fight.

As the Hospitallers and Wenshens reached the A.P. forces, the noise of gunfire seemed to escalate. Unfortunately, Dewey wasn't able to discern the direction from which it was originating. But he had his suspicions.

"SSgt Castro? We run into the enemy?"

"We have, Lieutenant. Both sides." A pause and Castro continued. "It looks like the flat-tails have come around the three sides of the A.P. There's a lot of them. A whole lot."

At that moment, Cpl Mitchell, who was next to Dewey, started firing short bursts back the way they'd just come. Dewey turned, bringing his weapon up as he did. One flat-tail was on the ground, its back, punctured by three rounds from Mitchell's weapon. Passing the downed flat-tail came a dozen more.

Dewey slapped the comm, speaking through it and the speaker. "Look alive, people. We've got company."

Down the line, the rest of Cpl Mitchell's fireteam had opened up, unloading short bursts that were wreaking havoc on the flat-tails. A few made their way through the slaughter only to be met by the Wenshens and their spears.

"Lt Tyler," SSgt Castro said over the comm. "We're bunched up. Tripping over each other."

"Understood." Dewey paused to fire at another flat-tail. He stepped back to reload. Pfc Schultz stepped into the gap, firing on the next advancing flat-tail. "Move the first line into the box and have them fill in gaps along the A.P. lines."

"Will do. Stay alive, Lieutenant."

"You, too, Castro. That's an order."

Then, as if to remind Dewey that his orders only went so far, Pfc Schultz went down, sliced across the knees and then his chest, separating him into three parts. Dewey aimed and fired at the flat-tail that had taken Schultz's life. The flat-tail collapsed, and two more moved into the space. Dewey fired on one. The second was dispatched by a Wenshen spear.

"Fall back," Dewey said so that Wenshen and Hospitaller could hear. "Connect with the A.P. With the apes."

They moved in a jagged line, stepping backward, mindful of each other, the deadly plants, and the numerous flat-tails.

Dewey had emptied a second clip and was on his third when they reached the A.P. forces and those brought in by SSgt Castro. Three more flat-tails brought Dewey to the end of his third clip. He stepped back as a Wenshen and Pvt Becker filled in the space, quickly dropping several more of the flat-tails.

While he loaded his fourth clip, Dewey contacted Cpl Garner at the lookout. "Any good news?"

"Actually, I think there might be," Garner said. "Neoklis says the number of flat-tails has thinned. Maybe two hundred still milling around you. But he said the count is rough."

"Two hundred? Is that all?"

Garner laughed. Dewey tried, but a flat-tail had grabbed a Wenshen. Just as quickly, they were slashed to ribbons by the creature's tail. Dewey fired, knowing it was too late to save the Wenshen. However, it was one less flat-tail.

"Keep me posted, Corporal."

Dewey stepped forward, filling the momentary gap left by Cpl Mitchell. His weapon was jammed. One of the Wenshens pulled Mitchell clear of a flat-tail. Dewey fired three rounds into the creature's back. It went flat to the ground, dead, as another one climbed over it. A spear suddenly appeared in the space between head and body and it, too, fell dead.

More of the flat-tails came. Dewey continued to fire three-round bursts, dropping the creatures as quickly as he could. To either side, Hospitallers were doing the same. In between them, Wenshens stepped forward to strike and then return to the temporary safety of the wall of Hospitallers.

Dewey's comm beeped. It momentarily distracted him, and he had to step back to fire on a fast-approaching flat-tail. He tapped the comm and continued to fire.

"Hospitaller? You still alive?"

"I am. Who have I been speaking to?"

"Captain Kingston Reeves, emergency expeditionary forces."

Dewey stepped back and dropped the empty magazine from his weapon. Two Wenshen stepped in to stab at an approaching flat-tail.

"I have it on good authority that the number of flat-tails is down," Dewey said. He'd slapped the next magazine into place, mindful of the fact that he only had three more. "You still got people standing?"

"More than I thought," Capt Reeves said. Dewey thought he sounded tired. It was understandable. Dewey felt tired, too. The A.P. captain was still talking. "They're not wall-to-wall anymore. The experiments - excuse me - the Wenshen have proven to be deadly with their spears."

"They learned the hard way," Dewey said. He pushed past the two Wenshen near him and quickly took down two more of the flat-tails.

"Well, it looks like we all have, Lieutenant."

"Agreed. We can talk more about life lessons after we've finished learning this one."

"Stay safe, Hospitaller."

Dewey was on his last magazine when he realized the flat-tails were no longer attacking his section of the line. Then, he became aware of an extended silence through the external microphone. He looked up and down the line. There were several more Wenshen down and at least one more Hospitaller. But the only flat-tails he could see were dead ones.

"Cpl Garner?"

"They're gone, Lt Tyler." Garner sounded as relieved as Dewey suddenly felt. "Neoklis said the last of them have scuttled off. Nothing is moving around you and the other fighters."

"Understood. Tell Neoklis we lost a few of his people and that I'm sorry."

"He knows." Cpl Garner's voice suddenly had the tightness of someone who'd had enough bad news for one day. "He saw it all."

"Right. Please ask Neoklis to keep watching, just in case the flat-tails are as tricky as we are."

"Will do, Lieutenant."

Around Dewey, the others had slowly realized that the attack was over. The Wenshens smiled, but they also looked tired, too. Several of the Hospitallers were on their knees, heads tilted back as far as the evac helmets would allow.

Dewey tapped for general comm. "Stand easy, but alternate watch. Let's not assume it's over."

His words brought several Hospitallers to their feet.

Dewey clapped Cpl Mitchell on the shoulder and then started walking toward the A.P. lines, looking for their captain. Capt Reeves was near the far side of the box. He was either chatting amiably with several Wenshens, or things were about to get a different kind of complicated. Not wanting to see another battle so soon, Dewey waved his arms to draw attention before saying through the speaker, "Is everything okay, Vasilios?"

Vasilios turned to Dewey. His eyes were narrow with anger. "The ape said it's over for us. For you, too."

"Stand by." Dewey tapped the comm. "Capt Reeves, we had a deal. Unconditional surrender."

Capt Reeves turned in Dewey's direction. Despite the scratches and dirt on his face shield, it was clear he was smirking. "That deal is null and void, Lt Tyler. You need to consider your position and surrender."

Dewey's comm beeped. He could see on his screen that the call request wasn't coming from the surface of the planet.

"Why is it voided, Captain? And why should we surrender?"

Capt Reeves laughed and pointed up. "Our reinforcements are arriving."

Dewey looked up. Just visible in the atmosphere were six dropships. That would explain the captain's sudden turn in attitude. Unfortunately, it was misplaced.

"Captain, those aren't yours."

The smirk faltered for a second. "Nonsense."

The comm went dead. Dewey could see Capt Reeves speaking into his comm. Was he attempting to connect with the dropships? Or was he trying to hail the carrier he'd likely come into the system on?

While he struggled with the situation, Dewey pinged back to the comm that had requested to speak to him.

"This is Lt Tyler. Go."

"Lt Tyler, the is Maj Dorothy Halloway. Do you need us to come in hot, or do you have the situation under control?"

Dewey almost laughed as he saw the defeated look on Capt Reeves's face.

"Situation under control, Major," said Dewey. "But it'll be good to see a friendly face."

"Thirty minutes, Lieutenant."

Dewey switched the comm, connecting to Capt Reeves. "About that surrender?"

32

The light over the airlock indicator winked green. The hatch clicked and began its slow journey. Dewey waited just long enough for the gap to allow him to slip through. He turned sideways and stepped past. Outside, Neoklis and Vasilios were standing a few meters away, talking to each other. They turned as Dewey cleared the airlock.

"Lt Tyler?" asked Vasilios.

The only problem with changing into a fresh, clean evac suit was that Dewey was now mostly identical to every other Hospitaller and civilian still on Wenshen.

"Yes, it is." For emphasis, he tapped the digital name tag that he'd adhered to the exterior of the suit. He wasn't sure how long the electronics would hold up to the Wenshen atmosphere. Hopefully, Neoklis and the others would be used to any landmarks of this particular suit by then.

Neoklis also had a question, but not for Dewey. "Theophilus, how was it?"

Dewey turned to watch as Theophilus struggled with the latches on his helmet. Theophilus was wearing an EVA suit. As no one was sure which suit would best contain the Wenshen atmosphere, they erred on the side of caution.

Once it was clear that Theophilus needed help, Dewey stepped over and pulled the helmet latches for the elder Wenshen. They removed the helmet together, and then Dewey showed Theophilus where the release locks for the rest of the suit were located.

"Theophilus?" Neoklis asked once more.

"Interesting," said Theophilus as he stepped out of the suit. "I don't know how the Hospitallers stayed in these for days at a time."

"They're Hospitallers," Vasilios said. To him, based on conversations Dewey had with Vasilios, Hospitallers were the pinnacle of stoicism. Dewey also had the impression that Vasilios would have liked to be a Hospitaller if it were ever possible.

Since the capitulation of the A.P. forces on the planet and those on the lone ship above the atmosphere, Dewey and Maj Simmons had been able to really talk with the Wenshens. The Wenshen had also been shadowed continuously by several of the civilians who also wanted to understand the Wenshens and their culture.

They'd learned that there had been several times where children had been orphaned on Wenshen. But unlike a planet with hundreds of millions on it whose orphans exploded in numbers during war, the Wenshen were still small in numbers. They lovingly took in the children suddenly deprived of parents. There wouldn't be a need for a Hospitaller orphanage on Wenshen for a century, at least. But perhaps the Wenshens, because of their genesis, would beat the odds and be a more peaceful world, a more unified world.

While Theophilus described what it was like to be locked in a suit, Dewey hung the suit on a peg recently installed on the exterior wall for this purpose.

"I almost wish we could put our atmosphere inside the buildings and live here," Theophilus said. He paused and shook his head. "But the ghosts are still here, so let the others keep them."

One of the things they'd found in the second research building was the specimen storage. The Hospitallers didn't think the Wenshens would want to see what was in the storage room. Theophilus had insisted. Since it was their world, Maj Simmons and Maj Halloway, pulled the Hospitallers aside and let Theophilus see how the A.P. had truly seen the Wenshens.

"In time," Theophilus said to Neoklis, "we should see about a way to respectfully handle the remains of the ape victims."

Dewey's smile was partially hidden behind his face shield. The A.P. had sent for reinforcements, bringing three more ships into the system. Unfortunately for them, by the time they arrived, so had Free World and United Planet contingencies. The arrival of all parties resulted in a week of meetings and inspections.

The Wenshen had quickly tired of it and told them all that they would now leave. The elders, Georgia being one of the more vocal, insisted that they would only deal with the Hospitallers. After some pleading by the civilians, it was agreed that some civilian scientists and anthropologists would be allowed limited visits.

"All of our dead are brought back to H.Q. and cremated," Dewey said. "All of the ashes are collectively stored in large urns."

"We still haven't figured out how to keep a fire going," said Neoklis.

"No reason that we can't treat them like we do our people now," Theophilus said.

The Wenshen had unknowingly adopted an ancient tradition of letting the flesh rot from the bones, often with the help of animals, and then storing the bones. The Wenshen had a chamber outside of the village, down a side canyon, where they interred the bones, wrapped and tied in bundles.

"If you're relying on the local creatures to consume the flesh, being in preservatives may have an impact on their ability to do their job."

"Agreed, Lt Tyler," said Neoklis. "But that's a flat-tail we can battle another day."

"Speaking of another day," said Vasilios. "Will you ever be back here?"

Once the A.P. had agreed to keep away, the other governments were happy to wash their hands of the Wenshen, too. Despite what the A.P. scientists had done, no one seemed willing to pull on that thread to see what unraveled.

For their part, the Hospitallers had established a semi-permanent liaison with the Wenshen. A ship with attack capability was now stationed over the planet. A company of soldiers and scientists occupied the research facility.

A rotating squad and one officer stayed with the Wenshens to learn their ways and what technology the Hospitallers could adapt to their environment. It was Georgia who suggested they start with a hotplate.

Dewey's platoon and Maj Simmon's ship crew were leaving now. They would reunite with the rest of their battalion in the Gran Maitre system where they'd been before receiving the mayday call.

"It's always possible," said Dewey. "I've been told that the rotations will be short. No more than six months. I would certainly like the opportunity to return."

"It would be good to see you and your people once more," said Neoklis. "We appreciate all that you've done for us."

"Especially showing us that not all others are apes."

"Time will tell." A movement drew their attention.

One of the first things the Hospitallers had done when they had enough people and supplies was to fortify the research facility. Substantial barriers, weighted with local rock and dirt, now circled the buildings. Several small gates and one large gate were the only ways through the barricade. The large gate was opening now. Just outside of it, a rapid response vehicle was waiting to enter.

Several times, the RapRes vehicles had been attacked by flat-tails. They'd proven to be impervious, unlike an EVA suit. Now, no one moved on the plain without being inside a RapRes. Even the Wenshens had taken advantage of the availability of safe passage from the research facility to the trailhead in the foothills. There was talk of establishing a callbox so the Wenshens could call for a lift if ever they needed.

The engines of the RapRes growled as it rolled past the gate and into the yard. It pulled a wide u-turn before coming to a stop. The back hatch on the RapRes lowered, accompanied by the whine of hydraulics already being affected by the Wenshen atmosphere. Equipment was taking a beating on Wenshen, but already the Hospitaller scientists and engineers were deriving solutions.

Once the hatch had touched down, becoming a ramp, people emerged. First came several Wenshens who'd taken the trip out to the dropships for fun. Behind them came several Hospitallers in combat evac suits.

Dewey's comm chimed for attention.

"SSgt Castro?" Dewey asked over the comm.

"Lt Tyler." The first suited Hospitaller approaching saluted. "We're all loaded and ready to lift."

After returning the salute, Dewey turned to the Wenshens. "That's my ride," he said. He offered a hand to Neoklis. "It's been an honor to meet and work with all of you."

Neoklis shook the offered hand, saying, "And thank you for showing us that we are not alone."

Dewey shook hands with the other Wenshens present. Then, with a final wave goodbye, he followed SSgt Castro into the back of the RapRes. He stood at the opening, one hand on an overhead grab rail, watching until the rising hatch cut off the outside view.

He sat just as the RapRes lurched forward. SSgt Castro offered a steadying hand until Dewey was safely in his seat and was applying the harness to keep him there.

"Can't say I'm not going to miss the people," SSgt Castro said.

"Agreed," said Dewey. "But I won't miss having to wear an EVA suit for a whole week at a time."

"Funny, I thought it was a good look for you."

"Thanks, Castro."

"You're welcome, Lieutenant."

The silence was illuminated by a smile on each of their faces. Dewey was actually looking forward to getting back on a ship. They'd be getting new orders since the Shnel Shnek was permanently out of commission. Hopefully, they'd get a nice quiet post. Perhaps they'd get a post where Dewey could finally finish reading his book...or at least start it!

The End

Hi.

If you're reading this, I'm assuming you either liked the book or you were punishing yourself. I certainly hope it was the former. There are a lot of other books to read in the Hospitaller Universe.

And there's more to come.

So, if you'd like to read more about the Hospitallers, you can get a short story, Two From the Ashes, by joining the newsletter. Unfortunately links don't work on paper. However, if you go to www.earltroske.com you can sign up on the first page. As an alternative, type this into your web browser:

https://www.facebook.com/EarlTRoske

And you'll find the link to sign up in the page banner.

Still here? Cool. You must really have liked the book. Maybe you could do me a solid and leave a review? It helps the book find more readers.

Why should you be the only one to have all the fun, eh?

Until the next book,

Earl

www.ingramcontent.com/pod-product-compliance
Lightning Source LLC
Chambersburg PA
CBHW030321200626
46816CB00006BA/1883